FOUL HOOKED

Islay Manley

BROWN
DOG
BOOKS

Contents

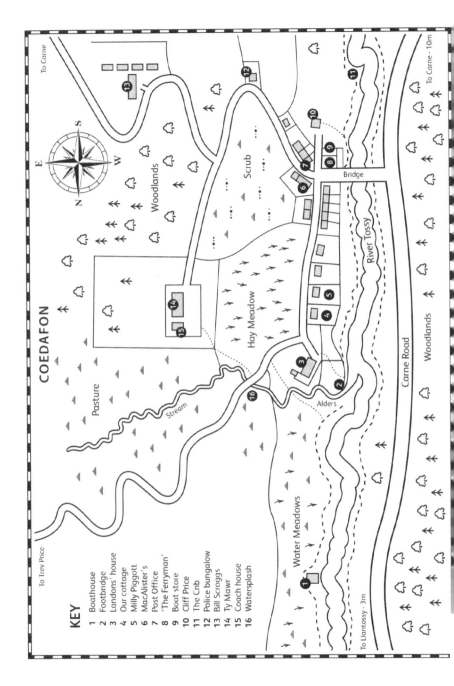

COEDAFON

KEY

1 Boathouse
2 Footbridge
3 Landons' house
4 Our cottage
5 Milly Piggott
6 MacAlister's
7 Post Office
8 'The Ferryman'
9 Boat store
10 Cliff Price
11 The Crib
12 Police bungalow
13 Bill Scroggs
14 Ty Mawr
15 Coach house
16 Watersplash

To Trev Price

To Carne

To Carne - 10m

Woodlands

Scrub

Pasture

Stream

Hay Meadow

Alders

Bridge

River Tossy

Carne Road

Woodlands

Water Meadows

To Llantossy - 3m

Chapter 1

THE NEWT

If Andy, my husband, were telling this tale he would do it in quite a different way. He is a tidy-minded man, and his method would be to collect all the facts, note all the events, arrange them in proper order and then write them down, one by one, just as they must have occurred – one fact arising out of another and one event following logically upon another. He would, in fact, begin at the beginning, wherever that was – perhaps at Newton's birth – then go on to the poor boy's death and so to the final scene last Sunday morning when the body of the third victim was pulled out of the river. That would be the proper way – the way Andy would do it. But I am afraid that, unlike Andy, I am not very methodical. I should be sure to forget the most important things and then have to put them in out of their proper order, and the result would be a pretty awful muddle. So I mean to tell you everything just as it happened to *me*. That way, I certainly shall not forget anything and, although, in the course of the story, you may, perhaps, be as much at sea as I was while the events were taking place, still, in the end you will understand it all, just as I did. In fact, you may even understand it long before the end, as you – whoever you are – are almost certainly much cleverer than I am. That would not be difficult, as Andy would say. Poor darling! He often makes remarks of that sort, but only since his dreadful accident. He was in a plane crash three years ago and was badly burned down his left side. He is a little deaf and quite blind on that side now, and his left leg, too, was affected, so that he walks with a pronounced limp. So you see, he has good reason to be soured and, when he is a little bit irritable and makes tart remarks, I take no notice because I love him dearly and he is fond of me, too, I know, in his undemonstrative way.

Now, just to put you in the picture, I must tell you how we came to be at Coedafon at all. After Andy's dreadful crash and his years in hospital, he seemed to have no interest in anything and, besides that, became very sensitive about his appearance, although the plastic surgeons have made a wonderful job of him. He could not even read much – a thing he has always been very fond of – as his right eye, too, had been affected. The only thing left to him really was fishing. So, since we both luckily have a little money of our own, we decided to buy a cottage on one of the Welsh rivers where the fishing is cheap. We heard of just the thing at Coedafon. So here we are, Andy Marsden and I – my name is Margaret, but I am known as Meg – and our two dogs, Curly and Squelch. Curly, who plays quite a part in events, is an Irish water spaniel with tight, liver-coloured curls all over her body, a curly topknot and a long, whippy tail. Squelch is a fool of a black cocker spaniel. Actually, it was Curly who got us mixed up in these strange happenings in the first place, as you will see. In fact, without her it is almost certain that a murder would not only have gone unsolved, but even unsuspected.

The village of Coedafon – hardly more than a hamlet really – lies along the left bank of the River Tossy and a bridge over the river connects it with the main road to the spa and market town of Carne, ten miles away. Three miles in the other direction, upriver, the road leads to the somewhat larger village, Llantossy where there is another bridge – but this is only a footbridge. For about ten miles up and down river on the Coedafon side of the Tossy there is only one man-made road and that is the road that leads from the bridge, through the village, and then steeply uphill, past PC Jones' modern bungalow and Ty-Mawr, the Big House, into thick forest where it meanders around for about fifteen miles or so, connecting one forest village with another until it also comes out, eventually, at Carne. So you see, we are pretty isolated. There is one other short road possible for cars and this is the lane which leads from the village to Trev Price's farm about a mile away. At first it runs parallel with the river, past a row of cottages of which ours is the last, and then, at the doctor's house, it trends away from the Tossy and climbs to the farm. There is a footpath on each bank of the river. The one on our bank runs from Llantossy through forest and water-meadow, past a deserted boathouse which once belonged to the owners of the Big House, past the end of the doctor's garden, along behind our cottages, under the bridge and so to Coedafon salmon pool, where it ends. The footpath on the other bank runs all the way from beyond Llantossy to Carne. I have drawn a plan of all this so that you will not get too muddled.

Well now, there is only one more thing I must tell you before we begin, and that is that the village of Coedafon, by immemorial right – just why I do not know – owns three quarters of a mile of fishing from just above Ty-Mawr boathouse to just below the salmon pool beyond the bridge. This is really what brought us to Coedafon. The fishing is mainly for trout, of course, but the one salmon pool is quite productive and, besides this, there is a place in the river just below the doctor's garden where a solitary salmon often lies. A small stream joins the Tossy at this point and is spanned, where the footpath crosses the stream, by a plank bridge. This is the best position from which to cover the salmon lie.

So there we are.

We had only been about a month at Coedafon when the event occurred which first involved us in this story, although we did not, of course, realise its significance at the time. It was on a Monday at the beginning of May, the month when a cooked prawn is usually the most rewarding bait for a salmon. It was a beautiful day such as you only get in early May, with leaf buds breaking on all the trees and bushes, and chaffinches in full song. No day for dark thoughts and cruel actions, one would have thought. The date, Andy says, was 3 May and I know it was a Monday because it was washing day. I shall give all the facts in detail because later they became of some importance. After lunch, at about ten minutes past two o'clock, I went out into the back garden to collect the dry clothes from the line and Curly, our Irish water spaniel, followed me out. She went snuffling off down the garden and disappeared through the hedge at the end, beyond which lies the river and the footpath along it. Suddenly I heard a yelp of pain from Curly, followed by a stream of really filthy language in a boy's voice, and then the sound of scuffling and snarling.

I dashed down to see what all the trouble was about and, as I scrambled through the hedge, I came face to face for the first –

and last – time with the boy, Newton Landon. He was standing with a salmon gaff raised above his head and a look of quite frightening malevolence on his face.

'What are you doing to my dog?' I shouted. 'Stop it at once!'

'He bit me,' the boy said in a voice choked with rage.

'I'm sure she never did,' I said. But then I noticed that, indeed, one knee of his blue corduroy trousers was torn as though by a dog's teeth.

'He did, he did!' shouted the boy.

'You must have provoked her,' I said.

'I didn't do anything,' he asserted furiously. 'He was eating my prawns.'

I saw then that the ground around the boy's feet was littered with prawns which had obviously spilled from a jam jar with a broken string which lay on its side amongst them.

'All the same, you shouldn't have hit her,' I said. 'You did hit her, didn't you?'

'I wish I'd killed her,' he said venomously.

'Put down that gaff,' I said, 'and come with me. We'll have a look at your leg and see what we can do about that tear in your trousers.'

A little to my surprise he obeyed and, shovelling the prawns back into the jar, he followed me sullenly into the house.

'What's your name?' I asked, as I sat him down on a chair and started to roll up his trouser leg.

'Newton,' he mumbled.

'Newton what?' I asked.

'Newton Landon. They call me "The Newt". They think I don't know – but I do. I'll "Newt" them,' he muttered darkly, nodding his head.

The Newt. The name suited him exactly. With his black, greasy hair, his curiously pointed head and receding chin, his small, reptilian eyes and permanently half-open mouth he did, indeed, remind one irresistibly of a newt. Even his large hands on the ends of arms too short for his body and his clumsy, gum-booted feet which called to mind the webbed paddles of a newt contributed to the likeness. Later I was to learn that he resembled his namesake in yet another respect for, it seems, he was practically amphibious, as much at home in the water as out of it. Much good it did him, poor creature!

'Newton Landon. Then you're the doctor's son,' I said, remembering that Landon was the name of the doctor whose house lay just beyond our own.

The boy grunted assent.

'Well, there's nothing much wrong with your leg,' I said, rolling down the trouser leg once more.

'He bit me, though,' said the boy. 'My trouser's torn.'

'I'll mend that for you now,' I said. 'Sit still.'

While I searched my sewing box for some blue cotton to match the corduroy the boy sat glowering at me with an un-childlike malevolence which made me feel quite uneasy. I could find no blue cotton and decided in the end to make do with black thread.

'You better make it good,' said the boy, as I started on the tear, 'or my dad will get you.'

'You'd better leave strange dogs alone in future,' I retorted, 'or one of them will get *you*.'

To my surprise he seemed to find this remark highly amusing and burst into a sudden cackle of laughter.

'Not likely.' He grinned. 'Not when I got a gaff.'

'Mind you don't gaff yourself one of these days,' I said. 'It's easily done, if you slip when the point is unprotected like yours is.'

'Yah,' was all the answer he vouchsafed to this.

A singularly unattractive child!

At last the tear was cobbled up and, the moment I had cut the thread, the boy rose from the chair without a word, and made for the door where he gathered up his tackle and then shambled off down the garden. Then on an impulse and because my conscience was a little uneasy about that tear, I snatched up a handful of toffees from a bag on the table and ran after him. As he got through the hedge I pushed the toffees into his trouser pocket. After all, he was only a child!

'Here, here's something to sweeten you a bit.'

All the thanks I got was a scowl, and I stood and watched his newt-like head bobbing away along the river path to the village.

When I turned to go indoors again our neighbour, old Milly Piggott, who lives in the cottage next to ours, was leaning over the fence. She is old and half blind with a cataract and, perhaps for that reason, is a passionate gossip. In spite of her poor eyesight, little that happens in her vicinity escapes her notice.

'Wot's 'e want?' she enquired, jerking her head towards the retreating boy.

'He and Curly had a bit of an argument,' I said.

'Argiment!' she scoffed. "E's a bad un, that boy is. No animals isn't safe from 'im. I know 'oo started the argiment – and it weren't Curly, bless 'er. Bleedin' like a pig she were when she come up the gardin afore you.'

'Bleeding!' I exclaimed in horror. 'Curly bleeding! He must have hooked her with the gaff!' and I ran towards the house to find my precious dog. She was lying in the front room beside Andy's chair, licking a gaping wound in her haunch. Squelch was helping enthusiastically but half-blind Andy, absorbed in making up prawn tackles for an evening's fishing, had noticed nothing. The blood flew to my head with rage – against Andy, quite unjustly, for not observing the dog's state and, more reasonably, against that horrible boy. If only I had known I should have boxed his ears and certainly he would not have gone off with my toffees in his pocket.

After bathing the wound I went out, still in a rage, to get some disinfectant from MacAlister's, the village shop, and as I left I glanced back at the French clock in the sitting room in order to check that the shop would be open. The time was 2.30.

Like most country stores, MacAlister's stocks a little of everything, from nylon blouses and pig buckets to Beechams Powders and fish hooks but, unlike many, our shop is efficiently run and anything stocked can be found in a moment. Dougal MacAlister, the proprietor, is a Scotsman from the west coast. He found himself in these parts during the war when he fell in love with and later married lively, dark little Gladys Rhys whose widowed mother kept Coedafon shop in those days. When the war was over Dougal returned to Gladys and soon after that old Mrs Rhys died and the shop was theirs. They have one son who has now left school and is going to follow in his parents' footsteps. He is little and dark and round and lively, like his mother, and is always referred to as 'the Boy', or 'MacAlister's Boy'. His real name is Ian, as I was to discover on a very official occasion but, except on that event which I shall recount later, I have never heard it used.

When I reached the shop Gladys was alone in it, Dougal presumably being away on his afternoon delivery round and the Boy out on some errand.

'Mrs MacAlister,' I asked, when my disinfectant had been found and I had paid for it, 'can you tell me anything about a boy called Newton Landon?'

'Oh, the Newt is it?' said Gladys in her Welsh sing-song. 'And what devilment is he at now?'

'So he's well known round here?' I asked.

'Oh yes, indeed, Mrs Marsden. Wicked he is. Only for being the doctor's son, look you, he'd have been shut up by this.'

'You think he's mad, then?'

'Well, mad – no. More wanting, like, and wicked with it. Now, young Leslie, him as is nephew to Evan Jones, policeman, and his cousin, Billy, along over the farm, now they're a bit wanting too but soft, like, and not a bit of wickedness in them. But Newt – it's wicked he is *and* wanting, look you. A special teacher they have from Carne to teach him to read and write, but as well try to teach a jungle tiger, I say, though turned fourteen he is. All he do care about is tramping the fields and tormenting the beasts and frightening the life out of Les and Billy. And fishing. Fishing mad he is.'

'He's gone fishing today,' I said.

'And every day, look you. Many's the time Cliff Price, bailiff, has rued the day he learned him to fish. For his father's sake it was, he did it. Dr Landon saved Cliff's life with the appendix, so 'tis said, and he feel he do owe him something.'

'Why should he rue the day?' I asked. 'Fishing should keep the boy out of mischief.'

'Ah, so you might think indeed, only that he don't know the difference between where he can fish and where 'tis poaching if he do. Don't know, or don't care, whichever. Cliff done all he can to stop him. No go. Then at the last he said as he'd take him before the magistrate next time he caught him and a night or two after – in March it was – Cliff was doing a night round, look you, and coming over the plank bridge by the doctor's garden someone pushed him in the river. Banged his head, Cliff did, as he went in and God's mercy he weren't drowned.'

'Was he sure it was the boy pushed him?'

'Su-er, no. But sure enough. Who else indeed?'

'Can't his father keep him in order?'

'The doctor? No. He do go in a dream, Dr Landon do. Not in this world the half of the time. Mind, a good doctor he is, though.'

'Well,' said I, taking up the bottle of disinfectant, 'I must be careful not to get myself pushed in the river, too, like Cliff Price.'

'What's he been at then?' asked Gladys.

'He hit my dog and I told him off. Tore her with a gaff.'

'Dee-oo, no! Well, well!' exclaimed Gladys, round-eyed. 'Look you don't fall in the river, then, one dark night.'

'I'll be careful,' I said laughing.

When I got home it was ten minutes to three and I found that Andy had made Curly comfortable on a rug in the living room and I kissed the back of his head as he sat peering at his tackles. He didn't move but smiled his lop-sided smile and I knew I was forgiven for my bad temper. Then I bathed Curly's wound with the disinfectant and put the iron on again that I had set aside when I brought Newton Landon into the house. Soon after, I went out into the back garden once more to bring in the washing from the line. I was gathering in the last armful when, looking towards the river, I saw a now familiar head bobbing along above the hedge. It was Newt making his way upstream again. I was half inclined to run after him and give him a piece of my mind but then thought better of it.

Afterwards I tried to remember what time it would have been when I saw that distinctive head above the hedge and the nearest I could get to it was that it must have been about a quarter past three.

I finished my ironing then, and Andy went out and sat in the shade of our pear tree which was a mass of bloom that week, with the bees so busy among the blossoms that I could hear their humming from the kitchen. At four o'clock, or just after, I began taking the tea things out where he was and, as I came and went, I told him of the afternoon's happenings and what I had learned about the Newt from Gladys. But Andy was sunk in his thoughts, as he so often was in those days, and his only remark was 'Gossip, gossip, clack, clack. You and Milly Piggott are a pair.'

When I came to cut the bread and butter I found that the butter was finished and I called out to Andy to tell him I must go to the shop again, but he shouted back, 'No. Stop here, Meg, and rest yourself a moment. You've been on the go all day without a minute's let-up. I'll go for you.'

'Let me go with you,' I said, knowing his dislike of going alone among strangers.

'No, no. Stay here,' he said irritably. 'I don't need you always at my elbow.'

So I let him go. It was good for him, I know, to see people and do as much as he could on his own.

I had scarcely turned round from seeing him out of the door when I heard a car coming fast up the lane and then there was a cry from Andy and the screech of brakes. I flew out with my heart in my mouth and before my mind's eye a vision of my poor husband writhing in the dust. But at once I was reassured as I heard him call out: 'It's all right, Meg! No harm done. The doctor here just grazed me with his car!'

When I got to his side, however, I could see that he was shaken. I led him into the house and Dr Landon followed us, apologising as he came.

'I really am most dreadfully sorry, Mrs Marsden,' he was saying. 'I don't usually go so fast down the lane but I was kept late on my rounds and was hurrying home for a cup of tea before going on to Carne. I've got an appointment at 4.30. I am on the

Hospital Management Committee, you know,' he continued, somewhat unnecessarily I thought, because no-one was interested in his appointments at that moment, 'and we meet every first Monday in the month at that time. However, it will do me no harm to miss my tea. Let me have a look, Mr Marsden, please. Just to make sure that there is no harm done.'

'No need to miss your tea,' I said – a little grudgingly I must admit. 'We had just put the kettle on. You can join us in a cup.'

'Well, that's very kind of you, Mrs Marsden, very kind. I certainly do not deserve it.' Turning to Andy, he added, 'Now Mr Marsden, if you will be so good as to sit in this chair by the window we shall soon see whether there's anything amiss.'

'I'm perfectly all right,' muttered Andy.

'Nevertheless, just to set my mind at rest ...'

I left them there and fetched the tea and, when Andy had been pronounced unscathed, we sat around somewhat stiffly, sipping from our too-hot cups and making constrained conversation.

It was the first time I had seen the doctor close at hand. I judged him to be about forty, a tall, fleshy man with a slight stoop, already nearly bald and slow in his movements. I could see what Gladys meant when she described him as being 'not in this world'. His pale eyes had an unfocused look as though he were absorbed in the contemplation of some picture – a not too pleasant picture – in his mind. He was nervous, too, for some reason, perhaps from the shock of the accident, and his hand shook as he lifted his teacup to his lips. However, he contributed his share to the small-talk.

Remembering that we were not yet registered with any doctor

under the National Health Scheme, I asked him whether he could take us on.

'Or, perhaps,' I added, 'you already have more patients than you can deal with?'

'No, no,' he said, quickly. 'My colleague Dr Brading, at Llantossy, and I now share a practice which was at one time managed alone by old Dr Wakes who died some years back. So we're not so hard-pressed as some GPs.'

As he said this I noticed with surprise that he was blushing – or perhaps it was the hot tea bringing a flush to his face.

'I can quite well fit you in,' he added, 'and if you will come round to my surgery at six this evening I will see about your cards.'

I thanked him and a silence fell. Then on a sudden impulse, I said, 'We made the acquaintance of your son this afternoon.'

The words seemed to galvanise him and, for the first time, he looked at me as though he really saw me, his eyes scrutinising my face. He opened his mouth to say something, thought better of it, looked hurriedly at his watch and rose to go.

'You will excuse me, Mrs Marsden,' he said, 'but I am very late for my appointment. Thank you for the tea. Oh, and there is one thing. I wonder would you be so kind as to let my wife know why I have not been home this afternoon. The house is just down the lane.'

I said I would do that and he departed in a hurry.

'Well,' I said as soon as the door had closed behind him, 'what's wrong with him?'

'Perhaps running into me upset him,' said Andy. 'Or perhaps he's just killed a patient.' And we both laughed.

Some minutes later I set off to give the doctor's message to his wife. I was curious to see her for we had never yet, during the past month, happened to encounter each other in the village. As I strolled along in the sunshine between the springing hedges I pictured her in my mind's eye as a little, dark, dowdy, stay-at-home woman with the Newt's black hair and beady eyes, house proud and harassed and rather stupid. How wrong I was! The woman who opened the door to me was as beautiful a creature as I have ever seen. She was already not in her first youth – that is to say I judged her to be in her early thirties – and the Newt's age confirmed this – but her figure was perfect and there was not a wrinkle or blemish on her dazzling skin. Her almost Grecian features were crowned by a mass of short curls of the colour of clear amber which gave her the look of an innocent boy, or of a young god from Greek mythology – Adonis, perhaps, or the young Apollo. But even more arresting than her classical features were her eyes which were large and of a dark, blazing blue and these, on opening the door, she directed on my face with an intensity that was embarrassing.

'Yes? What is it?' she asked brusquely and I noticed that her voice was slightly breathless as though my knock had brought her hurrying from a distance.

Then stumbling a little in my speech under her gaze, I introduced myself and gave her the doctor's message. I was adding a short account of the reason for it 'My husband, you see, is partially blind,' I remember I was saying, when she interrupted me in mid-sentence.

'Would you call your dog, please,' she said abruptly.

Then I noticed that Squelch, who must have followed me from the cottage, was nosing down the garden hedge, his ridiculous black tail wagging enthusiastically. I called him and, after pretending for a moment not to hear me, he came at last reluctantly.

'All right. Thank you,' said Mrs Landon.

The interview was obviously over and she turned to go back into the house. As she laid her hand on the panel of the door, I noticed that this was not one of her beauties. It was a large hand and, though white and shapely enough, was spoilt by curiously spatulate finger-tips. I have read somewhere that such hands denote a strong musical sense but, however that may be, they were certainly a blemish on Mrs Landon's perfections.

'Not a dog-lover,' I thought, as I walked slowly homewards. 'Not a lover of anything much, except perhaps,' remembering her hands, 'of music. We can certainly never be friends.'

However, in that I was mistaken.

Our little French clock was chiming the third quarter as I reached home. A quarter to five. I found Andy under the pear tree in the garden with Curly stretched contentedly at his feet, both seemingly little the worse for their adventures of the afternoon. I remember that above their heads a pair of bullfinches crept about among the pear blossom, whistling their hollow, plaintive notes and scattering the ground – and Andy – with white petals. Every now and then the sun caught the cock bird's breast so that there was a flash of scarlet overhead among the white. From beyond the hedge came the rippling sound of the river and the fresh scent of running water, altogether an idyllic scene, and I went off happily to plant a late row of peas in the kitchen garden. This led to other jobs and, before I knew, it was six o'clock and time to go to the surgery with our medical cards.

It was 6.15 by the time I arrived but there was no press of patients waiting. The only occupants of the wooden bench against the wall were a certain Mrs Blodwen Jones and her son, Leslie. Mrs Jones is the sister of the village constable, PC Evan Jones, and at first, because of the identity of surnames, I had taken her to be his wife. Both are incomers to Coedafon, it being police policy seemingly not to appoint constables to their native districts. They live in a new police bungalow on the hill above the village, whence PC Jones bicycles in daily to report for duty at Llantossy Station. The Joneses, though 'foreigners', nevertheless have connections in the neighbourhood, for their sister, Gwen, is the wife of farmer Trevor Price. Whether the 'Mrs' is a courtesy title accorded to Blodwen for Leslie's sake or whether there has in fact at one time been a Mr Jones – now defunct or departed – I have never been able to find out. She is a large, dark woman with protruding teeth and, now I know the relationship, I can see that she is very like her brother, the constable, a large, dark man – also with protruding teeth. Her son, Leslie, is a small, dark boy with – of course – protruding teeth, and it was he who was the patient. His mother was worried about him.

'He've been acting real funny,' she confided to me as I sat down beside her on the bench. 'I bin wondering is he sickening for a turn.'

It appears that Leslie suffers periodically from "turns" of an epileptic nature.

'This afternoon it was he began to act funny. We was up at the farm on account of me sister, Gwen, said for me to fetch down the cabbage plants she'd laid aside for Evan. Coming back down I thinks to step aside and have a word with Trev – me brother-in-law, look you, as farms Uphill Farm. He was harrowing molehills in the hay meadow alongside the lane. I heard his rattle as I went along up. So I turns in the field gate by the brook, see, but Trev weren't there though. Must have gone off a minute for something. Harrow was there all right. When I goes back into the lane Les is gone – clean gone. Can't see him nowhere. Cut off home, likely, I says to meself. But he weren't home and I got to worrying and, gone four o'clock, I goes out to look for him and I come on him by MacAlister's. Crying and shaking and carrying on he were but I couldn't get no sense out of him. So …'

But the rest of Mrs Jones' tale was cut short by the opening of the surgery door. It was her turn and she bundled her offspring before her into the inner sanctum. The child certainly did look queer, I thought, white as a sheet, with goose pimples on his neck and skinny wrists, as though from cold – this mild May evening. What had frightened him? I wondered.

As my thoughts wandered idly around the subject of poor Les and his equally unfortunate cousin, Billy, Gwen and Trev Price's eldest son at Uphill Farm, I heard a car come round the corner of the house and stop at the front door. Then through the open window of the surgery waiting room, which looked towards the front of the house, I heard Mrs Landon's voice in unenthusiastic greeting.

'Oh, there you are, Jo-Jo, so you've arrived.'

To which a man's voice replied, 'A truly sisterly greeting, Elise. You don't seem very pleased to see me.'

Then Mrs Landon's voice again saying, 'Don't be ridiculous, Jo-Jo. Of course I'm pleased. Take the car round to the garage while I mix you a short one.'

With that the car started up and, as it passed the waiting-room window, I saw that the driver was a florid-faced man wearing a natty business suit and yellow wash-leather gloves – notable details, these, in this out-of-the-way country district where even the doctor goes about in a duffle coat and tweeds. Mrs Jones came out of the inner room then, holding Leslie by the hand and it was my turn. My business with Dr Landon was soon despatched. He seemed quite recovered from his nervousness but was far from cordial and I had misgivings about our going on his panel, in spite of the convenience – for Andy's sake – of his nearness.

Going down the drive again on my way home, I remember I was feeling very low in spite of the beauty of the evening. Doctors and waiting rooms always affect me like that; we have had so much of them in recent years. But it seems to me in retrospect that I felt an extra depression that evening. Was it premonition, perhaps? Or, more likely, is it just a case of hindsight, my present knowledge tingeing the moment with a deeper gloom than it really possessed at the time. However that may be, it was as I reached the doctor's gate that I saw the figure of a small boy running towards me and at once I knew that it represented disaster or a crisis of some sort. It was Rodney Jones, Billy's younger brother and, unlike his brother, in no way slow – far from it.

'Is doctor in?' he gasped as he reached me.

'Yes. He was in the surgery a minute ago.'

''E's to come at once,' puffed Rodney.

'Why? What's happened?'

'The Newt!' Rodney called over his shoulder as he raced on. 'Drownded!'

Drowned! How terrible! Poor Mrs Landon I thought and hurried after Rodney with some vague idea of offering help or comfort, though why I should have considered myself capable of providing either, I don't quite know.

Rodney had gone round to the front for some reason and rung the house bell and I arrived on the doorstep as Elise Landon opened the door to the boy. She, too, must have had some premonition, for the moment her eyes – her blazing blue eyes – fell on Rodney every vestige of colour drained from her face and she stood there like a statue clutching the door jamb.

'Doctor's to come at once!' panted Rodney, urgently.

'There's been an accident,' I interposed hurriedly before the boy could go any further.

'What is it? What accident? What does the boy want?' asked Elise distractedly.

'He wants …' I began, but I was forestalled.

'Newt's drownded,' stated Rodney flatly. 'In the salmon pool.'

And then Elise Landon began to laugh, the pitch of her laughter rising higher and higher until it was no longer laughter but scream upon scream, which brought her husband and her brother running to her side.

Chapter 2

FOUND DROWNED

Well, there is no point in going into the details of the painful scene which followed on the abrupt breaking of the news of her son's death to Elise Landon. Eventually, she was quietened down and Rodney's message at last delivered to the doctor, its proper recipient. When Robert Landon had hurried off with set face to the scene of the accident, it was made quite clear to Rodney and myself that our presence was extremely unwelcome and we took ourselves off, leaving Elise in her brother's care.

'Now, Rodney,' I said when we were out of earshot of the house, 'tell me just what happened. Was it you who found Newton?'

'No, 'tweren't me, Mrs Marsden,' he replied. ''Twere Mac-Alister's Boy. Mighta bin me though. I was going fishing behind the Crib. Good place for eels. Then I see MacAlister's Boy standing on the Crib waving his arms and shouting and I starts to run and when I come up the Boy says there's a corpus other side of the Crib in the pool and it's the Newt and he hasn't got no clothes on and he's drownded, he reckon. I go to have a look and I seen him in the backwater, lying on his face in the mud he was with his legs floating out, like.'

'The Crib' of which Rodney spoke was a small, artificial promontory of rocks piled up at the head of Coedafon salmon pool to improve the draw of the water and also to provide a convenient stance for anyone fishing the pool. Newton must have fallen from it in some way, I supposed, though how he came to be naked I could not understand unless, perhaps, he had tired of fishing and decided to have a swim in the backwater which lay behind the Crib.

'Had he been swimming?' I asked.

'Dunno,' said Rodney.

'Were his clothes there then?'

'Didn't see no clothes.'

'I suppose you and the Boy pulled him out?' I asked then.

Rodney gave me a look of horror. 'What, *me* touch a corpus!'

'He might not have been dead.'

'He were dead, no kiddin',' affirmed Rodney.

'So then you came here,' I said.

'Ar. The Boy, he said as he'd fetch the police and for me to run and get the doctor.'

That seemed to be the extent of Rodney's knowledge. He was on tenterhooks to get back to the river so as to miss none of the excitement. Besides, it appeared that in the hurry of the moment he had carelessly left his precious rod on the Crib – a home-made rod as he proudly told me with a real eel hook on it from MacAlister's. No bent pins for Rodney. So he darted off and I turned in at the cottage gate.

Glancing at the clock in the living room, I was surprised to see that it was still only ten minutes past seven – under an hour since I had left with the medical cards. It seemed impossible. In the garden all was as I left it. Andy was still sitting under the pear tree with Curly at his feet. However, the sun was shining through the branches now and the bullfinches had departed. Only Squelch seemed to have any true idea of the length of time that had elapsed since he had last seen me. He greeted me with yelps of joy as though I had been gone a week, but then five minutes is a long absence for Squelch.

'Back already?' Andy looked up. 'Must have been an empty surgery.'

When I told him of all the happenings of the last hour his only comment was: 'Serve the little beggar right! He seems to have been a pretty nasty bit of work.'

It was hard indeed to interest Andy in anything in those days.

'You won't be able to fish the pool this evening,' I said.

'Why not?' he asked.

'Well, it wouldn't be decent,' I said, 'And, besides, the police will probably be there.'

'Damn!' was his only comment on that.

'Why don't we both go along to the Ferryman after supper,' I suggested. 'Hear what the village has to say about all this.'

The Ferryman is the local pub. Built on the site of the old ferry house, it nestles almost under the bridge, and the old jetty to which the ferry boats once tied up has been made into a small terrace just large enough to hold a couple of round, weather-worn, wooden tables, a bench against the wall and four green-painted iron chairs. From the terrace, a good but distant view can be had down river to the Crib above the salmon pool.

Andy thought nothing of my suggestion but I persevered, for it was not curiosity alone which prompted it. Andy had to get out and see people, and the sooner he made a start the better.

'Nobody will notice you,' I said, 'in all the excitement. Come on. It'll do you good – and me too.'

'Poor Meg! What a dull life you lead!' he sighed at last. 'All right. I'll come.'

Perhaps he was really more curious than he pretended.

It was nine o'clock when we entered the public bar and Cliff Price, bailiff – known thus to distinguish him from Trev Price, farmer – was holding the floor, a mug of hard cider in his right hand. Most of the male population of the village was there, except Dougal MacAlister, who is teetotal, and PC Jones who, from motives of prestige, does not frequent the Ferryman. All were intent on Cliff and his story; not an eye turned towards us, except the landlord's, briefly, as he served us with a glass of beer apiece.

Cliff Price is an unusual-looking man owing to an almost total lack of colour. His hair could only be lighter if he were actually an albino – which he is not – and his eyes are of a very pale grey, like rainwater. The sun and wind seem to have no power to redden or tan his thick, cream-coloured skin – an idiosyncrasy which gives him the unhealthy look of an etiolated potato shoot. In actual fact he is, I believe, as strong as an ox. He served as a commando in the war and, by virtue of his service overseas, is by Coedafon standards a much travelled man. Perhaps as a consequence of his travels he is a great deal more articulate than the majority of his fellow villagers.

'Well, there was his fishing rod, see,' he was saying as we came in, 'pushed in under the footbridge over the brook, the butt of it jammed between the end of the plank and the ground and the reel in the mud and I thought, 'Some silly b---'s going to have trouble with grit in the drum.' Then when I come to look close I see it was the Newt's tackle. I ought to know it! I've had it in me hands often enough, threatening to break it up and throw it in the river.'

'Like 'e threw you, Cliff, back in March,' came a bantering voice from the corner. 'And you a commando.'

'Shan't never live that down,' said Cliff, dolefully, but I noticed that his lips were twitching as he said it and to cover up his obvious desire to smile he buried his face in his cider mug.

'You keep your trap shut, young Harry,' bellowed old Tom Todd, the publican. 'It's a wonder your mam lets you out at night. Go on, Cliff, tell us.'

Thus encouraged, Cliff continued: 'Well, there was this rod, see, and the line was in the water – a thin spinning line, it was, and I could see it bellying out on the current and bending back up to where it was caught in summat in the bottom – rock or branch or summat. Then I seen the gaff laying under the bank and a jar of prawns by it and a fishing bag – Newt's bag – I reckernised it. And over beyond that a heap of clothes and a pair of gumboots. Well, then I knew the boy musta done what I seen him do many's the time. Musta stripped and jumped in the river to fetch up his hook as was snagged in the bottom. Swim like an eel, he could.'

'Ar, that's right,' came an assenting murmur. 'Like a newt he could swim.' There was a snigger from the audience.

'His dad kept him short of tackle,' continued Cliff. 'He'd do anything almost to get back a bit. Why, I seen him bare as a sucking pig diving around in the river and frost on the grass. So that's what happen, I reckon. Went in to fetch up his bait and drowned, I reckon.'

'Poor little b-----,' said soft-hearted Tom Todd.

'No loss, if you ask me,' said Farmer Trev Price. 'Used to torment our Billy something shocking.'

'Ar. He were a torment, sure enough,' agreed Tom. 'Led young Les Jones a life, by all accounts. One time I seen PC Jones give 'im a clout on the ear as near took 'is head off. Seems young Newt 'ad stuck a fish-'ook in the seat of Leslie's pants and was making 'im run up and down while 'e played 'im like a salmon. Cor, the constable didn't 'alf carry on. Talking of Jones, did you show 'im the rod, Cliff?'

'Ar. I was coming to that,' said Cliff. 'Arter I see the rod on the bank I goes on down river keeping a sharp look-out for the boy to see what devilry he's up to. No sign of him, of course, though, because he's dead by then. When I come to the bridge, there's the ambulance moving off and the doctor standing in the road looking after it and PC Jones standing beside 'im. So I goes up to the doc and I says, "Your boy's rod's sticking out in the river by the footbridge at the end of your garden," I says. "Better send 'im up to fetch it," I says, not knowing the boy was dead, see. The doc he just give me a look and then he turns around to Jones and he says "You'd better explain, Constable. I must get home at once."' And here Cliff put on a very refined accent, '"If it's the boy's rod collect it and take it back to the station with you. It may be needed at the inquest." Inquest? I says, all abroad. Then Jones, he steps up. "Young Newton's just been found drowned – at the Crib," he says. So then the doc turns sharp round and goes off through the village, and me and Jones goes upriver by the footpath.'

'Funny the doc didn't come with you,' said Tom. ''Twas all on his way in a manner of speaking. 'Tisn't no further for him by the footpath nor 'tis by the lane.'

'Well, he didn't,' said Cliff. 'Didn't seem to take no interest. Which is funny when you come to think.'

There was a pause for cogitation while Cliff emptied his cider mug and got a refill, free, from Tom.

'The shock it was, likely,' said Tom.

'Ar, shouldn't wonder,' agreed Cliff. 'Well, when me and Jones come to the footbridge, I tuk up the rod and begun to wind up the line. Reel was gritted up shocking, but 'twasn't my worry. Thought as I'd have a job to free the hook, seeing as 'twas snagged – might even have to break the line – but when all the slack was in the hook come up easy. One good pull and up she come.'

'How'd you reckon that was?' asked Dan.

'Well, it do happen,' explained Cliff. 'The current working on the belly of line that'll often work the hook loose – the pull coming from a different side, see.'

'So if 'e'd a waited a bit need never've drowned 'isself,' commented Tom.

'No, that's a fact,' assented Cliff. 'Funny ent it?'

'Cor! Makes you think!' exclaimed Trev Price. 'How d'you reckon he come to drown, Cliff? Him swimming so good as he done.'

'Reckon he got caught up in a branch,' replied Cliff. 'There's that big willow as come down in January, upstream side of footbridge. Bin aiming to get un shifted long enough. There's branches from that old tree underwater and some of 'em reaches almost up to where he was snagged. Big piece of rotten branch, there was on the hook when it come up. Reckon he got in among them branches and couldn't get clear. Then the current swep' 'im out after.'

'Ar, that'd be it,' agreed Tom. 'Poor little b-----,' he added, for the second time, for Tom – unlike so many others – had had no quarrel with the Newt.

Cliff Price, though he still had much to say, had little to add to the story. He and PC Jones had collected up the tackle and the clothes, which were quite dry except for the socks and gumboots. These last had water in them, Cliff said, as though the boy had gone over the tops of them – perhaps in his efforts to free the hook. Only when he had failed to free it from the bank had he stripped and gone into the water. That is what it looked like and everything hung together to support Cliff's theory of the course of events.

By now it was ten o'clock and closing time. We did not wait for the hurriedly gulped last round of drinks but slipped out into the dark spring night. There are no street lights in Coedafon – indeed no electricity at all as yet in the village – but the lamplight shining from cottage windows lit us sufficiently on our way. Andy put his arm through mine as though to guide and protect me as he used to do when we were first married so that, in spite of the tragedy of poor Newton – whom I scarcely knew – I was happy.

Andy, I felt, had taken the first step towards a return to living.

As we turned in at our gate, a car passed us going towards the village. I was almost certain that it was the one I had seen earlier in the evening arriving at the doctor's house. So Mrs Landon's brother had not stayed long.

Chapter 3

INQUEST

The next day Newton and his tragic end were, of course, the subject of much conversation, speculation and reminiscence in the village. Old Milly Piggott, to whom I applied for the loan of some butter for our breakfast, was full of exclamations of philosophic horror at the boy's sudden departure from this vale of tears. You never knew, did you, when you would be called! She, too, had seen Newton making his way upriver shortly after three o'clock on the previous afternoon, as I had.

'And to think, Mrs Marsden,' she exclaimed, 'as you and me is very likely the last as saw that boy alive.'

This was quite a new thought to me and I wondered whether I should report the fact to Constable Jones. Andy, however, pooh-poohed the idea.

'In the first place, you almost certainly were not the last people to see the boy alive. He wasn't found till half-past six and he must surely have gone home for his tea in the interval. And in the second place, it wouldn't matter a fish head if you were the last to see him because the boy died by accident and the exact time of his death is of no importance whatsoever.'

'How do you know it really was an accident?' I said. 'It might have been murder.'

'You've been reading too many thrillers, Meg,' was his only answer to that.

But I was not entirely convinced and decided to let my mind

settle the question for itself in the course of the day – as a mind will do if left to itself. Or my mind will, at any rate. By evening I knew that I should know what I had decided to do without ever having consciously thought of the problem again. (If Andy reads these words he will be finally confirmed in his often expressed opinion of my mental processes!)

In MacAlister's shop where I had to go in the course of the morning in order to replenish at last our depleted butter supply, I found Mrs Blodwen Jones retailing to Gladys the latest news from the police station. The post-mortem on Newton was to be carried out that day by a certain Dr Yorke of Carne and the inquest was fixed for Thursday at Carne Hospital. Her brother, Evan, would of course appear and other witnesses would be Cliff Price, bailiff, Gladys' Boy who had found the body, and Dr Landon.

'Seems Mrs Landon do feel too poorly to 'tend though, and that's no wonder,' said Mrs Jones. 'The doctor, he've said as he'll say her piece for her. Evan was up there first thing to take a statement, but seems she don't know nothing. Never saw the boy after two o'clock. Didn't come in to his tea, but that didn't worry her none. Seems he often gave his tea the go-by.'

'Pity 'tis Mrs Landon couldn't have worried herself more about the boy when he was in life,' said Gladys. 'Neglect him, she did, to my way of thinking. Like a wild animal, he was, for the want of a bit of worry from his mam.'

'Ar, wild is the word – cruel wild,' agreed Mrs Jones, 'and me and Leslie won't be sorry as he's gone.'

'Your Leslie better?' enquired Gladys, going off at a tangent.

'Yes, thank you, Gladys,' replied Mrs Jones. 'Doctor's pills done 'im good. Can't seem to find what set him off, though. Summat give 'im a fright, I reckon. Well, bye-bye for now, Gladys. Evan'll be down with the subpeeny for the Boy.'

So Newton had not been home for tea, I thought, as I bought my butter. Andy was wrong there.

At the post office, which was my next port of call, the talk was still of Newton. The post mistress – or to be more accurate, the sub post mistress – is, in name at least, one Mrs Rees but the work of the place is done by her daughter, Gloria. Mrs Rees is a stout, placid, elderly woman, in poor health, who is passionately interested in all telephone conversations – of which there are very few in Coedafon, as may be imagined – and in such telegrams and postcards as come her way. Gloria, a buxom, motherly spinster of about 40, regards her mother's curiosity as just another of those comic foibles to which the aged are prone and allows her to attend to all telephone business whenever possible. Gloria, herself, is an intelligent woman. She was a clever girl and got herself a good education at Carne Grammar School, after which she earned her living for years as a teacher. Her father's death and her mother's poor health eventually brought her back to Coedafon, where she seems perfectly contented.

'Mother's in the seventh heaven,' she told me, as I paid for a book of stamps. 'The phone's done nothing but ring since 6.30 yesterday evening. First it was poor Dr Landon ringing for the ambulance. He used the call box here because it was nearer than going home, and I must say I never saw a bereaved father look less bereaved. It was extraordinary, really. He smiled at Mother and thanked her for her trouble almost as though he were announcing the birth of a son rather than the death of one.'

'Shock takes people in funny ways,' I said.

'Well, it might have been shock, but his behaviour certainly shocked Mother all right. Then there was a call from the doctor's house booking a room at The George in Carne for Mr Ellis, Mrs Landon's brother. Then this morning calls have been flying to and fro between Carne and the doctor's house and the police station at Llantossy about the post-mortem and the inquest and I don't know what all. Mother never remembers being so busy before. She feels herself quite at the hub of affairs, I assure you. Poor dear! It gives her pleasure and it does no harm.'

A sentiment with which I was not sure that I agreed.

In the course of the day, from this bit of gossip and that, I gradually acquired a clearer picture of the Landon family in general. Robert Landon, it appeared, had come to the district some eleven years before as assistant to the old GP, Dr Wakes, and when that old gentleman died had taken over the large and very scattered practice and run it single-handed for some five years – a feat which nearly killed him. Some two years previously he had suffered a severe breakdown in health and this had brought home to him, at last, that he must take a partner and the partner selected was a certain Dr Brading. These two now shared the practice between them, the River Tossy forming the dividing line between their two spheres of influence. Dr Brading, it emerged, was a woman and her headquarters were at Llantossy, a much larger village than Coedafon and provided with both a church and a school, neither of which exists in our hamlet. On certain fixed days of the week the two doctors hold surgeries in outlying villages on their respective sides of the river.

As to the Landon family life, little was known of it. The doctor and his wife kept themselves very much to themselves. No help was employed in the house; indeed, there is no help available in the village to employ. Robert was well thought of as a doctor but he and Elise were neither liked nor disliked as persons. Having no non-professional contacts in the village – even household shopping being done in Carne – they simply were not known. Newton, however, was known and universally disliked. He was backward and was allowed by his parents, apparently, to do exactly as he pleased – and what pleased him pleased nobody else. He delighted, it seemed, in tormenting any creature weaker than himself, either animal or human, and the chief human sufferers at his hands had been the two cousins, Leslie Jones and Gwilym Price. Gwilym's father, farmer Trevor Price, had been heard to say that he would wring the young so-and-so's neck like a chicken's one of these days, and Leslie's uncle, the constable, had threatened more than once to have him put away where he would be out of mischief for good. In fact, it was the general consensus of opinion that his fate had been an unmixed blessing.

Now, in all this spate of reminiscence and gossip, when every person who had so much as glimpsed the boy on the previous day retailed the fact with relish, there was never a word of anyone having set eyes on him after about three o'clock. Farmer Price had seen Newton start off down the river at about two – although in what circumstances was a little obscure; Bailiff Price, walking up the far bank of the river, had seen him fishing from the Crib at about three o'clock, and had himself been seen by Tom Todd from the terrace of the Ferryman. After that the boy seemed to have remained invisible, except to Milly Piggott and myself, until the body was found just after 6.30. So we remained, as far as I could discover, the last people to have seen him alive.

By evening my mind, working in exactly the way I thought it would, had made itself up and I found myself determined to attend the inquest in Carne on Thursday. Then if my evidence was of the least importance, I could produce it; otherwise, I could remain silent. The time – ten o'clock, and the place – the committee room of the Carne and District Hospital, were easily obtained from MacAlister's Boy who was one of the witnesses to be summoned. Andy was very much against my decision, but for once I was stubborn.

So nine o'clock on Thursday morning found me waiting at the far end of the bridge for the bus into Carne. There were no other passengers from Coedafon and I was a little nervous about finding my way into the inquest. But I needn't have worried. In the hospital forecourt I ran into Dougal MacAlister and his Boy emerging from the shop van and I attached myself firmly to them, and so gained entry without difficulty. Cliff Price and Dr Landon had already arrived. I had seen Cliff's motor bike and the doctor's car parked in the forecourt. In the committee room, besides the witnesses, there were half a dozen women, all strangers to me, and two men, one of whom I recognised as Mrs Landon's brother. The other, who was talking to Mr Ellis, was a big, handsome man of about thirty-five with shining cap of jet-black hair. He was expensively dressed in a grey, long-jacketed suit and grey suede shoes and I caught the gleam of a gold signet ring on the little finger of his left hand.

The proceedings were exceedingly short. The coroner, who had dispensed with a jury, was obviously in a hurry to have done with the business as quickly as possible. The first witness called was the Boy. The formalities having been complied with, the coroner settled his glasses on his nose and, consulting a paper on the table before him, fired his questions as fast as he could formulate them.

'Your name is Ian MacAlister?'

'Yessir.'

'And your address: MacAlister's Stores, Coedafon?'

'Yessir.'

'On Monday, 3rd May, at about 6.30 pm, you found the body of Newton Landon?'

'Yessir.'

'You knew it of your own knowledge to be the body of Newton Landon?'

'Did I know 'twas the Newt, sir?'

'The Newt, the Newt!' exclaimed the coroner, testily. 'I'm asking you, boy, whether you knew the body to be that of Newton Landon.'

'Yessir, I knew 'twas him.'

'Did you touch the body?'

'No, sir,' with emphasis.

'You then fetched Police Constable Jones from his house?'

'From the Bungalow, yes sir.'

'All right. Thank you, you can stand down. Constable Evan Jones, will you take the stand, please?'

And a dazed Boy was pushed away by the usher while PC Jones took his place and was sworn.

'You are Police Constable Evan Jones of Llantossy Police Station?'

'I am, sir.'

'And you live at the Bungalow, Coedafon?'

'Yes, sir.'

'Please tell me what occurred after you had been summoned by the boy, Ian MacAlister.'

'I proceeded,' said PC Jones, enunciating carefully, 'to a part of the river about 200 yards below Coedafon. This part, 'tis known as the Crib, sir. There's a salmon pool there and a backwater and in the backwater I seen the body of Newton Landon. It was naked. It was lying on its face in the mud but the legs was floating in the water. I lifted the body out of the water onto the bank and wiped the mud off of the face. Then I done artificial respiration on it but 'twas too late. The boy was dead. Dr Landon come up then and he said …'

'All right,' snapped the coroner. 'If necessary, Dr Landon will tell me himself what he said. You may stand down, Constable. Now, Dr Yorke,' he continued, his voice mellowing somewhat, 'I know you are a busy man and I will hear your autopsy findings next.'

Dr Yorke, a tall, willowy individual with long, white fingers, told us in a bored voice what we all knew already: that Newton had died by drowning – only he put it less simply than that. Afterwards, the coroner had a few queries to put to him.

'In the course of your examination of the body of this boy did you,' he asked, 'come upon any physical defect or any external injury that might have contributed to his death by drowning – weak heart, contusions about the head – anything of that sort?'

'No, nothing. The boy appears to have been in perfect health and the only external mark on him was a slight abrasion in the lumbar region. It had been inflicted shortly before death.'

'At the base of the spine?'

'Yes.'

'How serious was this abrasion?'

'It was entirely trivial, a mere scratch, although there was a little bruising round it.'

'Might the scratch have been inflicted by the branch of a tree?'

'I suppose so, if there's a tree in the vicinity, and if the branch were sharp enough. Anything sharp could have done it.'

'Thank you, Dr Yorke. I needn't keep you any longer.'

The coroner hrrmphed, shuffled his papers and muttered to himself, 'Yes, well, let me see now. We'll take Mr Clifford Price's evidence next. Mr Clifford Price.'

And the rapid questions and answers started again: name, address, occupation, then:

'You saw Newton Landon on the afternoon of his death?'

'Yes, sir.'

'What was he doing when you saw him?'

'Fishing the Crib.'

'That is the point on the river at which his body was later found?'

'Yes, sir.'

'At what time did you see him fishing the – ah – Crib?'

'Must've been around three o'clock.'

'He was fully clothed then.'

'Yes, sir.'

'And afterwards you found his unattended rod at a different point on the river bank?'

'That's right.'

'About what time would that be?'

''Bout 6.30 – thereabouts.'

'It was at some distance up river from the Crib?'

''Bout half a mile up, at the footbridge over the brook.'

'You found other things besides the rod, I believe?'

'Yes, sir.'

Cliff described the rod, tackle bag, gaff and jar of prawns, and pile of dry clothes and the wet gumboots.

'Are these the articles you found?' asked the coroner, pointing to a pathetic array laid out on a small table by his side.

'That's them,' said Cliff, giving them a rapid glance.

'Do you recognise the articles as belonging to Newton Landon?'

'I reckernise the rod, sir, and the blue cords.'

And I, too, recognised the blue corduroy trousers on the table. Had they been unfolded, I thought, my black thread cobbling would have been seen on the knee of one leg.

'Describe the exact position of the rod.'

Cliff described the rod, jammed into the plank bridge; the bellying line with its end obviously caught in some obstruction on the river bottom; the fallen willow with its tangle of underwater branches.

'The clothes were dry, you say, with the exception of the gumboots, which had water in them?'

'That's right.'

'What did you deduce from that?'

'What did I think, sir? Well, I thought as he'd got his gumboots wet trying to loosen the snag, but the hook was too far in and he couldn't shift un by pulling on the line, see, so he stripped out and dived in after un, as I'd seen him do many's the time.'

'You had seen the boy retrieve his bait in this manner on other occasions?'

'Oh, yes, sir, a score of times.'

'How near were the branches of the fallen willow to the place where the hook was hung up?'

'Hook was right in among 'em almost, you might say.'

'Thank you, Mr Price, that will do. Now, Dr Landon, if you will be so kind, I have a few questions – a very few – which I should like to put to you.'

Robert Landon made his way slowly to the coroner's table. His head was bowed and he looked older than he had done four days ago and very shabby compared to the elegant Dr Yorke. Nevertheless there was no sign of grief on his face, on the contrary. As he passed my chair it seemed to me that his eyes were lowered and his head bent, not in sorrow, but in order to hide a quite inappropriate expression of countenance – an expression that I could have sworn was one of amusement. The impression was fleeting and I may have been mistaken. Certainly as he stood before the coroner his features were decorously composed and he answered the questions put to him with the somewhat absent-minded air that seemed to be habitual to him.

'I understand,' said the coroner, 'that Mrs Landon was unable to attend today.'

'That is so. The shock of this affair ...'

'Quite, quite. But, doubtless, you will be able to supply any information we need. Now. Your son was of school age?'

'Yes, he was fourteen.'

'Yet he was not, I understand, attending any school?'

'No. He was unfortunately a little backward and we had a special teacher from Carne who gave him lessons in the morning. The boy had difficulty in learning to read and write.'

'Ah, that clears that up. Now, secondly, did you know that your son was going fishing that afternoon?'

'I did not, but I believe that my wife saw him leave the house with his rod shortly after 2 o'clock.'

'And neither you, nor she, saw him again?'

'Never again, alive.'

'Were you not anxious when he did not return in the course of the afternoon?'

'My wife was not anxious. He frequently missed his tea if he were fishing. We didn't object. As for me, I was not at home and knew nothing of his absence.'

'The footbridge where the rod was found is close to your house?'

'At the end of the garden.'

'So the boy may have been on his way home when he stopped at that point for a last cast or two?'

'It is possible.'

'Was your son a good swimmer?' The coroner changed tack.

'More than good. He swam like a fish.'

'Nevertheless, as regards this practice of diving into the river to free tackle, did you not think it a most dangerous practice?'

'We did.'

'You knew of it, then?'

'Certainly. And warned Newton against it constantly. In fact, I went further and threatened to confiscate his rod if there was any more of it.'

'Yes. Very proper. Are you satisfied in your own mind that it was this unfortunate habit that led to the boy's death?'

'Perfectly satisfied.'

'I agree with you. I think there can be no doubt that the boy, Newton Landon, was accidentally drowned while attempting to retrieve his tackle from the river and I shall record a verdict to that effect. There appears to be no blame attached to anyone in the case and I must extend my sympathy to you, Dr Landon and to Mrs Landon. Hrrmph.'

And the coroner blew his nose loudly, replaced his handkerchief in the breast pocket of his jacket and started to gather up his papers. The proceedings were at an end.

There had been neither opportunity nor, I thought, occasion for me to offer my shred of evidence. There seemed to be no doubt whatever of the manner of the boy's death and the exact time at which the tragic event occurred was of no importance.

Dougal MacAlister offered me a lift home in his van and I accepted gratefully. As we left the building the handsome stranger, who before the inquest had been talking to Mr Ellis, was now in earnest conversation with Cliff Price and I wondered vaguely what their business together might be. On the way home MacAlister's Boy was bubbling over with excitement at the morning's proceedings. For many a long day, I could see, he would be the village authority on the law and its processes, but his father, Dougal, a dour and downright Scot, had been impressed by one thing only – the coroner's despatch.

'Nae blether aboot yon coroner,' he remarked. 'A man o' few wurrds was yon,' and then addressing himself to his offspring, 'Let him be a sample to ye, boy.'

And we all three lapsed into the silence of our own thoughts. Dougal, too, like the coroner, was a man of few words and he had only one further reflection to make on the recent tragic events: 'Good riddance to bad rubbish,' he said with an air of finality as we ran over the bridge into Coedafon. And that, I think, was the general opinion of all who had known the unfortunate and unattractive Newton Landon.

Chapter 4

MR BROWN

So life returned to normal in the village of Coedafon. But Andy and I had one further reminder of the Newt, for it occurred by chance that on the day following the inquest – which happened to be a Friday – I was a witness of his funeral. On that day every week, if weather and water are at all possible, Andy and I and the dogs, taking food with us, are in the habit of making an expedition to Llantossy Church pool. This is one of the best of the Tossy's salmon pools and the fishing rights on it and on two and a half miles of river which lie between Llantossy bridge and Coedafon village water are owned by a rich industrialist – the maker of a famous brand of jam – who has a small country estate in the neighbourhood. Being a busy man and seldom able to indulge in his favourite sport, he was kind enough, when we first arrived, to let a rod to Andy on Friday of every week during the fishing season. The cost of the rod is not small so, in order to get every atom of value for our money, we make a day of it on Fridays, arriving at Llantossy Church pool early in the morning and fishing our way down river – now for trout and now for salmon – to arrive home at Coedafon just before dark. Llantossy Church, which gives its name to the pool, stands on a small, raised promontory of rocky land on the far bank of the river and the churchyard, which occupies the greater part of the promontory, is surrounded on three sides by water. The pool is best fished from below the churchyard wall on the downstream side, for the salmon rest under the bank on that side of the river in a series of lies, one behind the other, on the edge of the deep, fast water at the foot of the rocks. Below the churchyard a small, rocky island divides the stream and at this point two rickety footbridges span the river, using the island as a stepping stone.

On Friday after the inquest Andy, Curly, Squelch and I took the morning bus to Llantossy as usual and made our way along the river path to the pool. It was a perfect fishing day with sun and cloud and a light breeze at our backs. Heavy showers in the night had freshened the water and brought in a run of salmon. We could see them porpoising in lie after lie, their oily backs just breaking the surface in the exciting head-and-tail of a taking fish. Andy got busy without delay and was soon lost to the world in the only occupation which could make him, for a short time, forget his troubles. I waited until he had made his first cast over the fish at the head of the pool, then, taking the dogs I wandered off upriver, knowing that the screech of the reel as a fish took would give me ample warning to be ready with the gaff.

As I came to the end of the church wall I saw a little procession emerging from the west door of the church and proceeding slowly towards an open grave. Pall bearers carrying a small, flowerless coffin were followed by the curate of Llantossy and a man's figure which I recognised as that of Dr Robert Landon. Bringing up the rear was a tall, dark woman who was a stranger to me. It was Newton's funeral, of course. I did not want to see it. I did not want to think of death on this beautiful day, so I lay down on the grass under the wall in the shadow of an old yew tree to wait until the melancholy procession had departed. That was how I came to overhear a rather curious conversation.

I was watching Squelch's small, black tail waggling joyfully to and fro as he hunted moorhens in a clump of osiers when suddenly I heard Robert Landon's voice behind me saying, 'Rachel, I must talk to you.'

A woman's voice answered, 'Well, here I am, Bob, but you must be quick.'

'That's just it,' came from Robert Landon. 'I haven't time to say anything here. When can I see you?'

'What is it, Bob?' asked the woman – a little impatiently, I thought.

'It's Elise. I think she suspects ...'

'Suspects! There's nothing to suspect,' interrupted the woman quickly.

'No, no, of course not, but you know what Elise is. I must talk to you about it.'

There was a pause. Then the woman, called Rachel, said, 'There's a patient at Pentre I'm not satisfied about. I should like you to see him in any case. If you will meet me there at three o'clock you can take a look at him and afterwards we can talk. He lives in the cottage next to the pub.'

As she spoke it dawned on me that "Rachel" must be Dr Rachel Brading of Llantossy. Some mystery here, I thought. Were Rachel Brading and Robert Landon having some sort of an affair? However, it was none of my business and I was relieved when the sound of their voices receded and I was left in peace to listen to the pleasant sounds of purling water and of a blackbird singing in the yew tree behind me. Soon a sound even pleasanter than the blackbird's reached my ears – the song of the reel as a salmon stripped off the line in its first rush downstream – and I hastened to the scene of the battle to be on hand with the gaff when the fish tired. Robert Landon and his affairs were quite forgotten.

We landed the fish and another before the salmon went off the take. Then we crossed the river by the two rickety footbridges and made our way slowly down our bank, fishing for trout as we went. The two salmon in the frail were heavy on my arm but I would gladly have carried twice the weight to see Andy so happy. The trout were rather disobliging, to my secret relief, and soon after midday we settled ourselves in a sunny bay to eat our sandwiches. Since leaving Llantossy we'd had the river entirely to ourselves but now I saw approaching us from upriver two men. One, I could see by his breeches and gaiters was Cliff Price, bailiff; the other I did not immediately recognise.

'Morning, sir,' said Cliff as he came up. 'Any luck?'

So we showed him the contents of the frail.

'Ar, nice pair of fish,' commented Cliff. 'Clean run hens, the both of 'em. Fifteen pounds apiece, I reckon. Come and take a dekko, Mr Brown,' he called over his shoulder.

The stranger so addressed approached slowly – rather unwillingly, I thought – and threw a casual glance at our catch.

'Very nice,' he said and moved back again at once.

His face seemed vaguely familiar but I could not place it.

'Mr Brown is evidently not a fisherman,' said Andy, when that gentleman had strolled out of earshot.

'Well, that's funny,' said Cliff, scratching the back of his neck. 'From what 'e said, that's what 'e *is* – a fisherman. Come down to look at the fishing. Don't seem to fancy your fish, though, do 'e?'

'Who is he, Cliff?' I asked.

'Name of Brown,' said Cliff. 'Nobbled me arter the inquest yesterday.'

The inquest. The handsome man with the natty suit and shining hair and a gold ring on his finger! Of course! I had seen him talking to Cliff as we left the hospital; only now he was wearing brown sailcloth trousers and a sports jacket which altered his appearance. The gold signet ring was still on his little finger, though; I had seen it glint in the sun. So his name was Brown, whoever he might be.

'Did you know him before, Cliff?' I asked.

'No more than the man in the moon,' said Cliff. 'Funny thing, though, coincidence you might say. I seen him that day Newt were drowned. Walking up this 'ere bank, he was, along by Ty-Mawr boathouse.'

'Was he fishing?' I asked.

'No, jest walking,' replied Cliff.

'But you think he's a fisherman?' I asked.

'Ar,' assented Cliff. 'He asked me yesterday did I know of any fishing going hereabouts and I told un about that rod as is going in Anderson's syndicate. Seemed interested and asked would I show 'im the water and I says 'e can come with me on me round and welcome. Nice spoken gentleman. Knows summat of salmon all right, though yourn don't please 'im, seemingly.'

'Perhaps he wants his lunch,' said Andy, looking meaningfully at the sandwiches.

'Ar, might be. I'll be getting along,' said Cliff taking the hint. 'Tight lines!' And he departed to catch up with Mr Brown who, by this time, had wandered quite a distance down the river bank.

I give this small incident in some detail because it describes our first introduction to one of the chief characters in this tragedy.

The rest of the perfect day went by in a flash, as perfect fishing days do, and sunset found us passing Ty-Mawr's disused boathouse, about half a mile from our cottage. It is a solid brick building with a tiled roof, built out on piles over an inlet of the river. In the days when Ty-Mawr, the Big House of Coedafon, was occupied, a small row-boat was kept there and was used by the family for trolling over the salmon pools. But the war wiped out the family at Ty-Mawr and now the Big House lies deserted and slowly disintegrating into the woods above the village; and its boathouse, too, is empty and deserted. Farmer Price, who has the grazing of the water meadows in which the boathouse stands, is careful always to keep the door closed and has even fitted a small hasp and padlock to prevent entry. I had often wondered why he went to this trouble, so, when on this evening I noticed that the padlock was hanging loose, I pushed open the door in order to satisfy my curiosity. It swung half open, then came to stop against an old iron weight which had probably at some time been used to steady the boat as it was slowly drifted down over the salmon lies. The reason for Trev Price's care was immediately apparent, for I saw that the flooring extended over only half the boathouse, forming a landing stage; the other half was open water where the boat was once moored; obviously a most dangerous place for cattle should they stray in. It was dark inside when I peered in, for there was no window and the sliding door on the river side was closed, but on my left I could see the gleam of water in the dock and hear its stealthy lapping; a dank odour of rotting river weed rose from it. In the far corner on my right something glimmered in the gloom – something white – and such was the depressing atmosphere of the place that my blood froze and I thought instantly of corpses. But it was only a pile of paper sacks of the kind that are used to contain fertilisers and, no doubt, Farmer Price had stacked them tidily there after spreading the contents on his meadow. Nevertheless, I shuddered and backed hastily out again into the rosy light of the sunset. It was a sinister place and I had seen enough of it.

'What's the matter?' asked Andy, surprised at my precipitate retreat. 'Did you come face to face with a tiger?'

'Not a tiger,' I said, laughing, 'but a ghost, perhaps.'

And perhaps I spoke more truly than I knew.

Chapter 5

THE BIRTHDAY PARTY

Next day, I remember, we sold one of the salmon to Dougal MacAlister at the shop, and the other we cut up and, with no ulterior motive, gave the pieces round to our acquaintances in the village, thereby gaining for ourselves a sort of standing in Coedafon. After this, we were no longer merely strangers from London but neighbours whose generosity – according to the unwritten law of such country places – demanded a return. So our salmon came back to us in the form of 'a pint on the house' from Tom Todd, 'a coupla sticks of me favourite rhubarb' from Milly Piggott and a bowl of Jersey Rose's double cream from Mrs Trev Price. But the best return of all was that from that day Andy began to feel himself a part of the community and no longer skulked around the village like an outcast.

The fat middle cut of this productive fish I set aside for Dr Landon and his wife, as a token of our sympathy and as a gesture of friendship which, I hoped – social life being scarce in Coedafon – would lead to the better acquaintance of Elise Landon and myself. In the afternoon I decided to deliver the fish myself and so, for the second time that week, found myself walking up the drive to the doctor's front door but, this time, remembering Mrs Landon's apparent dislike of dogs, I left both Curly and Squelch at home. It was again Elise Landon herself who opened the door to me and, once more, I was struck by her Grecian beauty – the beauty rather of an Adonis than of a Venus. Her greeting this time, too, was scarcely more cordial than on that first occasion.

'Did you want the doctor?' she said. 'Because, if so, he's out.'

'No, no,' I stammered. 'I just came to offer our sympathy – my husband's and mine. Our name is Marsden and we have recently come to live in the cottage nearest to you. We have met before, but only very briefly,' I bumbled on under her blank stare, 'but I expect you've forgotten, and I thought you might like this,' I finished, thrusting my damp parcel into her hand.

'What is it?' she asked, looking at it with distaste.

'A small piece of salmon,' I said apologetically. 'We caught one yesterday. But, perhaps, you don't eat salmon?'

'Salmon? Oh – oh, I see. It's a present? Well, that's very kind of you. Thank you,' she said without warmth.

There was a short but awkward pause before she added, 'Won't you come in for a moment, Mrs … I'm sorry, I didn't catch your name.'

'Marsden,' I said. 'Meg Marsden.'

'Well, come in, Mrs Marsden,' she repeated, a little more cordially. 'I'll just put this in the larder and be with you in a minute.'

And, having shown me into a room on the right of the hall, she hurried off with the parcel held before her as though it were something putrescent brought in by the dog.

It was a pleasant room in which I found myself. The southward-facing French windows gave onto a small, paved terrace with steps leading down to the drive. To the west another large window looked out onto the forecourt of the house and, beyond it, to the garden. Both windows gave tree-framed glimpses of the river which here forms a loop around the grounds. The north side of the doctor's property, which extends to about an acre of land in all, is bounded by the small stream at whose junction with the river young Newton's abandoned rod was found. The fatal plank footbridge, however, was not visible from the west window of the house as an orchard of apple, pear, cherry and plum – now just bursting into bloom – obscured the view in that direction. As I turned from admiring the blossom I noticed that a grand piano was the main feature of the room itself. So Mrs Landon was, perhaps, in fact a musician and her spatulate fingers – which I had noticed at my first meeting with her – were possibly a true indication of her tastes. It would, at any rate, make a subject of conversation, I thought, as I heard her returning footsteps.

'I think you must be fond of music, Mrs Landon,' I said, indicating the piano as she entered.

'Yes, I am,' she agreed eagerly, her face lighting up for the first time. 'Are you musical, too?'

'Yes,' I replied, 'but I am only a listener, not a performer.'

'I play the piano,' she confided. 'When I was a girl it was my dream to become a concert pianist, but my father had other ideas. He was a very determined man, my father. Thought I was clever and sent me to London University to take a science degree instead of allowing me to study music as I wanted to do.'

'So you are BSc?' I asked.

'No.' Then after a pause, she added: 'I never sat my degree.'

'You got married instead,' I guessed, thinking what a lovely girl she must have been.

'Yes,' she answered flatly and all the animation died out of her face.

I had said the wrong thing and an uneasy silence fell which she broke by rising abruptly to her feet.

'Well, thank you, Mrs Marsden, for your kind present. I – my husband and I – shall enjoy it.'

Somewhat astonished at the shortness of the interview and at the fact that not so much as a cup of tea had been offered I took my leave, saying politely that I hoped she would look in on us sometime and have a talk about music and listen, perhaps, to some of Andy's records played on an ancient portable gramophone. I felt, as I said it, that the entertainment offered was not exactly hilarious and I was, therefore, not at all surprised at her non-committal reply. I never expected to see her again, except to nod casually in the village.

However, a few days later, to my surprise, she appeared at our door around tea-time. It was another perfect May day and I took her out to where Andy was sitting under the pear tree. The dogs rose to greet her as she approached, but she shrank from them and seemed nervous even of silly, fat Squelch.

'They're very friendly,' I said soothingly. 'As soon as they have made your acquaintance they will go and lie down.'

'I hope so,' said Mrs Landon with her usual ungraciousness. 'I am allergic to dogs.'

Not a propitious opening to her visit, and it was with some misgiving that I left her and Andy together while I went to prepare the tea. I hoped that Andy, too, would not relapse into boorishness, as he was apt to do in those days, but would exert himself a little to entertain his guest, for, in spite of her unattractive manners, I was sorry for Elise Landon and willing to be friendly. She must lead a lonely life, I thought, especially now that Newton was gone. I needn't have worried. When I returned with the tea I found the two of them in deep conversation. Mrs Landon shared, it seemed, Andy's passion for Bartok and, when that subject was exhausted, they turned their attention to concerts in general, to operas and the ballet and, finally, to London, the home of all these joys. It was obvious at once that to Mrs Landon London was a holy city – the Mecca towards which her thoughts turned with longing and I could not wonder at it after a dozen years or so in Coedafon. She was all animation now and, as I studied her smiling face with its blazing eyes and crown of shining curls, I wondered, not for the first time, how she could possibly have been the mother of the Newt, that dark and ugly youngster. And yet, there was something about the nose and mouth and, especially, something in the timbre of her voice which proclaimed the relationship.

A curious thing about her was that she seemed quite unconscious of her looks. She employed none of the small airs and graces that almost any attractive woman, however virtuous, will produce in the presence of a man – even of so battered a specimen as my dear Andy. I formed the opinion that afternoon – and have been confirmed in it since – that she was so entirely engrossed in herself that other people, even men, were no more than shadows to her. However, even her self-absorption was interesting and the afternoon passed pleasantly enough, and at the appropriate time she took her departure – quite graciously, for her.

'What do you think of the beautiful Mrs Landon?' I asked Andy when she had gone.

'Is she beautiful?' he wondered.

'Andy! Of course she is. She has simply everything,' I said. But he disagreed.

'Her hands are ugly and her voice is hideous,' he insisted.

'Not hideous,' I protested. 'Just rather flat.'

'No, it's more than that,' said Andy reflectively. 'I got to know about voices when I was blind; it was all I had to go on with strangers, and Mrs Landon's is downright disagreeable.'

'You seemed to enjoy listening to her voice all right this afternoon,' I remarked.

'Yes, she's a clever piece,' said Andy, 'and pretty enough. But not my cup of tea,' and he put his arms round my shoulders and gave me an affectionate squeeze.

'Be careful! Milly Piggott will see us,' I warned him.

As if in answer to an incantation Milly Piggott's face did in fact appear at that moment above the fence.

'Cooee!' she called.

Reluctantly I moved over to speak to her.

'Mrs Landon bin to see you?' enquired Milly with artless curiosity.

'Yes, why?' I said shortly, annoyed for once by the blatancy of her approach. But Milly's hide is thick.

'Thought I 'eard 'er voice,' said she, with satisfaction. 'Enjoyin' 'erself, too, by the sound of it, and 'er pore boy not 'ardly cold yet, as you might say.'

'She's lonely,' I said. 'Everybody needs friends at a time like that.'

'Lonely!' exclaimed Milly. 'Oo says? You ask Mrs Rees, post office, if she's lonely.'

'What has Mrs Rees got to do with it?' I asked.

'She got ears,' said Milly meaningfully.

'Ears?' I was quite at sea.

'Ah. *And* she uses 'em. *And* she works the telephone. There bin a man ringin' that Mrs Landon each and every day this week past, *and* it ent 'er brother. Lonely! Oh, yes, indeed!'

'Miss Piggott!' I exclaimed, shocked. 'You shouldn't say such things, and Mrs Rees shouldn't listen in to private conversations.'

'Ears was give us to 'ear with and tongues was give us to speak with and if you don't like it you can lump it,' said Milly, and retired in a huff which lasted many days. In fact, it took a brace of fat trout to bring her round again. I didn't believe a word of it or, if there was a man, it was probably Elise's solicitor or some relative or even, in spite of Mrs Rees' assertion, her brother. But I was to remember this conversation later.

That afternoon's call led to a friendship between the doctor's household and our own and, especially, between Elise and myself. We were, after all, the only people of our kind for miles around. I soon found that Elise could be most entertaining when she chose. In character we were complete opposites. She was everything that I should have liked to be but was not – tall, slim, elegant, beautiful, clever and talented and most attractive of all to me, a placid, down-to-earth sort of individual – she had a passionate vitality. There was an undertone of excitement about her always and I often wondered how she bore the uneventful and spiritually and mentally arid life of this small border hamlet. I soon became quite dominated by her and a day seemed dull when we did not meet. We were all soon on first-name terms and Elise would drop in most mornings for a cup of tea while Robert was visiting his local patients. On these occasions, if Andy were not present, she would talk endlessly, but to me fascinatingly, of herself. If Andy were there she would confine herself to more general topics and it was then that I realised how intelligent she was and saw what Andy had meant when he called her a "clever piece". She was hungry for conversation and talked with passion about books, music, art, philosophy, science – any subject that cropped up. But she never gossiped. Humanity, apart from herself, did not interest her enough.

In the afternoons we saw little of her, for then, wet or fine, she would take a book and accompany Robert on his more distant rounds – to her husband's surprise, it seemed, for this apparently was a new habit. Before Newton's death, Robert told us, she had never once come with him on his visitings, but now he could not get her to stay at home, however tedious his round. The house, doubtless, was haunted by the boy and she could not bear to be alone in it.

In the evenings, however, we often met again. Once or twice a week Andy and I, when weather or water or lack of salmon made fishing unprofitable, would drop in at the doctor's house for a cup of coffee or a drink after dinner. On these occasions Elise would seat herself at the piano and play for us. She was a really accomplished performer and Andy, who had at first consented to come with me only with the utmost unwillingness, soon came to enjoy these musical evenings and I rejoiced for his sake.

We saw, of course, considerably less of Robert than of his wife and he remained a bit of an enigma. He was always perfectly pleasant, but neither Andy nor I ever seemed to get any further with him. When Elise played the piano he frankly slept, to his wife's ill-concealed contempt. When the music stopped he would waken, quite unrepentant.

'I am a busy man,' he would say, 'out in the fresh air most of the day and by evening I find it hard to keep my eyes open. And, besides, music always sends me to sleep.'

It was at the morning sessions, alone with her over a cup of tea in the garden or, if it was wet, in the kitchen, that I learned most about Elise. I would ask some question about herself or her family and she would be off.

'I have one brother,' she told me once, 'but for all the good he was to me as a girl I might as well have been an only child. He is five years older than I am and was his mother's darling. She used to call him Jo-Jo – his name is Joseph. He hated that but bore it from Mother. When I called him Jo-Jo, though, he used to get in a rage – in such a rage as to make him almost dangerous, I can't think why. I used to do it to tease him. I still do, and it still makes him angry.'

'What does he do for living now?' I asked.

'Oh, he's in some business,' she said vaguely, as always when it was a question of some matter that did not directly concern herself. 'Something to do with electrical gadgets. He must be rolling in money, but none of it comes my way. You'd think Jo-Jo might be a bit generous seeing that Father left him a good whack when he died and I got nothing. But Jo-Jo's mean. Was as a boy, still is, and always will be. He loves money like a miser.'

'Is your mother still alive?' I remember asking on another occasion.

'Mother? Oh, yes. She married again when Father died. At her age! Imagine! But, of course, she was quite a catch – a rich widow and still not bad looking. She lives in Jamaica somewhere. I never hear from her.'

'I was my father's favourite when I was a child,' she told me another time. 'He was a selfish man who liked his own way but I used to think that I could twist him round my little finger until I came up against him about studying music. I still don't know why he was so determined that I should not. I think it was some notion he had that all artists, of whatever kind, led dissolute lives; he was a terrible prude. All my scenes and cajoling had no effect and to the university I had to go. He was a rich man – a stockbroker – but he kept me very short of money, so I had no choice.'

'What year did you go up?' I remember asking on that occasion, thinking that she might have known my sister, Pat, who had also been a student at London University. However, it appeared that she had been up three years before my sister.

'And for how long did you stick it?' I asked.

'For over a year.'

'Until you met and married Robert?'

'Yes,' she said abruptly, and again, as once before, I found myself up against a brick wall. About Robert, her courtship and marriage she would say nothing.

Thinking over this conversation later, in a desultory way, I suddenly came on what I believed to be the explanation of her willingness to talk of this particular period of her life.

'Why, of course!' I remember exclaiming, as the reason flashed into my mind.

'Of course what?' asked Andy, who was busy tying salmon flies at a table nearby.

'I was thinking about Elise,' I explained, 'and the way she never talks about how she first met Robert.'

'Why should she?' asked Andy.

'Why shouldn't she?' I replied. 'When she's so ... so garrulous you might almost say, about her life up to and after that time.'

'Well, why shouldn't she? You tell me,' said Andy.

'It's Newton, don't you see? If he was fourteen when he died and she was still a student and unmarried two years before Pat went up to London University, that is, just under fourteen years ago, it means that Elise and Robert must have taken a little on account and Newton must have been born either before or just after they were married – too soon, in any case. And, perhaps, that's why Elise's prudish father left her nothing in his will.'

'Oh, you women!' was all Andy's comment.

Apart from these family titbits, the main burden of Elise's talk at our morning tea sessions was the boredom of life at Coedafon.

Robert had taken the assistantship with old Dr Wakes almost immediately after becoming qualified, so that nearly the whole of their married life had been spent in this backwater. Elise hated the country and loathed housework – though she was a good cook – so there was nothing to keep her happily occupied. As long as Newton was alive I suppose he had provided a certain interest, but she never, except by inadvertence, mentioned his name and it was difficult to make out just how fond she had been of him or whether, indeed, she had been fond of him at all. Robert seldom mentioned his son's name either but, when he did so, there was no doubt as to what his sentiments towards the unfortunate boy had been. Robert had, quite obviously, detested his dim-witted son.

One day at the end of June we were invited to a more formal meeting with the Landons; a meeting which in the event gave us a better insight into the situation in that household. The occasion was Robert's birthday and we were invited to evening dinner. It was a Saturday, I remember, and Elise's brother, Joseph, was staying over the weekend. He had come down on business of some sort. To make numbers even – or, perhaps, for some other reason known only to herself – Elise had invited Dr Rachel Brading to be the sixth member of the party. It was a curious evening and by no stretch of the imagination could it have been called enjoyable.

To begin with, Andy made difficulties about going. The evening was perfect for fishing. It had rained on that day and on several days before but, about five o'clock, the rain had cleared off and the whole earth sparkled in the June sunshine. The recent showery weather had brought a run of grilse into the Crib pool and

Andy was champing to try them with a new greased-line fly which he had concocted. Finally, Andy had got wind that there would be strangers present at the dinner, and that always frightened him. However, I was adamant for once and even managed in the end to get him into a tidy suit. Owing to all the argument we were a little late in starting but, even then, Andy would not hurry and, in my impatience, I could not prevent myself from going on a little ahead of him. So it was that I arrived on the doorstep alone and, without pausing, opened the front door to walk in, as I had been in the habit of doing for some weeks past.

I was about to call out that we had arrived when I heard Elise saying in a low voice, tense with fury, 'I don't know how you dare talk to me like that considering ...'

She was at the telephone in the far corner of the hall with her back to the front door but, at that moment, she must have heard me, for she turned her head sharply and for an instant I saw her face above the receiver contorted with rage. For a second she glared at me then, turning her back once more, banged the receiver down on its rest. When she came to meet me her face was once more quite composed but her head and hands were trembling.

'These damned, dunning trades people,' she said. 'You'd think they'd leave one alone on a Saturday evening.'

It seemed a lot of emotion to expend on a grocer. But I had no time to wonder or question, for at that moment Andy arrived and Elise told us to go on into the sitting room and get ourselves drinks while she attended to the dishing-up of the dinner. The company in the sitting room had a far from festive air. Robert, with the preoccupied look on his face which was habitual to him, was pouring himself a stiff gin and tonic at a small table by the door. Rachel Brading, whom I recognised instantly as the woman I had glimpsed in Llantossy churchyard at Newton's funeral, was standing in front of the west window, with the light of the declining sun shining full on her face. She slowly swirled the sherry in her glass as she gazed into the garden and her thoughts were obviously far away. I saw now that she was an attractive woman – not beautiful but well, if somewhat generously, built, with large, dark eyes, filled at that moment, it seemed to me, with a look of profound unhappiness.

The only person completely at his ease was Elise's brother, Joseph Ellis, a pompous, fat man in a navy blue business suit who was swigging pink gin and discoursing loudly on the vagaries of the stock exchange. No wonder Dr Brading looks so sad, I thought to myself, if that's the best "Jo-Jo" can do to entertain her.

Our advent cheered things up a little but not much, for Andy was still sulking and Robert seemed even more silent than usual. However, Dr Brading, Joseph Ellis and I managed to make some show of animation until dinner was announced. Once we were all seated at the table things went a little better. Elise seemed in high spirits; all traces of her rage at the telephone quite dissipated. When Robert had been round filling our glasses with wine she raised hers in the air with a little excited laugh.

'To Robert!' she said and then, looking round the table at us all, 'You must all wish him happiness, one by one. Rachel, you first.'

And Rachel Brading, who was sitting at Robert's right hand,

turned her dark eyes on his face and, raising her glass, said softly: 'To your happiness, Bob.'

Then a curious thing happened. As their glances met it was immediately and embarrassingly clear that these two were head over heels in love. One could almost hear them, in the tension of the moment, crying out to each other, 'I love you, I love you.'

I glanced quickly round to see whether Elise had noticed what was to me so obvious. She had. There was no mistaking her comprehension as she stared at her husband and, once again, I was struck by the intense blue of her eyes. Her expression, however, was not one of surprise, nor of hate, nor rage, nor jealousy; it was an expression, I could have sworn, of glee – I can use no other word. She was amused and pleased with herself, like a child at a practical joke. She laughed again on the high, excited note as before.

'Now you, Jo-Jo,' she said.

And Joseph Ellis, too, raised his glass to Robert, and then Andy mumbled his good wishes and I echoed them and, finally, Elise, spacing and emphasising each word, said, 'And … many … happy … returns to you, Robert,' and, with that she swallowed down her glass of wine at one draught as though it had been spring water on a thirsty day.

The wine had one good effect on us all in that it loosened our tongues and the hitherto dreary party began to show some signs of animation at least, if not jollity. Joseph Ellis, who was on my left, turned out to be a talkative man with something of his sister's egotism, and he regaled me with tales of himself, his house, his car, his wife, and his children. The order of importance of these subjects of conversation appeared to be as listed above and all, of course, were of superlative quality although the expense of their upkeep, it seemed, was appalling. I gathered that, to meet the expense complained of, he was in the habit of playing the stock market and he gave me details of some of his clever coups. Stocks and shares, in fact, were obviously his favourite preoccupation. To me, however, they were not so interesting as to prevent my attention wandering from time to time to the conversations of other members of the party. Andy, I was glad to see, had got over his self-consciousness and ill-temper and was explaining to Elise, at whose left hand he sat, the theory and practice of greased-line fishing for salmon. Elise, though she had every appearance of listening to his discourse, was more interested, it seemed to me, in the low-voiced conversation of Robert and Rachel at the other end of the table. She was stretching her ears, I thought, to catch what they said. Her eyes kept flickering towards them and her comments to Andy were not always very apropos.

'At the instant of taking you must give them line,' I heard Andy say at one moment.

'Give them line?' queried Elise with an appearance of interest.

'Yes, instead of tightening at once you must drop the rod tip and let out the loops of line you've been holding in your hand. In that way, the fish hooks itself as it turns back to its lie.'

On which Elise's rather random comment was: 'It's better to let them hook themselves.'

As for Rachel and Robert, they were deep in reminiscences of their young days, for it appeared that their families had once been next-door neighbours.

'Do you remember my thirteenth birthday?' I heard Robert asking, during a lull in Jo-Jo's stock exchange saga. 'It was the last before I went away to school.'

'Yes, of course,' answered Rachel in a low voice, 'but why do you remind me of that day of all days?'

'You were so angry with me and I've never understood why.'

'Because you were so cruel.'

'Little boys are cruel creatures.'

'Yes, I know that now.'

'I believe you haven't forgiven me, even yet.'

'I have forgiven you, Bob, but I haven't forgotten and I don't believe I ever shall.'

'Was it so terrible?'

'Yes, it was terrible. Don't remind me of it, Bob, please.'

At that moment they suddenly realised that I was listening and both fell silent. Feeling as guilty as though I had been caught eavesdropping behind a door, I rushed in to fill the silence with the first words that came to my tongue.

'So you and Dr Brading are old friends,' I said.

'We were neighbours as children,' said Robert. 'But my family moved to another district when I was fourteen and we lost touch with each other entirely after that.'

'Until Dr Brading came here as your partner,' I said, brightly.

'Yes, that was quite a coincidence,' said Rachel. 'When I answered Bob's advertisement for a partner I had no idea that he would turn out to be the boy next door. I never thought of connecting little Bobby Landon of long ago with Dr Robert Landon, LRCP, of Coedafon.'

She turned a tender look on Robert and their glances met and held for a long moment.

'Was Robert as surprised as you were?' I asked.

Incredulity must have sounded in my voice, for Robert turned quickly to me and said, 'You are thinking Rachel Brading is not so common a name that it could easily be forgotten, but, you see, Rachel's maiden name was not Brading. It was Smith.'

'Oh, oh, I see,' I said. 'I'm so sorry. I had no idea that Dr Brading was married.'

Robert considered me with his cold eyes and seemed about to make some tart rejoinder when Rachel, just touching his hand with a restraining forefinger, leaned across him and said, softly, 'No, of course not, Mrs Marsden. Why should you? You see, my marriage was not a very happy one and two years ago I divorced my husband.'

Then to cover my confusion, she turned the conversation to my own affairs.

'I hear you have taken the cottage next to this house,' she said. 'I hope you are not finding it too primitive.'

I said that both Andy and I rather liked a primitive life and she agreed that there were many compensations for the lack of electricity and piped hot water.

'That, for instance,' and she waved her hand towards the window with its view of trees and meadows, bathed at that moment in evening sunshine and unblemished by a single building.

'Where do you live?' I asked, emboldened by her friendliness to show my interest in her, once more. 'In Llantossy, I suppose, since that is your headquarters.'

'No, unfortunately,' she said, 'I have found it impossible so far to find a decent house in this neighbourhood. My surgery, of course, is in Llantossy but I can't live there because it is just a small, two-roomed lock-up affair which I was allowed to put up on a piece of waste ground beside the police station. The police keep an eye on it for me to see that it isn't broken into and my drugs stolen. But I live and sleep, temporarily at least, in a small cottage on the river bank a mile and a half this side of Llantossy. You must come and see it sometime.'

'I should like to,' I said, and meant it. There was something warm and sincere about Dr Brading which was very attractive. I could not understand how she had ever come to fall in love with that cold fish, Robert Landon.

After dinner we had coffee on the west corner of the terrace in the red light of the setting sun, while a thrush sang to us from one of the orchard trees and, afterwards, Rachel and I helped Elise to clear everything away and wash the dishes. By then it was dusk and, while Rachel and I drifted out again to join the men folk on the terrace, Elise lit an Aladdin lamp in the sitting room, set it on a stand by the piano and sat down to play. I remember that she selected first a Chopin study whose rippling background and plangent chords conjured up images of rivers rushing and plunging through gorges and then broadening out into shallow, purling rapids. Like the Tossy, I thought. After the Chopin she played a lovely thing which I did not know. It brought to mind a summer evening with a crimson sunset, such as we had just seen but, instead of a thrush, a bell seemed to toll in the distance – the Angelus, perhaps. I noticed that tonight her playing did not send Robert to sleep. It bored Joseph, though, and soon he got up and went into the house. His passage through the sitting room must have disturbed Elise, for she stopped playing then and came to the French windows and called to me, 'Meg, Andy tells me you have a lovely voice. Come and sing a song for us.'

'Andy said that!' I exclaimed, surprised and touched that he should have praised me to strangers.

'Yes. Why didn't you tell me before? Come on and do your share of entertaining.'

'Shall I?' I asked Andy.

'Yes, yes, girl. Go on,' he said testily.

So reluctantly I joined Elise.

'What shall I sing?' I asked her.

'Do you know "Drink to me only"?' she asked.

'Yes, of course,' I said, 'but nobody sings such old-fashioned stuff nowadays – and, besides, it's a man's song.'

'I want you to sing it, please,' insisted Elise. 'I would ask Robert,' she added, staring into my eyes, 'but he has a voice like a crow.'

So, thinking with a good deal of embarrassment of the two on the terrace, I embarked on that hardy evergreen to Elise's accompaniment. Before I had finished Joseph opened the door from the hall and stood just inside it waiting, rather impatiently, I thought, for the end of the song and, the moment the last note was sung, he addressed himself to his sister. 'Elise, it's getting late,' he said. 'We must get our business done tonight, because I can't spare another day. I must be off first thing in the morning. I've lit the lamp in the dining room and brought down all the papers.'

'How impatient you are for your money, Jo-Jo. Can't you even wait until my guests have gone?'

'It's your money, too – and don't keep calling me Jo-Jo,' said Joseph irritably.

'All right, come on. Let's get it over,' said Elise, and the two of them went off together into the hall.

It was black dark beyond the light from the windows when I rejoined the party on the terrace.

'Thank you, Meg,' said Rachel's voice out of the darkness as I approached. 'If I may call you Meg,' she added. 'Your name ought to be "Mavis". You sing like a thrush.'

I was ridiculously pleased at the compliment and would have liked to sit and talk with Rachel for a little but, at that moment, a small, dark shape bounded up the terrace steps and into the lamplight. It was Squelch and close on his heels came Curly, and then I remembered that in the hurry of our departure we had forgotten to close the kitchen window. Well, that ended the evening and I left Andy, who had a torch, to start homeward with the dogs while I went to find Elise to make our adieus.

'I know she's in the dining room,' I told Andy, 'attending to some family business with her brother.'

As I opened the dining room door I heard Joseph saying, 'Your share of the capital comes to about nine thousand pounds. You can have it in a lump sum or ...'

'Is that all?' interrupted Elise, and then, suddenly becoming aware of my presence at the door: 'What do you want?'

I seemed to have put my foot in it again and confusedly I explained about the dogs and that we were on our way home and that I had come to thank her for the party.

'Well, goodnight,' she said ungraciously. 'Shut the door when you go out.'

So I did that and took my departure, calling goodnight to Rachel and Robert as I went down the terrace steps. They called back and I knew that, as soon as the darkness had swallowed up my retreating form, they would be in each other's arms.

'Curious piece to choose for a birthday party,' said Andy as I caught him up.

'Which piece was that?' I asked.

'Why, the second piece Elise played, of course. Didn't you recognise it?'

'No,' I confessed. 'What was it?'

'It was that macabre thing by Ravel – supposed to represent the body of a hanged man, illumined by the setting sun, slowly turning on a gibbet, while a passing bell tolls in the distance.'

An odd choice, certainly, for a birthday party!

Chapter 6

THE BLUE TROUSERS

We did not see either of the Landons on the next day, Sunday, but on the Monday morning Elise came in for her usual cup of tea. I remember this occasion particularly because, after it, there was a considerable gap in our almost daily meetings. She seemed in good spirits when she arrived and quite gracious, for her. We talked a little about Saturday's party and then I made the unlucky remark which led to a temporary breaking off of our friendship.

'By the way, Elise,' I said, 'who was the unpleasant tradesman you were talking to when I arrived on Saturday evening?'

To my astonishment, the innocent question seemed to annoy her.

'Mind your own business, Meg Marsden,' she said. 'Of all the nosy parkers in this world you are the worst.'

'It's not just curiosity,' I said, angry too, for once, because my conscience was not quite clear as to this statement, 'but I thought you might not know about Mrs Rees. Not everyone wants their quarrels with tradespeople broadcast to the village.'

'What do you mean? Who's Mrs Rees and what has she got to do with it?'

'Mrs Rees at the post office,' I explained. 'If you were more friendly in the village you would know that she listens to all telephone conversations and probably did to yours on Saturday evening.'

I thought for a moment that Elise was about to pass out with sheer rage. Her eyes blazed and every trace of colour drained out of her face.

'We'll soon see about Mrs Rees,' she said furiously and, leaving her cup of tea unfinished on the kitchen table, she flung out of the house.

I heard the sequel later from Gloria Rees. There had been a terrible scene at the post office with Elise raging at the iniquity of Mrs Rees and the old lady herself reduced to floods of tears.

'If I ever catch you listening in to my telephone conversations,' Elise had stormed, 'or even if I ever learn that private affairs of mine, which could only have been heard of that way, are being discussed in the village I shall have you and your precious daughter removed from here. You have been warned, and don't forget it. And you, Miss Rees,' she continued, turning to the luckless Gloria, 'you are even more to blame than your mother, because she is old and silly, but you ought to know better. You keep your ears and your mouth shut where my affairs are concerned and see that your fool of a mother does the same, or the consequences to you both will, I assure you, be most unpleasant.'

Gloria, submerged under this torrent of rage, had not had a word to say for herself and, as for poor old Mrs Rees, she had taken to her bed, more in mortification at being called a silly old fool than from any feeling of guilt at her misdoing. I must say that my sympathies were a little with Elise and I strongly advised Gloria to keep this episode as quiet as possible and to attend to the telephone herself in future.

Usually Elise did not bear malice, nor did she easily take offence; she was too insensitive to the feelings of others to realise how rude she often was, and too sure of herself and her own righteousness to be much affected by answering rudeness. It was difficult to quarrel with Elise, but this time I seemed to have succeeded, for there was an interval of several weeks before we saw her again – to my regret.

Meanwhile, an event occurred which altered the whole atmosphere of our life at Coedafon and overshadowed our carefree days with uneasiness and, even, fear. It was a small happening but it gave rise to a sinister suspicion which grew and grew until, at last, amid scenes of violence and horror, it turned into a terrible certainty.

The weather was the cause of it. May and June had, on the whole, been months of abundant sunshine and such rain as had fallen had been light and sporadic, so that the river, throughout those months, ran low and clear with only a slight rise occasionally after a day of showers. At the beginning of July, however, a persistent wind from the south-west brought weather more typical of autumn than of midsummer. Day after day black clouds came rolling up over the Welsh mountains and heavy rain drove up the valley of the Tossy, lashing the surface of the river into white spume, flattening the ripe hay in the water meadows and shattering the roses in the cottage gardens. Every salmon in the river was on the move, running upstream to the spawning grounds. At the beginning of the bad weather it was still possible to catch an occasional fish as it rested briefly in the Crib pool but, later, as the river rose and became more and more discoloured by floodwater from the hills and by washings from the banks, all fishing came to a standstill. For more than a week Andy never had a rod in his hand but sat, a dog on each side of him, glowering at the kitchen fire. At last, however, the wind blew itself out and, suddenly, on an evening about the middle of July, the clouds broke and a glorious sun shone out on a dripping and glittering world.

'The sun, Andy!' I called from the kitchen door. 'Come out and have look at the river!'

In a moment he and the dogs joined me and we made our way down the garden to the river bank. The Tossy was a sorry sight, its dark brown waters swirling bank high and strewn with debris. As we watched, the corpse of a chicken swept by, preceded by an empty petrol tin and pursued by a large tree branch. Foam-edged rafts of dead grass and twigs, mixed with every kind of refuse, revolved slowly in the backwaters. Then a running fish porpoised suddenly in midstream.

'We'll go fishing tomorrow morning early,' decided Andy.

A fateful decision.

'The fish'll never see anything in this,' I protested.

'I'll try them with a big gold minnow,' said Andy, 'or, better still, a couple of fat worms trundled along the bottom over their noses.'

He went off, happy as a schoolboy, to dig for worms in the compost heap, while the dogs and I hunted the banks for rats.

We were out of bed at first light next morning and reached the Crib pool just as the sun topped the steep and wooded eastern slope of the valley. A thick, white mist still shrouded the river when we arrived but the first rays of the sun soon dissolved it, and we saw then that the water, though it had gone down and cleared a little in the night, was still so thick and high that a successful morning's fishing was extremely unlikely. However, there were salmon in the pool, as was proved by a splashy rise on the edge of the backwater behind the Crib.

'If the fish are there,' said Andy, 'you never know but that one might be silly enough to get itself hooked. So here goes.'

With that, he put his spinning rod together, selected his brightest gold minnow and made his first cast, well above the neck of the pool. The dogs and I sat and watched him make his slow, methodical way down river: three casts from each stance and two steps down between the stances, letting the minnow linger a little at the end of each cast before reeling in for the next. The neck of the pool brought no result and he walked out onto the Crib itself in order to cover the rest of the pool from that position. His first cast was a short one, round the point of the Crib and into the backwater behind it. At the end of the cast the minnow, with its triangle of barbed hooks at the tail, dangled for a moment at the edge of the stream, and then Andy raised the rod point preparatory to retrieving his bait. But, at that moment, I heard the scream of the reel and saw the line streaming out down the current.

'He's on!' shouted Andy.

The dogs and I ran down to the water's edge to get a closer view, Curly, as usual, wild with excitement. But there was something wrong. The fish was not behaving as it should.

'Is he foul-hooked?' I shouted.

'No, blast it!' Andy called back. 'It isn't a fish at all. It's a snag of some kind.'

As he started to reel in his line a dark, inanimate object was forced up to the surface of the water by the drag of the heavy current. Just as the object reached the backwater, the hooks came away and it began to drift back into midstream. This was too much for Curly and, with a yelp of excitement, she plunged in after it.

'Curly, you damn fool, come out!' yelled Andy.

But Curly was past reason. She is a strong swimmer and soon she overtook the object, which now had a long, snaky appearance, and, fastening her teeth into one end of it, proudly brought it ashore and laid it at my feet.

'What is it?' called Andy.

'I think it's a pair of trousers.'

'Chuck 'em back in, but don't let that damn dog go after them again. I'm going to have another try and let's hope all the salmon haven't been frightened to hell.' And Andy prepared once more to cast across the pool.

I was holding the dripping garment at arm's length by the waistband and was just preparing to comply with Andy's instructions when my eye fell on a long rent in the right knee, carelessly cobbled together with thread. There was something familiar about that rent and that cobbling and, in a flash, I realised that the trousers I was holding in my hand were the same as those I had mended for the Newt on the afternoon of his death. That was my mending, I could swear it.

'They're Newt's trousers,' I called out.

'What of it?' shouted Andy, absorbed in his fishing.

What of it? Well, I wasn't sure. But, it was queer, and I wrung the trousers out and laid them on the grass, determined to make certain that they really were the Newt's. The material had certainly at one time been blue corduroy, such as Newt had been wearing that day; the colour could still be seen in streaks and patches. It was a fairly uncommon colour for corduroy but not, of course, unique. The coarse pack-thread holding together the edges of the tear seemed to be similar to that I had used, though its original colour was a little uncertain. The tear was the same shape. But it was when I put my hand into the right-hand pocket that I got my final proof, for I drew out from the bottom of the pocket a small, sodden wad of toffee papers, and immediately I had a vision of myself running down the garden path and thrusting a handful of toffees into the boy's trouser pocket as he went through the hedge. How many toffees had I given him? About half a dozen, I thought. Carefully, I sorted out the little wad in my hand. There were four papers, empty and flat, of course, the toffee all dissolved by the water, but still twisted at each end. He must have eaten two, at least, of the sweets before he died. The other pocket yielded three little lead squares of different sizes, such as are used to weight a salmon spinning line, and a small tin of the kind that cough lozenges are sold in, now much rusted by the water. Forced open, this disclosed four sodden and rusty salmon flies. Here was proof that the wearer of the trousers had almost certainly been a salmon fisherman – no common thing among boys of this size, even on Coedafon water, where the fishing itself is free. The finances of small boys do not usually stretch to the purchase of the necessary licence, let alone the expensive tackle needed for the catching of salmon. So these had been the Newt's trousers; there was no shadow of doubt in my mind. But, how came they to be knocking around in the backwater behind the Crib – not ten yards from where the boy's naked body had been found – when I had last seen them, as I thought, lying neatly folded on the coroner's table in Carne? What happened to his clothes after the inquest? It seemed a queer thing for anyone to do to throw them in the river. I had got so far in my cogitation when Andy joined me with a dejected air.

'No good,' he said. 'The water's too thick. Might as well pack up and go home.'

But he was obviously unwilling to leave.

'The fish are there all right,' he mused, 'and some whoppers among them. The one in the lie behind the Crib must weigh thirty pounds if he weighs an ounce. Think I'll just try bobbing a worm on his nose before we go home to breakfast.'

He sat down and, pulling his fishing bag towards him, started to change his tackle.

'Look, Andy,' I said, 'those trousers definitely belonged to the Newt.'

'Trousers? What trousers? What are you talking about, girl?'

'The ones Curly retrieved from the river.'

'Good God, you're not still brooding over those, are you?'

'It's jolly queer, Andy, you must admit.'

'Queer? Why?'

'The boy was wearing those trousers the day he was drowned

and they were found afterwards by the plank bridge. How do they come to be in the Crib pool now?'

'How can you possibly know that they are that wretched Newton's trousers?'

I explained about the rent and the toffee papers.

'The boy probably threw them in the river himself. He was a queer fish, by all accounts.'

'But I tell you, they were found on the bank and I myself actually saw them at the inquest after he was dead.'

'Perhaps Elise dumped them in the dust-bin and some nosing dog pulled them out and dragged them to the river. It isn't far from the house.'

'There are no dustbins here. You burn your rubbish, or you bury it.'

'Well, search me,' said Andy. 'I'm going to try this whopper with a worm.'

He limped off, his thoughts already back with his beloved fish. Oh, well, I thought, there must be some explanation, but what does it matter, and I found myself a comfortable seat under the bank and settled down to watch the progress of the fishing – if you could call it progress. The sun was well up by now but, even so, it was chilly sitting on the damp grass, and the dogs were getting restless, so I rose presently and strolled up and down the bank – upstream from the pool so as not to scare Andy's fish. Still thinking of breakfast, I looked at my watch: it was eight o'clock and, punctual to the minute, I saw Cliff Price, bailiff, leave his cottage beside the Ferryman to start his daily round. At first, he made to go upriver, but then turned and came in our direction, obviously to pass the time of day and enquire after the fishing. We met on the bank above the Crib.

'Lovely day!' I called out.

'Ar, that'll be hot in a coupla hours. River's a proper mess, though. Your good man fishing for eels?'

'For a big fish lying behind the point,' I said.

'What, in that there!' indicating the river. 'Fish wouldn't see a blinkin' battleship.'

Cliff gazed in astonishment at my husband's fanatic figure still plying his rod from the point of the Crib. But, even as we looked, the rod bent into an arc and we heard a short screech from the reel.

''E's into summat!' exclaimed Cliff in an unbelieving tone. 'No, 'e ent though,' he added, as we saw the rod being shaken to and fro. ''Tis a snag. River's full of rubbish today. Flood's shifted a lot of muck – and muck's about all as 'e'll catch if you was to ask me.'

I thought of the "muck" that he had already caught that morning and my eyes turned automatically to the trousers spread under the bank to dry. I saw Cliff's eyes follow mine, but, for some reason – I do not know why – I made no comment on them. It did, however, occur to me that Cliff Price might know something about those trousers.

'Cliff,' I said. 'You remember the day young Newton Landon was drowned?'

'Ar,' said Cliff, and to my surprise a wary look came into his eyes.

'It was you who found his clothes on the bank, wasn't it?'

'It was.'

'Did you, by any chance, look at them closely?'

'Ar, I looked at en.'

'Do you remember what the trousers were like?'

'Blue corduroy, they was.'

'With a rent in the right knee that had been mended?'

'Rent? Weren't no rent as I seen.'

'No rent?' I asked in surprise. 'Are you sure?'

'What are you getting at Mrs Marsden?' he asked, uneasily. 'Weren't no rent in them trousers. Good as new they was. That I'll swear.'

No rent! The mystery deepened. Was Cliff Price lying? His manner was certainly not expansive – almost as though he had something to hide – and very different from what it had been when he was telling his tale that first evening in the Ferryman. Then he had been only too willing to go into every detail. But, what possible reason could he have for lying?

'What you want to know for?' I heard Cliff asking.

Rapidly I debated in my mind whether or not to show him our find and decided against it. I wanted to think things out a little further and, also, I was unwilling to start rumours in the village.

'Just curiosity,' I said.

Cliff looked at me searchingly and seemed to be about to ask something further but, finally, all he said was: 'Well, I must be getting along,' and, turning on his heel, he strode off towards the village.

When I looked back to the Crib I saw that Andy was packing up his tackle at last.

'No good,' he said, gloomily, as he joined me. 'We'll have to leave it until tomorrow.'

The trousers were still lying on the bank where I had left them. The sun had dried them out considerably and, as I started to fold them up, I came on the still sodden toffee papers lying under one leg. I put these into the little rusty tin with the salmon flies and shoved the tin into one of the pockets of the trousers.

'You're surely not going to take that old rag home, are you, Meg?' asked Andy, noticing my activities.

'Yes, I am. There's something jolly fishy about it. I want to discuss it sensibly with you, Andy. No joking.'

'Still worrying how they got in the river?'

'Yes. And it's even more mysterious than you know, because Cliff Price says the trousers he found on the bank definitely weren't torn.'

'I saw you talking to Cliff and wondered what you were nattering about so earnestly. So you were telling him about your treasure trove?'

'No, I didn't tell him, though I'm afraid he may have guessed. And, Andy, I don't think we should mention it in the village.'

Andy laughed.

'Meg, you really are priceless. It would never have entered my head to mention to anyone that I'd foul-hooked a pair of old trousers. How did you get round to the subject with Cliff, if you didn't mention your find?'

'I just asked him about the clothes he found on the bank.'

'Apropos of nothing?'

'Yes.'

'He must have wondered what on earth you were getting at. The Landon boy's death is no longer what you might call red-hot news.'

'As a matter of fact, Cliff acted pretty queerly, I thought.'

Andy laughed again. 'My God! More mysteries! No wonder he acted queerly. He must have thought he was talking to a lunatic.'

'All right,' I said in a huff. 'Have your fun. I know you're not interested in anything but your damned fishing. I'm just something to be laughed at and everything I do is excruciatingly funny. Granted.'

I started to walk briskly homewards with the trousers under my arm. I had not gone far, though, before my heart misgave me and, when I turned and saw Andy limping after me, dejected and laden with tackle, the last trace of my huffiness vanished and I waited for him to catch me up.

'Sorry, old girl,' he said as he came up. 'I didn't mean to hurt your feelings.'

'I know,' I said, and we smiled at each other, and everything was all right.

The trousers were not mentioned again until the evening. I had them out drying in the sun all day in a place old Milly Piggott could not see them and, after tea, when Andy was comfortably settled with a book under the pear tree – no tackle-making today, for once, and no more talk of fishing – I had another good look at them. It was then that I noticed another odd detail. In the middle of the waistband at the back there was a second tear; a small ragged puncture pierced through both thicknesses of the material as though something sharp and pointed had been pushed through at that place. As I looked at the small, frayed hole I suddenly seemed to hear Dr Yorke's languid voice at the inquest saying 'The only external injury was a slight abrasion in the lumbar region,' or words to that effect, and I wondered whether that scratch at the base of the spine would have corresponded to this puncture in the waistband of the trousers. I remembered that the coroner had then asked whether a tree branch could have caused the abrasion. Dr Yorke had thought that it might have done so if the branch were sharp enough. Sharp enough. It would have had to be a very sharp branch indeed and a very strong one for its small diameter to have caused the hole in the trousers. Well, where was all this leading? Either the scratch and the tear had both been caused before the boy had entered the water, which seemed unlikely as it was queer place for an accidental injury on dry land, or else the boy had been wearing the trousers when the branch, or whatever it was, had caught him while he was swimming in the water. But, the trousers on the bank had been quite dry and the boy's body, when found, had been quite naked. It was all beyond me.

Suddenly I made up my mind. I would take the trousers up to PC Jones at the Bungalow and the police could decide whether there was anything worth investigating. Jones would be at home by now, unless he was on late duty and I preferred to go to him rather than to the police station at Llantossy; partly because I thought I might change my mind before morning, and partly because I was afraid of looking a fool in the eyes of the forbidding sergeant at Llantossy. So I bundled the trousers up and put them in a large brown paper bag and called out to Andy that I should be back in half an hour or so and to keep the dogs from following me.

'Where are you off to, Meg?' he shouted.

'Tell you later,' I shouted back. I did not want Milly Piggott to know my business.

At the Bungalow the door was opened to me by the constable's sister, Mrs Blodwen Jones. Her brother was in the back garden, planting out cabbages and she said she'd call him. Having done so she returned and showed me into the "front room", in this case a room facing to the side of the house and quite uninhabited from year's end to year's end, except on very special occasions. It was – or, rather, is, because although I have never seen it again, it must still be there, dozing its useless life away behind its lace curtains – furnished with a sitting-room suite upholstered in bottle green plushette with the matching cushions covered, against possible contamination, with squares of white crochet work, the labour of Blodwen's hands. In the hearth a fan of white paper hides the evidently shocking nakedness of the grate and on the mantlepiece above stand two white alabaster figures, decently draped, and a black marble clock. On the walls hang photographs, much enlarged and brown-spotted with the years, of former Joneses and, as a focal point of interest, an enormous print, coloured in blue, black and orange, of Vesuvius in eruption. A depressing spot.

'Set down, do, Mrs Marsden,' said Mrs Jones, moving a chair cushion an inch or two off the straight and obviously all set for a good gossip.

'Evan won't be no more than a minute or two. Just so as he can wash 'is 'ands and get 'is uniform.'

'How's Leslie?' I asked her, casting around in my mind for something to talk about.

'Ever so well, thank you, Mrs Marsden. That turn he had – back in May, 'twas – never come to nothing and doctor say now he'll mebbe grow out of 'em. Never bin so long afore without a turn. Evan, he say 'tis along of that Newton Landon being gone. A torment he was to our Leslie. They do say, speak no ill of the dead, but that Newton – well – set us all by the ears 'ereabout, he did. Not one but wished 'im out of the way.'

'I think, perhaps, he was not quite right in the head,' I said placatingly.

'Ar, you're right, he wasn't. The things 'e done up at the farm – me sister's place – you wouldn't credit. Cut the tails off of the old sow's farrow, one time, and tormented their Billy just like 'e done our Leslie. Trev, though, 'e caught 'im that time with the piglings and give 'im a thrashing as near took the hide off him.'

'Well, I daresay giving him a good hiding taught him more than taking him before the magistrate would have done,' I commented, 'but didn't Dr Landon complain?'

'Not that I heard of. Evan, though, he carried on about it. Said as Trev coulda bin took up for assault, or summat. Not but what I seen Evan give the boy a clout one time he was tormenting our

Leslie. Got our poor lamb 'ooked through the pants with a fish-hook and makin' 'im run up and down like 'e was a fish. My! Evan weren't 'alf mad!'

At this moment a heavy footstep sounded at the door and Evan himself appeared buttoning his uniform tunic. Mrs Jones tactfully vanished and, the necessary civilities exchanged, I started to unfold my tale to the constable. I found it very difficult and the further I went in it the thinner it sounded. I got no help from PC Jones. He listened impassively and made no comments.

'You got those trousers with you?' he asked when I had come to the end of my story.

'Yes,' I said, indicating the paper bag.

'Well, let's have a look at 'em. I can tell you if it's the same ones as was found on the bank. I took 'em off Cliff Price and kept 'em till after the inquest when I give 'em to Mrs Landon.'

So I produced my exhibit and the constable looked it over with care.

'These here are some old rubbish,' he said finally. 'Them as the boy was wearing was near new. Different pair altogether. Threw these in the river himself, likely.'

'But I saw him in these that very afternoon,' I protested.

''Bout two o'clock, you said? But he weren't found till half-past six. Plenty of time to go home and change 'em.'

'And the tear in the back?'

'Could 'ave 'appened any time.'

'Yes, I suppose so,' I said doubtfully, and was going on to object that no-one had seen him at the doctor's house that afternoon although Mrs Landon had been at home, when the constable interrupted me abruptly. 'You want my advice?' he asked.

'That's what I came for,' I said.

'Then you leave this lot with me and go you home and think no more about it.'

'Perhaps I will – but I'll take the trousers with me,' I said firmly.

Suddenly, to my astonishment, PC Jones was angry.

'You much better leave me burn 'em,' he said, getting up from his chair and towering over me. 'Wat you want stirring up trouble for? That Newton was a wicked limb. He drowned and he's buried. Let 'im lie.'

'I expect you're right,' I said, rising too, 'but I'll take the trousers,' and I packed them roughly back into the paper bag.

I thought for a moment that the constable was going to snatch them from my hand and his prominent teeth seemed to snarl at me with rage. For a moment I was frightened, but he made no attempt to prevent me as I pushed past him to the door. As I reached it, however, he suddenly called: 'Stop,' and I turned to face him with my hand on the door-knob. 'If I hears any slanders going round the village,' he said in a low, furious tone, 'I shall know who started 'em. There's a law against that kinda tattling and don't forget it. And another thing. I'm off duty at the present minute and there's no note made in my book of what's bin said in this room. So don't think to go making trouble for me at Llantossy. Reckon they'd take my word afore yours.'

'I'll remember what you say, Constable Jones,' I said and made my exit with as much dignity as I could muster.

Andy was full of curiosity – for once – when I arrived home, out of breath and indignant, but still clutching my brown paper bag.

'Where have you been, Meg? he asked. 'You look upset. What's the matter?'

'Come inside,' I said, 'and I'll tell you.'

In the kitchen, safe from prying eyes and ears, I told Andy about Constable Jones.

'He threatened you, did he!' said Andy grimly.

'Yes, he definitely did.'

'Now, I wonder why. You'd certainly think that a village constable would be quite pleased, rather than the reverse, to have something more exciting to investigate than a case of sheep-running or shooting without a licence. Most unnatural!'

'So you do admit at last that there is something a bit unnatural about all this?'

'Well, I'm beginning to think perhaps you're right, Meg. Tell me what Cliff Price said to you this morning.'

So I told him.

'Both the constable and Cliff agree, then, that these were not the trousers left on the bank. Cliff wasn't lying to you – unless the two of them are in collusion, but that seems unlikely, to say the least. Could the boy, I wonder, have gone home and changed, as Jones suggested, between the time you saw him and the time he was drowned?'

'Why should he do that?'

'He might have fallen in earlier in the afternoon and got wet.'

'Then Elise must either have seen him or, at least, found his wet clothes, and, surely, she would have mentioned that.'

'He might have thrown them in the river. He seems to have been pretty weak-minded.'

'Not so weak-minded as to throw away about a pound's worth of his precious tackle.'

'How do you make that out?'

'The tin box in the pocket. It had four salmon flies in it.'

'Perhaps Elise threw the trousers away after the boy's death.'

'Perhaps, but it seems a funny place to throw them.'

'Let's have another look at this famous garment.'

So I pulled out the trousers and laid them on the kitchen table. I pointed out the hole in the waistband, about which so far I had said nothing to Andy, and explained how it seemed to correspond to the scratch Dr Yorke had mentioned at the inquest.

'Did you tell the constable about this hole?'

'Yes.'

'That could be what he was worried about,' said Andy thoughtfully. 'What exactly are we working around to in all this?' he went on, thinking to himself. 'That young Newton was not naked when he was drowned, but was wearing these trousers. That, afterwards, he was stripped and dry trousers substituted for these and left on the bank. Why should he be stripped? How came it that there was a pair of blue corduroy trousers similar to these all ready to hand?'

'We don't know the answers to those questions.'

'No, nor to dozens of others, but we'll have to find the answers, because you see where all this is leading?'

'Well, no – not exactly.'

'*If* the boy was stripped, and *if* whoever stripped him was already equipped with a spare pair of trousers, then Newton Landon's death was no accident but – premeditated murder.'

Chapter 7

SUSPECTS

Premeditated murder! I looked at Andy, aghast. I suppose it was what had been at the back of my mind all along; ever since I had seen that rent, mended by my own hands, and those toffee papers; but put into words like that it sounded horrible and incredible.

'You'd better take this rag to the Llantossy police,' I said, suddenly anxious to get rid of the gruesome thing.

'And be the laughing stock of the village?' said Andy. 'Can't you imagine the story the good sergeant would make of it over a pint of ale? No. First we'll find the answers to some of our questions, then when, if ever, we have something of a case, we'll look higher than the sergeant and write direct to the chief constable. That'll put a spoke in Jones' wheel – if he's got a wheel to put a spoke into, if you see what I mean.'

'I can't believe a policeman would be mixed up in a thing like this,' I said.

'Perhaps not, but he bullied you and I mean to get my own back on him for that. Nobody's allowed to bully my wife but myself! Now, let's think of what questions we want answered.'

'Well, first of all,' I said, 'did Elise see Newton that afternoon after two o'clock, or did she find any wet clothes?'

'Yes, that's the first query. Then what happened to the boy's clothes after the inquest? That's two. Now, thirdly, did Newton have a second pair of blue corduroy trousers?'

'Those are all questions to ask Elise,' I said. 'They're a bit awkward, because she never talks of Newton, but I daresay I can work round to the subject somehow – if I ever get friendly with her again. She doesn't seem to have got over her huff yet.'

'Meg, for heaven's sake be careful how you ask your questions,' said Andy earnestly. 'Don't go ram-stam at it like you did this morning with Cliff. Remember, there's probably a murderer about in the village. And don't tell anyone – anyone at all – about finding these trousers. It's a pity Jones knows, but it can't be helped. And possibly Cliff Price knows, too, if he noticed the things spread out on the bank. Now, what else do we want to know? What about motive?'

'There's plenty of that around,' I said. 'Practically everybody in the village seems to have wanted the poor boy out of this world for one reason or another.'

'For instance?'

'For instance, Cliff Price, because Newton pushed him into the river and nearly succeeded in drowning *him*, and because the boy was the bane of Cliff's life with his poaching. Then there's Trev Price at the farm. He's threatened the boy with violence more than once, and even gave him a good hiding on one occasion for cruelty to his animals and for tormenting his son, Billy. And, of course, PC Evan Jones and his sister, Blodwen, for the way he treated young Leslie. Those are some I know of and there are probably many more.'

'All pretty weak motives,' said Andy. 'You don't kill a boy for that sort of thing.'

'Not in a town, perhaps, but the motives of country people are queer, especially in a closed, inbred little community like this.'

'Perhaps you're right,' said Andy. 'I'll delve about a bit at the Ferryman and see if I can unearth anything a bit stronger there. What about family motives?'

'Well, Robert obviously disliked his son, but in this case I think you really might say that was insufficient motive for killing him. After all, Robert's a civilised and highly educated person, though he is a bit of a cold fish. Besides, being a doctor, he could have found a better way of killing him than drowning. Elise hasn't a vestige of a motive that I know of and in any case I can't imagine her, with her artistic temperament, going so barbarously about the murder of her own son.'

'Hmm, not much there. What about opportunity?'

'Do you realise, Andy,' I said, 'that we don't even know the exact time of the boy's death? It was never enquired into, let alone established, at the inquest.'

'Robert might know how long he had been dead when he first examined him.'

'He might, but who is going to ask him? Not me!'

'Um, yes. It would be a bit tricky. Let's see whether we can't work it out for ourselves. What time do you think it was when you and Milly Piggott saw the boy going upriver?'

'I think it was about three fifteen. I remember calculating it out before I went to the inquest in Carne, when everything was still fresh in my mind and Milly agreed with me.'

'A quarter past three – well that sets one limit, and he was found at half-past six. But he didn't turn up for his tea, though he was expected. Under the circumstances the likelihood is that he didn't turn up because he was dead. It's not certain, but it's likely. Tea at the Landon's house, when they have it at all, is at four o'clock. So that sets the other limit roughly.'

'I think we can narrow it even further,' I said. 'How long would you say it would take to fish the lie at the plank footbridge?'

'It depends upon how persistent you are, but I can't imagine a boy of that age and temperament taking more than about fifteen minutes. There's only one lie, after all.'

'He must have been killed while he was fishing that lie. So give him about five minutes to get from here to the bridge and the limits are now between three twenty and three twenty-five.'

'Clever girl! Just look where one can get by using a little common sense,' said Andy, and his face was alight with an interest and excitement I had not seen for years. He was Man, the Hunter, hot on the trail.

But as for me, I was frightened.

'I don't like it, Andy,' I said. 'It's all guesswork. Let's drop the whole thing and burn the beastly trousers.'

He looked at me in astonishment.

'But it was you, Meg, who were so insistent on starting this hare.'

'I know,' I said, 'but I thought it would be a matter for the police to deal with. It's horrible to think of going about the village suspecting everyone and trying to hunt them down – by guesswork – some probably perfectly innocent person. It gives me the creeps.'

'Not guesswork. Perfectly sound deduction, though perhaps the premises are a bit shaky,' he conceded. 'Let's leave it for the moment. Don't think of it any more but come out with me and see if we can pick up a couple of trout for supper.'

So I packed the trousers away, wishing, I must confess, that I had never set eyes on the troublesome things, and got my trout rod and accompanied Andy down to the river, which had fined down considerably in the course of the day. However, whether because the water was still too thick or because our minds were not on the job, we caught nothing and soon I was overcome by an intolerable sleepiness and insisted on returning home to supper and to bed. It had been quite a long day!

In the sober light of the following morning our suspicions began to look a little silly, but Andy managed to persuade me in the end that we ought, nevertheless, to try and find the answers to our questions if we could and, also, by discreet inquiry, attempt to establish alibis for some of our suspects for the crucial period between 3.20 and 3.25. Andy had by this time become a fairly regular customer at the Ferryman, dropping in most evenings about opening time for a pint before supper. Now he changed his habits slightly and timed his visits for the half hour before closing time when tongues would be apt to be loosened and distrust of "London gentry" at its least acute. It was not difficult, apparently, to get Tom Todd's customers, and especially the few women who frequented the pub, to indulge in reminiscence of the Newt and his ways. He had become, it seems, a legend of juvenile delinquency in the village and tales of his unpleasant pranks were legion. None, however, indicated a motive for killing the boy any stronger than those we already knew of – indeed, none was so strong. On motive the Trevor Price/PC Jones family – Mrs Price, remember, is the sister of Mrs Blodwen Jones and her brother, the constable – seemed to head the list of suspects. The two children in these households, young Billy Price and Les Jones, indicated at least that mental instability was in the Jones' blood and, in other members of the family, it might come out in a murderous form. A sane and sufficient motive need not then be looked for. This argument, of course, did not apply to Trevor Price himself, but there might conceivably, we thought, be some sort of family conspiracy in which Trev was involved.

As Andy was outlining this theory to me one night in bed, a long-forgotten encounter came suddenly into my mind. It was the meeting with Mrs Blodwen Jones and young Leslie in the doctor's waiting room on the evening of Newton's death. It was the evening, too, of Leslie's last "queer turn" and I remembered Mrs Jones' account of it. She and Leslie had been returning from a visit to her sister at the farm and had reached the point where the stream that enters the river at the plank footbridge crosses the lane when Leslie had disappeared from her side. Later he had been found crying in the village.

'Andy,' I said in sudden excitement, 'do you think Leslie could have seen the murder? It's not far from the water splash in the lane to the river bank. You've only to follow the stream down the side of the doctor's garden. When he disappeared perhaps that's where he went. And another thing. The "turn" never came to anything, so it looks as though it may have been more of a fright than a fit.'

'What time did all this happen, do you remember?'

'The time must have been about right. It was in the afternoon, I know, and I seem to remember Mrs Jones saying that she had gone out to look for the boy about four o'clock, when he had been missing longer than it would have taken him to get home from the lane.'

'What was she doing to mislay her precious offspring like that? The boy can't have just de-materialised from her side suddenly.'

What was she doing? I tried to think back to that casual conversation, and suddenly remembered: 'She had stepped aside through the gate by the brook to have a word with Trev who was dealing with mole hills in the hay meadow. But he wasn't there.'

'Who wasn't there?'

'Trev wasn't.'

'But he should have been?'

'Apparently.'

'So perhaps he was down on the river bank murdering the Newt.'

'Perhaps.'

'And Leslie saw his uncle so occupied?'

'Could be. It's possible.'

'But not very probable,' Andy decided, after a pause for thought. 'How did Trev know that Newton would be fishing at the plank bridge? And what about the spare pair of trousers?'

'Trev knew that the boy had gone fishing that afternoon,' I said. I remember that in all the talk before the inquest it was mentioned somehow – I'm not sure by whom – that Trev Price had seen Newton leaving the Landon's house with his fishing rod about two o'clock. In what circumstances, I don't know. He may have lain in wait for him afterwards on the river path.'

'And the trousers?'

'They don't fit in anywhere. All the same, I feel sure that Leslie's "turn" had some connection with the murder – if there was a murder.'

'I wish we could make the boy talk.'

'You never will. He's perfectly inarticulate.'

Another odd circumstance about the talk in the pub, Andy told me on another occasion, was that only Trev Price and his namesake, Cliff Price, bailiff, of those who had suffered at Newton's hands had now no anecdotes to contribute concerning the boy. This was the more curious in that these two had, apparently, before Newton's death been the loudest and longest in their complaints. The bailiff, who we had once heard describing in great detail the finding of the Newt's rod and line, now even went to the length of leaving the bar as soon as the boy's name was mentioned.

'The two Prices both behave as though they have guilty consciences. Each has something to hide, I feel sure,' said Andy.

Cliff Price, bailiff, was, of course, quite an acquaintance of ours since we ran into him constantly on the river bank and, before my early morning encounter with him at the Crib pool, had always gone out of his way to stop and pass the time of day if he saw us in the course of his rounds, but after that encounter he seemed to avoid us or, if he met us face to face, he would pass on with no more than a polite 'Good day'.

Of the bailiff's private life we knew nothing until Andy

visited the Ferryman before lunch one day in order to replenish our supply of bottled beer. Cliff Price was in the bar – the only customer – but when he saw Andy he quickly drained his glass and went out with no more than a curt 'Good morning'.

'What's biting our bailiff? Seems to be in a bit of a mood these days,' said Andy to Tom Todd, who was behind the bar.

'You don't want to take no notice of him. He'll work it off,' said Tom. 'Allays was a rum 'un. Up in the air one minute, laughing and joking and telling the tale and the next minute mum as a slug. Like it as a boy, he was, and hasn't changed none since for all his foreign travel and his commando capers.'

'You knew him as boy, then?'

'Yes, surely. Big family of Prices there was in them days – all as like as peas in a pod. Same tow hair all of 'em had, girls and boys. Cliff and Margy is the only ones left now, though. Margy married Bill Scroggs, chicken farmer, up by Big House there.'

'What happened to them all?'

'We-ell. there was a bit of a rumpus. First year of the war it was. Cliff's dad he took up with one of these here Land Girls. Big, handsome chap he was – farmed a hundred acres t'other side of the river. Missus caught the two of them at it and old Price he up and hit her over the head with a goat's tethering peg – near killed her. Run off with the girl and ent bin heard of since. Cliff's mam, she wouldn't prosecute and, after, she went back to Worcester, where she come from, and took the kids along of her – all bar Margy, that is, who was Mrs Scroggs by then, and Cliff, who was in the army.'

'Any relations of Trevor Price, farmer?'

'Well, not to say relations. Second cousins or summat of that. You've nobbut to look at Trev Price to see as there's no near blood. Little and dark is Trev: a proper little Welsh runt,' said Tom, who is six-foot tall and weighs sixteen stone..

'Is Cliff married?' asked Andy.

'No, does for 'isself in the cottage alongside of here. My wife she've offered to pop in and do his chores and that, but seems he don't hold with wimmin. Where there's wimmin there's trouble he do say. Fond of kids, though.'

'But not, by all accounts, of the doctor's son that was drowned?'

'The Newt? No. Learned the boy to fish, though, he did and never got no thanks for it.'

'Cliff was patrolling this stretch of the river on the afternoon of the accident, wasn't he?'

'Ar, down t'other bank. I seen him go on up around three. Boy was fishing the Crib then.'

'Pity he didn't go up this bank a little later. He might have saved the boy's life.'

'You might say 'twas a pity,' said Tom Todd, 'or you might not.'

'So you see,' said Andy, reporting the conversation to me later, 'Cliff Price knew that the Newt was fishing that afternoon, and he was in the vicinity. On the far side of the river, it's true, but he could easily have doubled back over the bridge, picked up the dry trousers from his cottage, and gone up to the plank bridge to waylay the boy on his way back to tea.'

'What! and not be seen – in broad daylight on a fine May afternoon?'

'He may well have been seen on the bridge, but nobody would think anything of it. After the bridge, if he avoided the footpath and kept under the river bank, he'd be quite invisible from the village. And, another thing, he knew better than anybody about the Newt's habit of diving for his tackle. His motive is the strongest, too. An ex-commando can't enjoy being tipped into the river by a half-witted small boy. His pride would be hurt, and life was cheap to those lads. He may have thought that the Newt would be no loss to anyone. Or, he may not have intended to kill him, only to give him a fright.'

'He must have meant to kill him if he really came prepared with a pair of dry trousers.'

'True.'

Once again the horrible certainty came over us that among our acquaintances there was one who was a murderer, a deliberate killer. Was it Cliff Price? There was no possible proof as far as we could see.

While Andy was keeping his ears open at the Ferryman and unobtrusively directing conversation to the subject of the Newt, I was doing the same – with less success – at MacAlister's shop, a hotbed of gossip. Here, too, tales of Newton's unpleasant pranks were not wanting, but few new facts of any importance emerged, though I did learn that Cliff Price's brother-in-law, Bill Scroggs, was another of the boy's avowed enemies. The wretched child had apparently been in the habit of chasing the chicken farmer's pedigree poultry, and especially his Old English game cocks – which were the pride of Bill Scroggs' heart – and pulling out their tail feathers for use in the making of salmon flies. Bill Scroggs had gone to the Llantossy police and the boy had been cautioned by Constable Jones. Nothing much there, especially as Bill Scroggs did not seem to enter the case at any other point.

One item of information which I did pick up came from Dougal MacAlister. I was in the shop one day with Curly when Dougal's eye fell on the scar left on her by the gash from Newton's gaff. A small piece of fur and hide had been ripped clean away and a black and white triangle of naked skin now marred her curly haunch.

'Yon was a sore wound,' said Dougal, indicating the scar. He is fond of dogs and himself owns a melancholy Scottie whose main function is to guard the van when it is left unattended.

'Was it fighting she was?'

'It was Newton Landon did that,' I said, 'with a salmon gaff. Did you not hear of it?'

'Och aye, I mind now. Gladys was saying something of that.'

'Of course,' I said, remembering the afternoon I had gone to the shop for disinfectant to put on Curly's wound, 'you were out that day – with the van, I believe. It was the day that Newton was drowned.'

'Aye, aye. I mind I wasnae in the shop being as 'twas me afternoon for Llantossy.'

'Oh, so you must have been on the Llantossy road where you can get a good view of the river almost all the way. Did you see Newton fishing that afternoon?'

'No, I did not. I mind when the Boy came skeltering in with his tale o' the Newt drowned at the Crib I got to casting me mind back had I seen him. But never a body did I see but the constable on his bicycle.'

'The constable? Constable Jones you mean?'

'Aye. He was riding hell for leather along yon wee path by the river.'

'What would he be doing there?' I wondered.

'Och, 'twould be the licences, nae doot.'

'The licences?'

'Aye. Gun licences and the like. He'd be after checking up on the farmers.'

So here was a piece of information, indeed. But in my excitement – carefully concealed from Dougal – at having established that Constable Jones was on the river path on the afternoon of Newton's death, I quite forgot to ask at what time Dougal had seen him, a lapse which drew sarcastic comments from Andy when later I recounted this conversation. However, as luck would have it, the question which I had forgotten to put to Dougal was answered by Milly Piggott, and the dogs, again, provided the lead-in to the conversation from which this information emerged.

One evening I was in the middle of preparing the dogs' dinners when Milly arrived requesting – not for the first, nor the last time – the loan of "a pinch" of tea to "set her past" until the shop opened next morning. She came into the kitchen with me and, as I was searching for a packet of tea to "lend" her, her eyes fell on the dogs' bowls. Curly is a big dog and Squelch a small one and their feeding bowls are of correspondingly unequal sizes.

'You pay the same for both of them dogs?' enquired Milly, indicating the bowls.

'You mean the licences?' I said. 'Yes, of course. There's only one rate.'

'Don't seem right, do it? That Curly do eat twice what poor little Squelch do.' Squelch is her favourite.

I could think of no comment to make on this and she went straight on with her own train of thought: 'Reg – me nephew Reg, you know 'im?'

Yes, I knew him. He often came to see his Aunt Milly. He was a smallholder on the far bank of the river and a keen sportsman – too keen for the prosperity of his holding.

'Well, they cop 'im for 'is gun licence the other day – and 'is dog licence, and Trigger (Reg's gundog) no more than a pup reely. But that Evan Jones 'e says you can't call 'em pups after two years and 'e do remember when Trigger was born, worse luck, and that was two years gone last April. You'd 'ardly credit 'e'd remember. 'E's a sly one, is Evan.'

'When was this, Miss Piggott?' I asked, with Dougal's story very much in my mind.

'Oh, 'twould be a coupla months back,' said Milly. 'The day as that Newt drowned 'isself it was. I seen the constable riding 'is bike along the foot of the garden there, just after that limb 'ooked poor old Curly with the gaff. There goes Evan after the licences, I thinks to meself. There couldn't nothing else bring 'im down along the river path and, sure enough, it were the next day Reg tole me 'e'd bin copped.'

'It's clever of you to remember the date after so long a time,' I said.

'Ar, well, you see,' said Milly, 'it was in me mind that time to call after the constable and tell what that Newt done to your dog, on'y by the time I thought on it Jones was gone beyond.'

So the constable had definitely been on the river bank that afternoon – but too early. At the time when he must have been crossing the plank bridge on his bicycle Newton Landon was sitting on one of our kitchen chairs and still very much alive.

As to the last "suspect", Trev Price, we could find nothing to add either to his possible motive for murdering the Newt, nor to what we already knew of his movements on that fatal afternoon. The meadow where he had been working was near enough to the river for him to have slipped down at any moment and done the deed and he had, in fact, been absent from the meadow at around the time of Newton's death; but it was almost certain that no-one on earth knew where Trev Price had gone, nor what he had done during his short absence – except Trev himself. Both Andy and I found ourselves unable to probe further in this direction.

So here our discreet enquiries seemed to come to a dead end. There was plenty of suspicion, but no shadow of proof against any of our "suspects". Only those questions which we had wanted to ask Elise remained unanswered, but even if the answers were to confirm our suspicions, still there would be no proof.

'Let's give the whole thing up,' I suggested.

'I'm damned if I will,' said Andy, but he ceased to talk of the affair, at least to me.

Chapter 8

RACHEL

At about this time we had a small piece of personal good fortune: I won a £500 premium bond and decided to use the money – or part of it – on the purchase of a second-hand car. On the Saturday morning after we had received this windfall I was in the village buying the weekend groceries when Dr Rachel Brading walked into the shop. MacAlister's, it seemed, stocked a certain kind of indestructible stocking, unobtainable in Llantossy or Carne, and Rachel had come to buy a second pair. She looked tired and harassed, I thought, but appeared genuinely pleased to see me, although we had only met once before at Robert's birthday party.

'It's Meg Marsden, isn't it?' she said. 'You have never been to see me, as you promised.'

I had thought of her often, as it happened, but had not been sure of the sincerity of her invitation and so had let the days drift past without doing anything about it.

'When can you come?' she went on with surprising eagerness. 'It would have to be in the evening after surgery. But perhaps that's awkward for you with the buses?'

'That's all right,' I said. 'By next week we shall have a car. I've just had a financial windfall – a premium bond – and we are off to the car mart in Carne this afternoon to acquire a vehicle of some sort. Old Tom Todd has said we may garage it in the old boat store beside the pub. Andy hasn't been able to drive for years, of course, but I still have my licence.'

'Well, come one day next week – say Wednesday, about 7.30. I shan't be called out as Bob and I have come to an arrangement about the night work – week and week about – and it's my week off from tomorrow.'

And so it was arranged. We bought our car that afternoon and drove away in it. It was a joy to be behind a wheel again and to feel free of the countryside and less pinned down to the village of Coedafon. Also, it was one more step forward in Andy's rehabilitation and re-entry into normal life. For long he had been nervous of cars.

So Wednesday evening found me walking down a flagged path to the door of Rachel's cottage, a tiny four-roomed affair – two up, two down – built of solid blocks of stone. Its name, Weir Cottage, indicates its position, for it stands, well set back from the road, actually on the weir itself, the east side of the cottage rising flush from the wall that was built to contain the swirling pool below the dam. The weir has long since fallen into disuse and the fast water some sixty yards below it now an excellent trout run – as we know from fishing it from the further bank on our Friday expeditions to Llantossy. The fish find many comfortable lies behind the blocks of masonry fallen from the disintegrating sill. The woods across the river come right down to the water's edge, but on the cottage side the rocky, overgrown bank rises steeply to the level of the containing wall of the weir pool and, along the crest of the bank, former occupants of the cottage have at one time cleared an acre or so of land for garden and orchard. Dr Rachel Brading, however, was obviously no gardener, for, with the exception of a rectangle of grass under the south wall of the cottage, the whole of the former clearing was a wild tangle of blackberry, nettle and thorn.

As I stood looking around me I noticed that a windy day had now turned to a stormy evening with gleams of sunlight shining out suddenly from beneath black, rain-laden clouds which a furious wind was hurling upwards from the south-west horizon. A huge sighing filled the air from the woods across the river and, as I raised my hand to knock at the cottage door, I was suddenly overcome by a sense of the loneliness of this isolated cabin among the trees. So that my first words when Rachel opened the door to me were to exclaim: 'You're a brave woman, Dr Brading.'

'What do you mean?' she asked with a startled look.

'To live here all alone in this wilderness, miles from anywhere,' I explained.

'Oh, that!' she said with a relieved little laugh. 'I like it. Complete silence, especially at night, is the only thing which makes me uneasy and you never get that here. Even if there's no wind and the trees are still, there's always the weir. Come and listen.'

She led me across the stone-flagged sitting room, into which the front door opened, through a door at the far end of it and so to a tiny tiled kitchen. Crossing this, she opened one half of a double casement window with low sills which extended over almost the whole of the opposite wall, and immediately an eddy of wind rushed in, flinging the curtains aside and banging the door behind us, and with the wind came a roaring sound, louder than the wind's whining and louder than the groaning of the trees; it was the noise of the weir. Standing beside Rachel at the window I looked straight downwards into the foaming cauldron of the pool and felt myself turning giddy at the swirling and rushing motion of the water and its overpowering roar.

'Isn't it a fascinating sound?' said Rachel.

'Well, everyone to his taste,' I said. 'If it was me on a dark night I should be straining to hear stealthy footsteps through the din.'

Rachel laughed.

'I love it,' she said. 'However, we'll shut it out if you don't like it.'

But, even with the window shut, the sound of wind and water and of tossing woodlands seemed to fill the little house with an eerie sighing.

Rachel had changed, in my honour, into a fashionably cut red dress and high-heeled shoes which were somehow incongruous in this back-of-beyond. She was looking very plain and the red dress, for all its flattering cut, served only to emphasise the greyness of her cheeks and the dark rings under her eyes. I was shocked at her appearance. At Robert's birthday party I had thought her a handsome woman but, from whatever cause – overwork or worry or illness – she had, in the few weeks since that occasion, lost all pretension to good looks. She even seemed to have shrunk in size. Only her dark eyes remained as attractive as ever.

Conversation at supper, which we ate in the kitchen, was on trivial subjects. Rachel was surprised that Andy was not with me – I had noticed that a third cover was laid at the table – but I explained that he was still shy of strangers on account of his disfigurement.

She asked after the fishing and told me how, though she herself was no fisherman, she often sat at the window over the weir when the salmon were running and watched the great fish weaving their way through the rapids and flinging themselves in flashing arcs up the cascade of water that fell over the sill of masonry at the head of the pool. The large double casement in the kitchen, she told me, had been opened up in what had originally been a blank wall by a former Tossy bailiff when he had occupied the cottage, and the windowsills had been made low so that he could sit and watch the running fish.

When we had cleared and washed the dishes we took our coffee into the living room and sat before the south window in the fading light. It was an impersonal room, more like a rented lodging than a home, as though the owner's mind and heart lived elsewhere, though her body lodged here. There were no ornaments and few books, and every article of furniture looked as though it had been bought cheap and second hand at some country auction sale. The chairs were comfortable enough, however and, as our eyes idly watched the stormy scene beyond the window – a tall ash tree bending and writhing in the gale; leafy twigs hurtling across the pane; a company of wind-blown rooks battling their way home to the rookery – our talk gradually took on a more intimate tone.

Rachel told me something of her work in the villages, smallholdings and farms. She loved it, she said. The long drives through the countryside in all weathers, the many extraordinary characters she met and, above all, the feeling of usefulness she had in this scattered community of, for the most part, simple and ignorant folk who, in times of trouble, had no one to whom they could turn but herself.

'But soon I may be leaving it all,' she finished with a sigh.

'Leaving!' I exclaimed. 'Leaving the district for good?'

'Yes, I'm afraid I shall have to go.'

'But why? If you like it so much?'

'My life here has recently become impossible,' she said, 'for certain reasons which I can't go into.'

She rose abruptly and went into the inner room, returning presently with a Primus lantern.

'It's getting dark – but don't go yet,' she urged as she busied herself with lighting the lantern and hanging it from a hook above the hearth. The low, wooden ceiling of the cottage was no more than a couple of feet above her head and, as she hung the Primus on the old bacon hook and started to pump it up, the white glare of its light fell full on her face giving it a corpse-like pallor. Looking at her it seemed to me that she was in as much trouble as any of her patients had ever been and that she, too, might like someone to confide in and to seek advice from. Perhaps that is why I had been so eagerly invited.

On an impulse I broke the silence which had fallen to ask: 'Is anything the matter, Rachel? I have an idea that something is worrying you. I know I'm practically a stranger, but strangers are often good people to unburden oneself to. One need never see them again afterwards. And if you are going away soon that applies particularly to you and me. It often does one good to talk of a trouble and I might even – bringing a fresh mind to the problem – be able to suggest some remedy.'

Rachel made no reply, but she left the lantern and came and sat down again in the chair beside me. It was almost dark by now and nothing could be seen from the window beyond the square of lantern light lying on the grass. Two moths fluttered up from the outside windowsill and were caught for a moment in the light, but a gust of wind took them and whirled them away into the darkness. The noise of the wind was everywhere. But still Rachel was silent.

'Is it Robert?' I said at last.

That roused her.

'How do you mean?' she asked sharply, flashing her eyes on my face.

'You and Robert are old friends, I know,' I said, 'but I wondered whether, perhaps, you were more than that.'

Rachel was looking at me intently and I could swear that there was relief in her eyes, and in her voice, too, when she said, 'You're right. We are more than old friends. How did you guess? Is it so obvious?'

'I think it's obvious to Elise.'

'Yes, damn her! I can feel her watching Bob and me when I am with them and for the last few weeks she seems to me to have been mounting guard over us to prevent us from ever having a moment alone together. She has even taken to accompanying Bob on his afternoon rounds, in case, I suppose, we should have some assignation in the country.'

I remembered the voices in Llantossy churchyard on the day of

Newton's funeral, arranging just such an assignation and thought that Elise had some reason for her suspicion; but I did not say so.

'Her latest trick,' Rachel continued, 'is, when Bob is called out in the evening – if it is not too late, to insist on his leaving her here and fetching her again on his way back from the case. She is afraid to be left in the house, she says. This never seeing Bob alone for a moment is nearly sending me out of my mind. I can't stand it any longer. Seeing him constantly but never being able to speak to him. That's why I must get away. But, Meg,' she added, looking at me earnestly, 'you mustn't get me wrong. I think you imagine that I am Bob's mistress, but I am not. I have fought for years against this infatuation – because infatuation it is. A sort of madness of which all his faults can't cure me. I know he's cold and sometimes cruel, but I love him all the same. Perhaps if I could once become his mistress I might be cured.'

'I remember that you spoke of his cruelty once before,' I said.

'Oh! When was that?' she asked, startled.

'At Robert's birthday party.'

'Yes, yes. I remember, and that is a case in point. It happened long ago, when he was only a boy, but is a sample of what he is capable of.'

'What did he do to shock you so much?' I asked.

'He killed my puppies,' she answered. 'Perhaps that sounds trivial to you, but I shall never forget it. Afterwards he said he had done it to please me – to solve my problem for me – and it may have been so, but for years I could not forgive him.'

'What happened?' I asked.

'When I was about twelve an uncle on my mother's side gave me a little cairn bitch as a present. I was fond of dogs and he thought all children should be brought up with them, but my family as a whole were not dog lovers, especially my father, who thought them unhygienic – he was a doctor, too. Soon the inevitable happened and poor Queenie produced five illegitimate pups on the drawing room sofa. My father was furious and an edict went forth that the litter must be destroyed forthwith. However, I was so thrilled with the puppies that I could not bear to have them drowned and I managed to smuggle them into the tool shed at the end of the garden where the noise they made could not be heard from the house. Bob, who lived next door, helped me to look after them. Dad was a busy man and for a month or so all went well. Then one fine Sunday, Dad, although he was no gardener, went down to the shed for some tool or other and came upon the litter. There was a terrible scene, Dad pointing out that the pups were now too old to be drowned and would have to be put down by the vet. It was the most miserable day of my whole childhood and it was Bob's birthday, too – a day I had been looking forward to. Of course I told Bob all about the rumpus and he told me not to worry. He would find a way out. He was always very resourceful and I put my trust in him, but his "way out" this time was to drown the whole litter in the water butt by the tool shed. That night, when I went to say goodnight to Queenie and the pups, I came on Bob in the act of drowning the last of the litter. I shall never forget his face. Although he explained later that his expression was one of horror at what he was doing, I could never see it like that. His teeth were clenched and his lips drawn back in a sort of snarl as he held the struggling creature under the water. He seemed to me the incarnation of wickedness. Around him lay the dripping, rat-like little bodies of the pups which were already dead and Queenie was running frantically from one to another, whining and licking each in turn. It was the end of our friendship and I never spoke to Bob again, nor heard of him until the day I answered his advertisement for a partner.'

'And yet, he may well have thought as he said, that he was merely solving your problem for you. After all, he was only a boy,' I commented, as Rachel fell silent.

'It's possible, but even so, what sort of mind must he have had to solve the problem in just that way?'

'Or what devotion to you to be able to force himself to such an action for your sake!'

'It might have been that. Bob is a strange, reserved creature and it's hard to know what he is thinking. I'm not even sure that he loves me – not as I love him. He says he does, but his protestations always seem to me to lack conviction. I have suggested many times that he should ask Elise for a divorce, but I don't think he ever has. What does he want? What *does* he want?'

'To have his cake and eat it, like many men,' I said.

'If only we could meet and thrash it out alone together,' Rachel continued, ignoring my comment, 'perhaps then I could find out what his real thoughts are and, if he doesn't want me, I could go right out of his life. And yet, now,' she continued, sinking her voice almost to a whisper and staring at her own wide-eyed reflection in the windowpane, 'I'm afraid to be alone with him.'

'Why should you be afraid?' I asked. 'If Elise finds you in a compromising situation surely that would force the issue. She would divorce Robert and that would make up his mind for him.'

Rachel turned her head towards me and gave me a strange look. For a moment we stared at each other – I puzzled and she intent – while the only sounds in the room were the hissing of the Primus lantern and the hollow booming of the wind in the chimney.

'How simple that would be!' she said, at last, and there was no mistaking the irony in her voice.

Suddenly I was annoyed at her tone. Rachel and her troubles, what were they to me? I had troubles enough of my own without trying to rack my brains over hers.

'Andy will have been alone long enough,' I said, rising abruptly. 'I must get home.'

Rachel seemed to be on the point of saying something further but, at that moment, the telephone on the windowsill rang shrilly, startling us both.

'Who can that be?' wondered Rachel, reaching for the receiver.

It was Robert. There had been an accident of some sort on the road beyond Llantossy, I gathered, and he was bringing Elise to Weir Cottage while he went on to see what he could do.

'There's a tree down on the river road,' Rachel told me as she hung up. 'The big elm in front of the Swan. It seems it fell across the courtyard as the men were coming out of the pub. It's a bit of a shambles, by Bob's account. He has rung for the ambulance.'

'Would it be of any help if I went along with Robert?' I asked.

'No, no. What could you do? But I ought to go. In fact I must go. I'll just change and be back in a minute,' and she hurried off into the kitchen, where I heard the scrape of a match as she lit a candle, and then the sound of her steps on the stair.

'What about Elise?' I called.

'Damn Elise!' came Rachel's muffled voice from the upper floor.

I went to the foot of the staircase – a short spiral of stone steps that rose steeply up in the thickness of the cottage wall – and called up again in the darkness. 'I could take her home with me.'

'Would you, Meg? That would be sweet of you.'

But, Elise, when she arrived with Robert some five minutes later, had other ideas.

'I'm going with Robert and Rachel,' she announced flatly.

'Don't be ridiculous. That's impossible,' said Robert impatiently.

'Come on Rachel, we must get moving,' and the two of them – Rachel now in her working suit with an emergency bag in her hand – were gone into the howling night before Elise could stop them.

For what seemed a long time Elise stood staring at the rattling front door, quite motionless, her hands by her side. The harsh, white glare of the Primus lantern at her back made a halo of her golden curls but threw her face into shadow, so that I could not see her expression.

'Take me home,' she said at last, abruptly.

So I turned out the lantern and, shutting the door firmly behind us, we battled our way against the gale to the car which I had left at the gate. It was a strange, wild drive. The little second-hand car rattled and squeaked as the wind battered it. On the open stretches of the road sudden squalls threatened to push us over the verge and on the wooded sections I fled through the tunnels of writhing trees with my heart in my mouth. The noise made conversation difficult and it was not until we were turning on to Coedafon bridge that a sudden feeling of pity for Elise made me turn my head towards her and shout, 'Rachel talks of leaving the district soon. Did you know?'

The effect on Elise was electric. 'Leaving the district!' she exclaimed. 'How do you mean? How do you know? Did she tell you so herself?'

Her excitement was really very odd.

'She was talking about it this evening,' I said.

'Where is she going? When will she be leaving? Not immediately, I suppose?'

I could have sworn that there was consternation, rather than the relief one would have expected, in her voice.

'I really know nothing more about it,' I said, taken aback and hedging suddenly as I realised how indiscreet I had been.

We were approaching our cottage now and I drew up at the gate and prepared to alight, but Elise stopped me.

'I'm not coming in,' she said in a hurried, excited voice. 'Please take me home – or I can walk.'

'Won't you be nervous till Robert gets home?' I asked.

'No, no. Take me home,' she repeated, and no arguments of mine could make her change her mind. So I drove her up to her house and, with mingled feelings of pity and exasperation, watched her, in the light of the head-lamps, run up the steps to the front door, open it and disappear through it into the hall beyond, where a dim light had been left burning. The door banged and she was gone without a backward glance.

Chapter 9

ENTER POACHERS

It was two days before I saw Elise again and then, as suddenly as she had terminated it, she resumed the day to day intimacy which she had broken off some weeks before. She spoke only once of the evening of the gale and then it was to say that the accident at the Swan had not been so bad as it had sounded; there had been no fatality and Robert had been home by midnight.

'You were wrong about Rachel,' she ended up this brief account, 'she is not leaving. It's simply that she is taking a holiday and going away for a fortnight. A locum is taking over from tomorrow.' Then fixing her large eyes on mine with a contemptuous look, she added, 'What a terrible gossip you are!'

Elise puzzled me; I could not make her out. In her way she was as great an enigma as Robert. On the one hand, in spite of her occasional rudeness, I was really very fond of her and also extremely sorry for her; she seemed, as a result I suppose of her intense egotism, so very friendless, and her home life was anything but gay. On the other hand, she did not seem to feel the lack of friends, wrapped up as she was in herself, nor did the crisis in her marriage appear to depress her unduly. She was restless and on edge, it is true, but it seemed to me that there was a sort of excitement behind her restlessness, very different from the self-pitying unhappiness one would have expected her to feel. Her blue eyes were brilliant with this inexplicable excitement and, on her face in repose, there often appeared a secret smile, as of pleasure at her own thoughts. I noticed, once again, how astonishingly beautiful she was.

About this time Andy began to take a real interest in Elise which, I confess, made me uneasy, especially when the thought crossed my mind, as it did occasionally, that the suppressed excitement which I noticed in Elise might have some connection with this new friendship between her and Andy. And yet, as I have said before, she was no coquette and she seemed no more conscious now than she had ever been of her own physical attractions. She and Andy held interminable conversations under the pear tree – for the weather had turned fine again after the great gale – but, whereas during our previous period of intimacy the chat between Andy and Elise had mainly concerned itself with matters of general interest, now the chief topic was Elise herself – as it had once been with me when I had been her confidante. I heard mere snatches of these conversations as I went about my chores in house and garden, for I had not the leisure, as Elise always seemed to have, to waste half the day in chat. But, from what I did hear, I was filled with astonishment that Andy, my husband, who has always been quickly bored by feminine confidences, should be able now to listen to Elise, not only with patience, but apparently with positive pleasure. He even seemed to seek her company and the climax came when he actually asked her to accompany him the next day on his Friday fishing expedition to Llantossy water. I was astounded, for his opinion of women – apart from his wife, and especially of non-fishing women as fishing companions – was well known to me and it was not, to put it mildly, complimentary.

'Meg can give us a lift up in the car,' he said calmly, 'and make us some sandwiches to take with us. Then in the afternoon she can walk up the bank and meet us at the boathouse with a thermos of tea.'

Elise looked doubtful for she was no lover of country expeditions.

'You will enjoy it,' Andy assured her, 'and it will do Meg good to have a holiday.'

'Who will gaff your fish for you?' I protested, annoyed at being arranged for in this way.

'There will be no fish to gaff. The salmon are dead off, as they always are in August, especially in a heat-wave like this. I shall take only my trout rod.'

'And what about Elise? Can she leave the house for a whole day like that? After all, hers is a doctor's household and there must be someone to answer the phone.'

This was a foolish objection to have raised, as I realised as soon as I had made it, for its only effect was to make up Elise's mind for her.

'My dear Meg,' she said, 'you don't really suppose, do you, that I am the slave of Robert's wretched telephone? When we are both out the phone is switched through to the Llantossy surgery, where the receptionist takes care of the calls. Thank you, Andy, I should enjoy a day on the river. But I hope you will leave your dogs with Meg.'

Andy said that he would do that, I made no further protest, and so it was arranged.

Friday morning was misty but the sun was hot behind the haze, giving promise of a scorching day. Elise appeared, looking cool and lovely in an apple-green linen frock and white sandals – a most unsuitable garb for the river bank, in my opinion. I drove the two of them up to Llantossy Church and watched them out of sight down the river path then, in an access of solitude for Andy, the sight of whose thin, limping figure following the lithe Elise, had suddenly brought a pang of love and pity to my heart, I hurried to the churchyard wall to see that he got safely over the two rickety footbridges by the island. I knew that Elise would give him no help; nor did she, I saw, but they were soon across, nevertheless, and I returned to the car, passing on my way the new grave where the unloved and unregretted Newt was buried. There was no headstone, as yet, but the turves that covered it had already begun to knit together and, in the place the stone would be, a large plant of the poisonous thorn-apple had found a home exactly to its liking.

I spent the day catching up on the garden work: cutting the grass, hoeing the vegetable garden and tearing up the old pea rows. By now the mist had dispersed and it was sweltering hot with not even a breath of wind to temper the heat. High up in a pale blue sky – so high as to be almost invisible – swifts wheeled and rocked, but in the garden not a single bird stirred or sang. Except for the sound of my own movements and the murmur of the river, the stillness was absolute. I might have been the last living creature on this planet; even the dogs lay in the shade like dead things. In the early afternoon, however, old Milly Piggott came and leaned over the fence, watching my activities with disapproval.

'It do bring the sweat out on me just to look at you,' she said.

'Best way to get slim – to sweat,' I said.

'Slimming! Lord love us, I dunno what wimmin is coming to nowadays! When I were a girl a man fancied a good armful – summat to get a hold of and plenty in front and behind – summat after your style, now. These 'ere vital sticks the gals do go on about, nobody never 'eard of 'em in my young days.' Then going off on another tack: 'Your 'ubby 'aving a lay-down?'

Milly was behind events, for once. She must have missed our morning exit. We had met Elise at the Ferryman boat store, where the car was kept, so she had missed her, too, I was thankful to realise.

'No, he's fishing,' I said.

'All be 'isself, poor lamb? Ent you ever afraid as 'e'll fall in the river, him seeing so bad?'

'He sees pretty well now, and better every day,' I said. 'I shall be going along to meet him soon with a thermos of tea.' No need to mention Elise.

'Caught any fish lately?' Milly continued.

'No salmon, no. The fish all lie like logs this weather. There's no tempting them.'

'Ar. Poachers' weather – that's what me nephew, Reg, do say. Come on 'em quiet as they lay under the bank and nip 'em out quick with a gaff afore they wakes up. Reg, he had a good un Wednesday. Sold 'em in Carne.'

'But it's illegal to sell fish in August, surely? How did he find a buyer?'

'Black market,' said Milly, with a conspiratorial leer. ''Ow d'you reckon them lorry gangs makes their living?'

'Lorry gangs?'

'Ar, en you 'eard? Night afore last, gang on the Tovey, over in Wales. Got off with a good lorry load, seemingly. London gang, they reckon. Poison,' said Milly with relish.

'Well, let's hope they don't come here,' I said. 'I must be off now to meet my husband.'

The rucksack with the tea things seemed to weigh a ton as I plodded up the river path. The heat was stifling and the sun on my bare arms was like a lighted match held against the flesh. The dogs panted languidly at my heels, too overcome even to hunt moorhens along the water's edge. I was glad to reach the boathouse and slip the rucksack from my back. There was no sign yet of Andy and Elise so I kicked off my sandals and dangled my feet in the backwater over which the boathouse is built. Blessed coolth! Presently the panting of the dogs got on my nerves and I pushed Curly into the river to cool down, and threw Squelch after her. Curly was outraged at the indignity of sudden immersion and, making a beeline for the bank, hauled herself ashore at once, but Squelch was delighted to find himself cool, at last. He started sniffing, nose in the air, along the lower branches of willow bushes where they hung over the bank, treading water meanwhile. This is one of his favourite sports, for these branches evidently smell beautifully of the birds that have perched on them. I watched him idly, and then noticed suddenly that he was in difficulties. His front paws threshed the water and his eyes bulged with fright, but his head seemed to remain above water and I saw that he had somehow managed to get himself suspended by his collar from a short willow twig. He was too far out for me to reach from the bank and I was just making up my mind to brave the snag-infested slime below the willow bushes when I saw the figure of Cliff Price coming down the river. He obviously had not seen me, for, when I shouted to him for help, he turned sharply towards me, as though startled. At first I thought he was about to ignore me and walk on but, after a short hesitation, he came slowly over to the boathouse. I explained the situation to him and he consented, somewhat grudgingly, to hold my hand while I leaned perilously out over the water and released the wretched Squelch, who thereupon made his way up the bank under his own steam.

Andy and I had hardly exchanged a word with Cliff since the morning when I had found Newton's trousers, but I now felt that I could scarcely do less than offer him a cup tea from one of the thermoses. He seemed, at first, to be about to refuse, but he was obviously very hot and very thirsty. His pale skin, which was normally unaffected by the weather, showed a dull flush and was beaded with sweat, and his checked shirt was sticking to his back.

'Don't mind if I do,' he said finally and seated himself in the shade with his back to the boathouse wall.

'I hear a gang of poachers has been at work on the Tovey,' I said conversationally when I had provided him with a drink. Cliff gave me a quick, searching look, hesitated a moment, and then, being a naturally talkative man, succumbed to the temptation to indulge in a little gossip.

'Ar,' he said, 'London gang, they reckon. Poisoned three pools. Must 'ave got off with uppards of a hundred fish. Taffy Evans – 'e's bailiff on that beat – he tell me the pools is packed on the Tovey. Fish is lying head to tail waiting for fresh to take 'em on up. Same like in the weir pool here.'

'I heard they used a lorry to take the fish away.'

'Ar. Leastwise 'twere a Land Rover, they reckon. Tyre marks there was on the bank, look, and the police reckon a Land Rover made en. And tracks of three men.'

'Have the police any idea who they are?'

'Damn, no! Nor ever will 'ave. They ent losing no sleep over it. Taffy Evans, though, 'e's in a bit of a spot. Seems 'is boss is creating and asking awkward questions – such as, where was Taffy to let a whacking great Land Rover go cavorting up the bank right past 'is front door? Seems it must 'ave passed his house, nigh the bridge there, but Taffy never 'eard nothing. Then again, summan musta done a recce afore the raid, Taffy he do say there 'asn't no strangers bin around that he seen.'

'Do you think they'll try the Tossy now they've been so successful on the Tovey?'

'Ar, they might, too. But me, I've me own notions. Won't catch me napping like they done Taffy.'

'Why? Have you seen anyone suspicious hanging around these waters?'

'Well, mebbe – and mebbe not. Got me eye on one as I don't

like the looks of. Gentry by his clothes and talk, but there's plenty bad'uns speaks nice and dresses dandy. Wouldn't be a friend of yours now, would 'e?' asked Cliff, darting a sly look in my direction.

'A friend of ours? No, there's no friend of ours in the district. Who is this man?'

'Calls 'isself Mr Brown – or did. And now I think on it, you and Mr Marsden seen 'im, too – that time back in May 'twas, and a Friday, like today. The mister, 'e'd just landed a couple nice fish and me and this chap, Brown, come along and 'ad a look at 'em.'

'I remember,' I said, 'and your Mr Brown was enquiring about a bit of fishing in this district. Did he ever find it?'

'Ar, there you are! No, 'e never did and never tried, aside from 'aving me show 'im the water. Saw 'im again in Carne, tother evening, 'aving a drink in the George. Very affable, 'e was to each and all till 'e seen me, then 'e done a bunk quick.'

'And you think he might be spying out the land for the poaching gang?'

'Could be. Nobody don't know what 'is business is. And another thing, I seen 'is car two three times on the Llantossy road and 'im in it. Parked one time, it was, near Weir Cottage where 'tisn't more'n a step or two down to the weir pool. Took 'is number and tipped the wink the to sergeant at Llantossy. And Constable Jones, I tell 'im to keep 'is eyes skinned, likewise.'

'So you're all prepared for the gang if they come here?'

'Ar, we got a nice surprise laid on, and so you might tell Mr Fancy Brown if so be as you get to passing the time of day with him.'

'Why should I ever be passing the time of day with Mr Brown? I don't know him from Adam – shouldn't even recognise him if I saw him again.'

'Well, mebbe not, but I'm just saying.'

'I believe you think he's a friend of ours. What gives you that idea?'

'It's nowt to me 'ose friend 'e is. All I asks meself is, what's 'e doing 'ere? That's what I'd like to know. And what might you be doing 'ere? London gentry, the both of you, and both come 'ere around the same time. Where's your jobs? Your 'ubby, now, 'e's a pleasant enough gentleman. I'm not saying as I ever caught 'im out in nothing, but all I say is, mind your step – and tell your friend the same.'

'So that's what you really think of us in Coedafon, that we're crooks of some sort?'

I was completely taken aback and, I must confess, hurt that people with whom we seemed to be on the best of terms should all the time be harbouring such absurd and unfriendly suspicions about us.

'You don't really believe that, Mr Price?'

But Cliff had risen to his feet and was preparing to continue on his way. He gave me a hard stare.

'Well, thanks for the tea, Mrs Marsden,' he said, without answering my question. 'I must be getting along,' and with that he strode off.

It really was astounding and so perfectly ridiculous that in the end I could not help laughing to myself. Poor dear Andy, with his one eye and gammy leg and I – I who am so honest as to be practically a cretin in the opinion of some of my friends – we two to be suspected of being crooks and professional poachers! No wonder Cliff had been a little short with us of late if that was really what he thought. I was still smiling to myself when Elise and Andy appeared, looking very hot and, to my secret delight, very, very cross.

'Any luck?' I called gaily.

'Too bloody hot,' said Andy, mopping his brow. 'One nice brace of trout early on and then nothing but parr. The silly little blighters kept hooking themselves as fast as I put the fly in the water.'

'For God's sake give us a cup of tea, Meg,' chipped in Elise, flinging herself down on the bank. 'I never want to see another fish or fishing rod as long as I live. How you two can go out day after day beats me.'

Her once immaculate white shoes, I noticed, were caked in mud and her linen dress crumpled.

'That's the end of that romance – if any,' I thought.

We lingered on the bank in desultory conversation, unwilling to leave the shade of the boathouse and the damp coolness of the water's edge to face the heat of the walk home. Although it was now late afternoon the sun still shone brassily from a cloudless sky and even the leaves on the osiers, which the least whisper of breeze will agitate, hung motionless in the breathless air. I recounted Cliff Price's tale of the poachers on the Tovey, although, for fear of Elise's ridicule, I said nothing of his absurd suspicions of Andy and myself. At first, Elise seemed to follow my tale with an interest which, for her, was quite unusual but, as I was embarking on an account of Cliff's suspicions of Mr Brown, she suddenly appeared to get bored with my long-windedness and scrambled to her feet.

'Why are we sitting here?' she exclaimed. 'Come on, let's get moving. I want to get home.'

So we packed up the tea things and followed her down the shade-less river path that here skirted Trev Price's twenty-acre water-meadow. As we approached the little stream that formed the boundary between the doctor's garden and the farmer's meadow, Elise hesitated. The quickest way home for her, at this point, would have been to follow the footpath through a small thicket of alder and blackthorn, cross the plank footbridge spanning the mouth of the stream, and turn up through a wicket gate in the hedge into her own garden. But, at the shady entrance to the thicket she stood still.

'It's too muddy in there,' she said abruptly. 'I shall go round.' And, turning left along the bank of the stream, she hurried off uphill without another word. We watched her as she toiled up the steep meadow side to the gate into the lane at the top. She climbed as though the devil were at her heels, in spite of the heat, and never so much as turned to wave good-bye.

'What's eating her?' asked Andy, with a thoughtful air.

'Search me,' I said.

The path through the thicket was bone dry after the drought of the last few days and, even had it been wet, Elise's shoes, already muddied to the ankle, could have taken no further harm on it.

Chapter 10

APPARITION

'Had a good day?' I asked Andy, as we strolled on our way after watching Elise out of sight.

'No, lousy.'

'The fair Elise not at her fascinating best?'

'Dear Meg! I believe you're jealous. What a lark.' And Andy went off into peals of laughter. 'No, but seriously, old girl, you don't really think I would spend a whole day alone with that egomaniac just for pleasure?'

'What did you go for, then? You took pains enough to get rid of me.'

'It was all in the interests of detection, Meg. We couldn't get cosy and confidential while you were buzzing around us all the time at the cottage. I thought if we were alone together I might get Elise onto the subject of her son and ask her some of the questions to which we haven't yet got answers. About the wet clothes, remember, and about what happened to the boy's belongings after his death.'

'Andy! I thought we'd dropped all that.'

'You may have done, but the more I think of it the more certain I become that the boy was helped out of this world.'

'All the same it's not very nice the way you've been leading Elise up the garden path this last couple of weeks. You may have put ideas into her head.'

'Darling Meg, take another look at your husband. Hardly a maiden's dream, you must admit.'

'You are to me.'

'More's the miracle.'

'All the same, Andy, I do think it's not quite nice to deceive Elise in that way.'

'Murder's not quite nice.'

There it was again, the horrible word, and I realised with a start that we were at that moment actually standing on the footbridge over the stream where Newton's rod had been found. It was in the sun-dappled water on our right that he must have drowned. I shivered, in spite of the warm evening, and the hair rose a little on my scalp.

'Let's get out of here,' I said. 'This place always gives me the creeps.'

When we reached home I set about preparing the supper while Andy, as he always does immediately on his return from fishing, busied himself in sorting and drying out his tackle, and there then occurred a small incident which has its place, too, in this story.

'Meg, have you seen my small trout reel?' I heard Andy call from the living room.

'No,' I called back. 'You took it with you this morning.'

'Yes, I know that,' said Andy, 'but I can't find it now. I know I had it at the weir pool because the water is so wide there that at that point, I remember, I changed over to the heavier rod and line.'

'Do you remember putting it away in your bag?'

'Yes, I remember distinctly doing that and then hanging the bag on a willow branch.'

'Well, it must have fallen out at some point,' I said. 'We'll go and look for it tomorrow. Nobody ever goes up there but Cliff Price so we're bound to find it.'

But, although I toiled up to the weir pool the next morning and on several subsequent occasions to look for it, the reel never turned up, and we came to the conclusion eventually that it must have been stolen. My suspicions in this connection, I must confess, fell upon the bailiff, Cliff Price, especially when I recalled that we had at various times missed other small pieces of tackle after leaving a fishing bag unattended on the bank of some remote stretch of the river where few people, other than Cliff, ever penetrated. If Cliff were a petty thief, a guilty conscience would go far to explain his rather odd behaviour towards us of late.

When, later, we were sitting under the pear tree eating our modest supper of grilled trout and a salad out of the garden, Andy returned to the subject of Elise.

'Don't you want to know what I found out today?' he asked.

'Your plan was successful, then,' I said. 'Well, what did you manage to worm out of the poor girl?'

'A lot of very interesting information. You know, she's a bit of a study, that woman. A complete narcissist, to begin with. She literally loves nobody but herself, but for herself she has an unbounded admiration. Have you noticed that when she passes the mirror in our living room she always turns her head to have a look at herself? And it's always an admiring look. Then she never wears make-up and I'm sure it's because she thinks lipstick and powder would spoil her own perfection. She's probably right, too. She certainly is astonishingly beautiful and needs no artificial aids. Then again, she's a man hater. Not only does she hate men but she is afraid of them.'

'Surely not, Andy. She's seemed keen enough on your company this last week or two.'

'Only because I am a disfigured cripple and, in her eyes, a neuter. Not dangerous, therefore. And a little, too, because she can talk to me about her music. You notice I say *her* music and not just music in general. Music, like everything else, is always related to herself: her virtuosity as a performer, her ambitions as a composer – did you know she composed? – and the way certain pieces of music affect her. When she is playing, and even sometimes when she is listening, she gets a feeling of power as though she were some sort of super-creature who could rule the world if she chose. She told me so. Pathetic, really, because, although she's good, there are many run-of-the-mill concert performers who are better than she is. Maybe she could have done something if her father had allowed her to study. Perhaps it was with him that her hatred and fear of men started.'

'And yet she married Robert and has stayed married to him for some fifteen years. She can't have hated him.'

'I'm not so sure, you know. I think she was trapped into that marriage. There's some mystery about it somewhere. Do you remember telling me once that you thought from something Elise had said that Newton was conceived, if not actually born, out of wedlock?'

'Yes, I remember. It was something she let slip once about the date of her marriage.'

'Well, I think it's true, and maybe that was how she was trapped. The old, old story of a flirtation, to use an old-fashioned word, that went too far. It seems rather uncharacteristic of Elise, though. She was very young then, of course, but a cold woman is more or less born that way and I don't suppose she was any more prone then than she is now to lose her head for love – or lust, if you like.'

'But Newton, surely, is the proof that she did lose her head?'

'Or was forced. I don't know, but I have a feeling that there was more to it than that.'

'Poor girl! She seems to have had a pretty raw deal, one way and another,' I defended Elise, 'and then the wretched child turning out a half-wit.'

'Well, not quite a half-wit. A three-quarter-wit. You know, I believe she was as fond of that boy as she could be of any creature outside herself. She certainly feels his death badly. There were actually tears in her eyes when I broached the subject today.'

'I don't know how you had the heart to do it.'

'Well, I did feel a bit of a brute, as a matter of fact, but I had to have the answers to my questions.'

'And you got them?'

'Yes. She found no wet clothes in the house on the day Newton died, so the boy didn't go home to change. She didn't see him at all that afternoon after two o'clock – as she would have been bound to do had he come back to the house for anything. It seems she spent the afternoon ironing the Monday wash. Newton had only one pair of blue corduroy trousers and they were the same ones – as far as she knows – as were returned to her after the inquest. All his clothes were packed up almost immediately after the funeral and sent to a refuge relief organisation. So they're gone beyond recall and can't be checked.'

'Did you tell her that you suspected that Newton's death was no accident?'

'Good heavens, no!'

'How on earth did you get all that information, then?'

'I brought up the subject of her son – rather abruptly, I'm afraid – and noticed at once that she was upset, practically in tears in fact, as I said. Then I apologised for my thoughtlessness and said the day of his death must have been a terrible shock to her. After that she told me all about it. Seemed eager to tell me. Couldn't find the words fast enough, as though she had gone over it all in her mind a hundred times before. She didn't say specifically that she found no wet clothes, but she did say that she was certain that the boy had not been back to the house in the course of the afternoon, which covers that point, of course.'

'Did you ask her point blank how many pairs of trousers Newton had?'

'No, there was no need. She gave me that information, too, without asking. She told me that, when the clothes were returned to her after the inquest, it was the sight of the boy's blue corduroy trousers that really brought home to her the fact of his death. She had not been able to take it in before. It seems that she had bought them on a recent weekend visit with Robert to her brother, Joseph. She had seen them in a shop window and had been taken with the rather unusual colour. On the morning of Newton's death she had laid out the trousers for him to wear and taken away his only other pair – which was brown – to wash. She seemed particularly affected by this small circumstance.'

'She was really fond of the boy, then. I used to wonder whether she had been, since she showed no emotion and never talked of him.'

'She was certainly very upset by his death.'

'That was the reason for her rather peculiar behaviour this evening, of course. She couldn't face passing the place where he was drowned.'

'I think that's very likely.'

We both fell silent, thinking our own thoughts. It was falling dusk by now in the garden and the swifts, which in the morning had circled so far above the earth, now fled in shrieking bands down the river, skimming low over the water. Two brown owls started a duet, one hooting from the woods above Ty-Mawr and the other answering from across the river. The evening was still and clear – no sign of mist now – and the scent of honeysuckle wafted up from the hedge along the footpath: the hedge through which young Newton had come that afternoon in May. I was filled with sadness for the boy whom everyone had hated – except, perhaps, his mother – and for Elise, who seemed to have got nothing out of life but frustration.

A dog's cold nose in my hand roused me from my meditations. It was Squelch reminding me that he had not yet received his post-prandial titbit. So he and Curly had the scraps from our plates, sitting neatly on their behinds with their front paws tucked up to their chests, and catching the flying bits most expertly, in spite of the dusk. Andy was still deep in thought but, when the supper things had been cleared and washed and the Aladdin lit in the sitting room, he broke his silence to say, at last, 'You know, Meg, I learned another rather interesting thing this afternoon.'

'What was that?'

'Joseph Ellis had quite an interest in Newton's death.'

'How do you make that out?'

'Old man Ellis, his father and Elise's, left money in trust for the boy, realising in all probability that he would never be able to earn his own living. Joseph was one of the trustees and, on Newton's death, the principal reverted to him. Elise seems to think that Joseph will be very pleased to get his windfall, as she suspects that, in spite of all his big talk, his finances at the present moment are not in too healthy a condition. She was very bitter that her father had not left the money directly to her to spend on Newton's behalf. It seems that the old man, Ellis, disliked and distrusted Robert and was afraid that he might get his hands on the money and I imagine that Elise's own little lapse from virtue also had some influence on the way in which her father chose to provide for his grandson. He seems to have been a pretty strait-laced individual who would have been unlikely to condone such a thing.'

'So you think that Jo-Jo might have pushed his young nephew into the river?'

'And held him under. He might have done. He had a motive and a good one.'

'*And* he was in Coedafon that evening,' I said excitedly. 'Don't you remember? I saw him arriving at the house when I was waiting in the surgery just before Newton's body was found.'

'Yes,' said Andy, thoughtfully, 'so you did. I had forgotten that. And another thing: Elise bought those trousers while on a visit to him. He could easily have got a similar pair and brought them with him.'

Silence fell again as we digested this. The night was heavy and quiet and the only sounds were the ticking of the little French clock and the tap and flutter of a big moth that flung itself again and again against the windowpane. To my mind's eye I called up the figure of Joseph Ellis as I had seen him on the evening of Robert's birthday party – paunchy and pompous, boasting of his possessions. Had I been talking to a murderer that evening? I remembered his cold eyes, his self-satisfied voice, his obsession with money, and the memory was so unpleasant that I could, indeed, almost believe him a murderer as well as a bore. But the method employed seemed out of character – too messy and too strenuous. Andy broke in on these reflections.

'You know, Meg,' he said thoughtfully, 'it could just as well have been Robert. He had an opportunity, too, to buy the duplicate trousers, and he hated the boy. There's no doubt about that. Then you remember what a state he was in that afternoon, before the body was found, mind you. At about four o'clock – just after the time at which we decided Newton must have been killed – he was so preoccupied by something or other that he ran me down at my own gate.'

Robert, now! There seemed no end to the suspicions aroused by the wretched garment we had dredged out of the river.

'Oh, no, Andy, I can't believe it,' I said. 'You don't murder a small boy just because you dislike him.'

'It's possible, though. He had the opportunity and, quite apart from his very obvious dislike of the boy, his tangled matrimonial affairs afford motive enough. Had Elise divorced him, he would have been liable for the boy's maintenance, and that, together with Elise's alimony, would have been a sore drain on his purse.'

'Forcible drowning seems a most unlikely method for a doctor to have used,' I protested. 'In any case, I simply don't believe it of Robert, the boy's own father – any more than I could believe it of Elise, and I'm not going to sit here any longer thinking of such horrors.'

I rose and called the dogs and went out into the lane to give them their last run before bed. It was a perfect summer night with a half moon just rising above the valley's rim, and so breathlessly still that I could hear distinctly the shrilling of field voles in the grass verges. The scuffling of the dogs and the sound of my own quiet footfall seemed almost a desecration of such stillness. As I walked down the lane through the black shadows of the trees which bordered it and the white interspersings of moonlight between them, a bat, following a beat as regular as a policeman's, hawked up and down the hedgerow on my left and, as in his erratic dartings he passed close to my head, it even seemed to me that I could hear his infinitely faint supersonic shrieking and the creak of his leathery wings. I walked through the sleeping village as far as the bridge and leaned over the downstream parapet. Here the quiet rush of water filled my ears and, as I looked towards the Crib, I could hear the plop of salmon jumping in the pool beyond. As I watched the moonlight on the water, my thoughts, in spite of my determination to put the subject out of my mind, turned once again to Newton and his tragic end. It seemed sacrilege to think of murder on this perfect night and, not for the first time, I cursed my own officiousness without which no suspicion of foul play could ever have been aroused. Why had I not wrapped the wretched rag of corduroy around a stone and flung it back into the slime from which it had come? Like some evil monster it had risen from the river-bed, covered with ooze, and in shaking itself, it had splattered all who came near it with the muddy drops of suspicion: first, our acquaintances among the village folk; Cliff Price whose talk of fish and fishing had once enlivened many a dull moment on the river bank; then, Trev Price, farmer, who had never been anything but pleasant to us and whose butter and eggs and milk we consumed daily; even Constable Jones on whose honest protection from the evil-doer we should have been able to rely; and now, finally, our friends – for in this restricted society where friendship grows quickly they were our friends, Robert, Rachel, even Elise. The mud of suspicion had fallen on them all, destroying our peace of mind and ruining our pleasant summer. And all on account of an unattractive child – a Newt, a creature of slime who, however you looked at it, was better out of this world.

As I called to mind the appearance of the Newt, so aptly nicknamed, my eyes were resting idly on the Crib from which the boy had so often fished. It was just discernible in the distance, bathed in moonlight and, as I looked, a figure seemed to rise up on it and so apt to my thoughts was the apparition that a shudder of superstitious fear went through me; for an instant it seemed to me that I had conjured up the spectre of the murdered boy. In a moment, as suddenly as it had materialised, the figure was gone. But now the summer night seemed full of menace. The blanching moonlight which drained the colours of life from everything it touched, the black shadows under the bridge in which an assassin might lurk, the rushing sound of the river which could mask a stealthy footstep – all seemed full of danger. In sudden, unreasoning panic I turned and ran for home.

I had not gone far, however, before the excited scampering of the dogs at my heels recalled me to my senses. What was I running away from, for heaven's sake? The figure on the Crib was certainly not that of Newton returned from the dead. There might, even, have been no figure on the Crib. Moonlight plays strange tricks, especially at that range. Even had there been in fact some person of flesh and blood standing above the salmon pool, what of it? There was nothing sinister in that; nothing, at any rate, more sinister than a little quiet poaching, perhaps – a quick dip with a gaff under the belly of an unwary fish, such as Milly's nephew, Reg, had recently indulged in. It might, indeed, have been Reg Piggott himself repeating his exploit of two nights ago; nothing more likely. I was quite reassured.

When I opened the cottage door, Andy was still sitting deep in thought, exactly as I had left him. He looked up as I entered and I noticed that his face was quite pale.

'Meg,' he said, 'I know how that boy was murdered. Someone came up behind him and, with his own gaff, hooked him through the band of his trousers and then pushed him into the water and held him there until he drowned. It was the gaff point that caused the abrasion on the boy's back and the hole in the waistband of his trousers. It must have been done at the salmon lie below the plank bridge, of course.'

'What a risk!' I said. 'And in broad daylight!'

'Not so risky, really. The pool is well secluded by trees in every direction and, if anyone did chance to come along the footpath, the drowning could be made to look like a rescue operation. Moreover,' Andy added, 'I know the name of the monster who did that. It came to me in a flash. It could be no-one else.'

'Andy!' I exclaimed, 'How awful! Who is it? What will you do? Can you prove it?'

He was silent for a long time, then he said at last, 'No, I can't prove it. I shall do nothing yet and, in the meantime, I think I shall keep the name to myself.'

I did not press him, because really I did not want to know.

'You've got those trousers still, I suppose?' he asked.

'Yes, they're somewhere about – in the kitchen, I think.'

'Good. Keep them safely.'

It was long before sleep came to either of us that night. The little cottage bedroom under the rafters, with its tiny window through which the moon cast a livid light, was as hot and airless as an oven. I tossed and turned and hung my bare feet over the edge of the bed in search of coolness but found none. Andy, at my side, lay without moving, but I could almost feel his thoughts circling and circling around his problem. At last, when the moonlight had left the window, I fell into an uneasy doze, broken by dreams of oozy, newt-like creatures that dragged themselves up from the river and shook their black and orange bodies at my feet, spattering me with drops – and the drops were of blood.

Chapter 11

THE TRAP

Next day, I remember, the fine weather, after holding up long enough for me to search for Andy's reel at the weir pool, broke temporarily towards noon in a series of thunderstorms which followed one another down the valley all afternoon and well into the evening, reducing Squelch to a trembling wreck of his usual cheerful self. The rumble and crash of thunder reverberating from the valley sides, the roar of sudden gusts of wind rushing through the woods above Ty-Mawr, the drumming of the thunder showers, all combined like the instruments in some gigantic orchestra into an elemental music which seems to me now, in memory, to have been a fit overture to the dramatic events which were soon to follow; for the curtain was about to go up on a drama which, for the time being, put all thoughts of Newton's death out of our heads. Elise opened the play on the following Monday during the course of one of our mid-morning sessions, and nothing could have been more prosaic than her opening words.

'Meg,' she said, 'will you come to a concert with me tomorrow in Carne? One of Robert's patients has presented him with two tickets and, of course, he doesn't want to go and has handed them to me. It'll be a pretty feeble affair, I expect: a summer season concert for the spa visitors, but anything for a bit of a change.'

I said I should be delighted, and it was arranged that I should take Elise in our car and pick her up at her own house shortly before 7.30 the following evening.

Elise was in high spirits that morning and laughed more than once, which was a rare thing for her. The undercurrent of excitement which I had noticed in her before was very much in evidence. When I remarked on her unusual cheerfulness she laughed again and said, 'Yes, it's true. I feel on top of the world today. It's the prospect of seeing the last of this lousy hole – for a short time, at any rate. Rachel's back and now it's our turn to go on holiday.'

'Where will you go?' I asked.

'Who knows,' she replied, laughing again excitedly. 'The whole world is open before me,' and she flung her arms wide in an exaggerated gesture. Then seeing my look of surprise, she explained, 'Robert and I will be going separately and I mean to try somewhere a little more exotic than the usual Little-Puddleton-on-Sea. Well, good-bye. See you tomorrow,' and she hurried off up the lane, humming to herself.

As I watched her retreating figure, MacAlister's van, I remember, came jolting slowly up the lane – on its way, most likely, to deliver poultry and pig feed to Trev Price's farm. At our gate it stopped and MacAlister himself leaned out from the driving seat.

'Hey, mistress,' he called, obviously addressing me, 'is himself at home?'

I said he was.

'I'm wanting a word with him,' said Dougal.

I called Andy and the two of them engaged in a low-voiced conversation of which all I heard was Dougal's final: 'Och, never fash. If ye canna do it, ye canna. I'll mebbe lay hands on one someplace else.'

'What was all that about?' I asked Andy as the van went grinding on its way.

'It was Dougal being mysterious about a salmon. He wants one cheap for some do that's on – a wedding reception I think. Not for himself, for some customer. I told him there wasn't a hope until August was out and the weather – and water – got cooler.'

Indeed, the heat was cooking up again after Saturday's storms. The fresh which followed them and emptied the pools of salmon had subsided as suddenly as it had risen, and now the fish were accumulating once more behind the Crib, under the old weir and in their other chosen resting places. But they would be quite uncatchable by rod and line. From now until September they would lie like logs in the tepid water, waiting for another fresh and only coming out of their enervated doze to leap high in the air and fall back into the water, broadside on, with a resounding smack.

I only mention this trivial conversation with Dougal because it went some way to prove that the moonlit figure on the Crib on Friday night whose identity had been exercising my mind for the last couple of days had not been a village poacher, for any local would almost certainly have come first to Dougal with his fish, though Reg Piggott had not done so, of course; he had gone to Carne to sell his salmon. And that reminded me to ask Milly whether Reg had made another foray on the Friday night, but she thought not; one sleepless night in the week would be enough for him, a busy farmer with the harvest just beginning.

I thought, then, that perhaps it had been Cliff Price making an extra night round in view of the rumours of lorry gangs at work. But this theory, too, was disposed of, for I met Cliff coming out of the pub on the following evening as I was fetching the car from the Ferryman boat store and he denied having left his cottage at any time on Friday night.

'Turned in early,' he asserted, 'and never stirred a finger till morning.'

'Oh, well, it was probably all my imagination,' I said.

However, at that moment I had unexpected confirmation that some prowler had indeed been abroad in the moonlight. Tom Todd heard my query as he stood at the pub door getting a breath of fresh air.

'Friday night, was it?' he asked. 'Ar, I seen summat, too. Jest drawing the curtain afore stepping into bed when I seen a chap dodging along by the side of the river, under the bank. Reckoned 'twas Cliff here.'

'No, 'twasn't me,' said Cliff shortly.

An urgent shout from the bar summoned Tom back to his duties at that moment and nothing more was said, but here was proof at least that the episode of the figure on the Crib had not been a figment of my imagination. Satisfied on this point, I put the whole thing out of my mind as being of no possible importance. The unidentified night prowler and the short exchange between Tom, Cliff and myself did, however, have their small place in the events that followed a day or two later.

To return to Elise: I extracted the car from among the junk in the boat store and bumped my way slowly up the lane to fetch her. Andy was standing at our gate as I passed, obviously waiting to waylay me. It seemed that he had suddenly got cold feet about my driving back in the dark.

'Are you sure you'll be all right, Meg?' he asked anxiously. 'I think I'll come with you after all.'

'Andy! Don't be an idiot,' I laughed. 'I'm not a learner driver, you know and, besides there's no ticket for you for the concert.'

'Well, if you're sure,' he said doubtfully, 'but be careful, Meg.'

'I will,' I said, laughing and letting in the clutch.

Elise was standing impatiently on the front doorstep when I arrived at the doctor's house. A little to my surprise she had made no attempt to dress up for the concert, but was wearing a creased pink cotton frock with an old coat thrown over her arm.

'I thought you were never coming,' she said ungraciously as she got in beside me. Altogether she seemed to be in a bad mood and squashed every attempt I made at conversation. So soon I, too, fell silent and settled down to enjoy the drive to Carne. It was a warm evening, but a mist was beginning to rise from the river and, in certain stretches, it lay already in thick, white blankets which concealed the water. The sun, like a ball of molten brass, seemed to rest on the western rim of the valley, throwing long shadows down the slopes, and the trunks of trees by the roadside were illumined in its ruddy glow.

We parked the car in Carne's main car park and set out to find the concert hall. Elise was still silent and preoccupied. In fact she had not opened her mouth for miles except to say that she was cold and to ask me to stop the car while she put on her coat. We had reached the door of the hall and she was fumbling in her coat pocket for the tickets when suddenly she turned to me and said, 'Meg, I'm sorry but I can't go on. I feel ill.'

And, indeed, I noticed then that she looked ghastly. Her face had a greenish pallor and she was shivering.

'What's the matter?' I asked her anxiously. 'Do you feel sick? Shall I get a doctor? Or something from the duty chemist?'

'No, no,' she said impatiently through clenched teeth. 'Just take me home. It must be something I ate at supper.'

So putting my arm through hers, I led her back to the car and we embarked on the homeward journey. The sun had dropped below the hills by now and dusk had fallen. The whole valley was full of shadow and tentacles of mist from the river were beginning to writhe across the road. About a mile from Carne, Elise was very sick by the roadside. Her hands were clenched and she was trembling when she got back into the car and I heard her mutter to herself, 'You would think someone was trying to poison me.'

My heart stood still at the words – conditioned as I had become of late to the thought of murder – and I put my foot hard down on the accelerator in a fever to get Elise home where she could get professional attention. But then a doubt entered my mind. Did she really believe that she was being poisoned, or was I taking her words too literally? Who could possibly want to poison her? Robert? Yes, yes, of course, and poison was a doctor's weapon. I was in a panic.

However, as we were crossing Coedafon bridge Elise said she felt much better and insisted that I should put the car away at the Ferryman and from there walk back to the house with her. The fresh air, she said, would do her good. When I protested that it would be better to drive her to her own door she turned on me in a fury, 'Do as I say, you little fool. I know best what's good for me.'

Under her spell, as I had been, I had put up with a good deal of rudeness from Elise Landon, not only that evening but for weeks past, but now, in a mixture of exasperation at her pig-headedness, rage at her lack of manners and shame at my own ridiculous and melodramatic fear that she was being poisoned by Robert, I suddenly lost my temper.

'Get out and walk, then!' I shouted. 'And be damned to you. But don't think I'm coming with you.' And I stopped the car at the turning into the lane.

She got out without a word but, when I had put the car away and was walking home, I found her still standing exactly where I had left her.

'Meg,' she said, 'I'm sorry. Please come with me.'

So then, of course, I was forced to go with her. She had won, as usual, and made me feel a brute into the bargain. Night had fallen by now and there was no moon so that in the lane beyond the cottage lights it was quite dark. I took Elise's arm and found that she was still trembling, which made me feel a greater brute than ever. As we approached the doctor's gate Elise said, 'We'll cut across the lawn and in through the French windows. It'll save fumbling our way round to the front door.'

So once through the gates, we took to the grass and made our way across it to the terrace steps. The lamp was lit in the sitting room and gleams of light filtered out as a slight draught stirred the long curtains behind the open windows. At the top of the steps Elise shook off my arm and started to run. In three strides she was at the glass doors and had wrenched back one of the curtains so that light flooded the terrace. For a moment she paused on the threshold, a black shape halo-ed in gold where the lamplight shone on her hair. Then she stepped into the room, at the same time uttering a low cry – a long 'Ah-h-h' – of rage, was it, or of triumph? As if what she saw in the room beyond the curtains was something which she had expected, though whether with dread or with hope it was hard to make out. I hurried to her side and the sight which met my eyes filled me with a furious embarrassment. Rachel Brading lay on the couch with her dress and hair in disorder. She had raised herself a little on one elbow and one leg, bent at the knee, was resting on the floor. Her face, drained of all colour, was turned towards Elise and her dark, melancholy eyes stared into Elise's blue, blazing ones with a look of horror. At the side of the couch knelt Robert and his head, too, was turned towards his wife, but on his face there was no expression, except, possibly, a mild surprise.

There was a long silence. Then: 'It was a trap, of course,' said Robert, rising slowly to his feet.

'A rat trap,' retorted Elise furiously, 'and clever rat walked right into it. Quite spoilt his fun and games, hasn't it?'

Rachel had now risen also and was standing by Robert's

side, her eyes still wide and frightened. Robert turned to her and, putting his arm round her shoulders, started to walk with her to the door.

'Go home, darling,' he said. 'None of this is your fault. I'll handle it.'

And I, too, made a move to escape through the French windows.

'Stop, all of you!' shouted Elise, beside herself with rage, and running across the room, she put her back against the inner door. 'None of you leaves this room until I've said what I want to say. You, Meg, you're my witness. You have already seen what I meant you to see, but I want you to hear the rest as well. You love gossip, don't you? Well, this will give you something to gossip about. And as for you, you putty-faced husband stealer,' she continued, almost spitting the words at Rachel, 'you'll stay and listen to what I think of you and to what I mean to do about you. And, to take the last point first, I mean to cite your name in my divorce action – make no mistake about that – together with a few details that will make that name smell pretty high, too high to be healthy for one of your profession. You don't really think, do you, that I haven't seen what was going on for years past? I could have put a stop to it long ago, but I preferred to wait until I had conclusive evidence. I had an idea that if I was careful to keep you two apart for long enough you would eventually lose your heads and deliver yourselves into my hands. And I was right; you have. But I suppose you know that before that I offered to divorce Robert quietly and decently but he refused?'

'That's a lie,' said Robert, flushing and losing his calm for the first time.

'And you know why he refused?' went on Elise, ignoring the interruption. 'Because he knows he can have you without marriage, so why let himself in for a lot of expense and, into the bargain, risk his position – such as it is – for the sake of second-hand goods, for another man's cast-off, for a woman who's no better than a whore?'

For a moment there was a stunned silence in which the word "whore" seemed to prolong itself like a great sigh, then Rachel broke suddenly away from Robert's side and ran blindly to the French windows and through them, and we heard the diminishing clatter of her footsteps hurrying across the terrace and down the steps and away into the night.

'You devil!' said Robert and, stepping deliberately up to Elise, he struck her, flat-handed, across the cheek. 'I could kill you for that.'

Elise was still standing with her back to the inner door and, when Robert struck her, she jerked her head away and it hit the panel behind her with a sickening crack, but her only movement thereafter was to put her hand to her injured cheek, spreading the white, spatulate fingers across the side of her face. I started forward with a cry, but they were too absorbed in each other to notice me and, already, Elise was speaking again. Her voice was quite calm now, but her face was the face of a Medusa, colourless and stony-eyed under the yellow, snaky locks. And Robert might, indeed, have been turned to rock as he stood motionless before her. His back was turned to me and I could not see his face.

'I shall make you suffer for this,' began Elise softly. 'I had intended only to divorce you, but now I shall break you, if I can. And I think I can,' she went on, her voice rising. 'You have played about with so many women in the last years that it will need only a very little research to turn up a patient who will serve my purpose. And then we shall see what the Medical Council thinks of your professional conduct.'

'You will find it very hard to prove non-professional conduct against me,' said Robert, 'because there never has been any such conduct.'

'You think so?' said Elise. 'We shall see. There was young Mrs Morgan, for instance, and that girl who came last summer to teach Newton.'

'I think you must be mad,' exclaimed Robert furiously, and I could see his fists clenching at his sides.

'Oh, you thought yourself very clever,' went on Elise, 'but I am no fool either, as you will soon find out. And I do not intend to be reticent when our case comes up in court. By the time it is over your name will stink and I hope your latest lady-love likes the smell of it – and of her own.'

'Two can play at that game,' shouted Robert.

'You can't bring anything up against me,' said Elise calmly.

'Don't you think so?' asked Robert. 'Cast your mind back to our wedding night. That was a trap, too, into which I fell. It's a tale which will hardly uphold any injured innocence act you may be intending to put on.'

'I have nothing to lose,' said Elise. 'Unlike you, I don't have to consider what people think of me. In any case you have no proof.'

'More proof than you can ever get concerning a non-existent affair with a patient.'

'But not more than I actually have concerning your affair with Rachel Brading. Meg, here, is my witness as to that.'

'My God! Is that woman still here?' said Robert, whirling round to face me. 'What are you doing here?' he shouted at me. 'Couldn't you see that this was a private discussion between my wife and myself? I thought you had gone with Rachel.'

'I'm sorry,' I said. 'I tried to go but Elise stopped me.'

'Well, get moving now,' said Robert, waving his hand towards the terrace.

'No,' commanded Elise, darting across the room and seizing me by the wrist. 'I need you to protect me,' and her left hand, which she had taken away from her face, went up again to cover the crimson mark on her cheek. Robert gave an angry laugh.

'Protect you!' he exclaimed. 'That's rich. That really is a fitting climax to this little scene, the cat asking to be protected from the mouse.'

'You have struck me once,' retorted Elise. 'How am I to know that next time you will not go further? Meg stays with me until you get out of this house.'

'So I am a prospective murderer now!' exclaimed Robert, and for a moment they glared at each other, naked hatred in their eyes.

'If you are afraid of me, as you pretend, you had better go home with your friend, Mrs Marsden,' said Robert at last. 'This is my house and I intend to stay in it.'

'If you stay, I shall ring the police and ask for protection,' said Elise, making a movement towards the door. Suddenly Robert's bluster left him.

'And where am I supposed to go at this time of night?' he asked mildly.

'Rachel will no doubt share her bed with you as she has done before,' said Elise.

All expression died out of Robert's face and a slow flush flooded upwards from his neck. Then, setting his jaw, he turned abruptly and made for the inner door. When he had opened it he paused and said, 'I am about to pack a bag. I should be obliged if you would put my letters in the surgery each morning and any communication that you or your solicitor wishes to make to me should also be delivered at the surgery. I have my key to the side door and the rest of the house I leave to you, in the meantime.'

He closed the door and we heard the sound of a match striking as he lit a candle in the hall and then the thud of his footsteps as he slowly mounted the stairs, then the banging of the door and silence. To all this Elise listened intently; then, turning to me, she gave a great sigh.

'Ooof, that's the end of him. Thank goodness! I shan't need you any more for the present, Meg. You can go home now.'

'That's very kind of you!' I said, but the irony was quite lost on her and she continued as though I had not spoken.

'Of course, I shall want you again when the divorce comes up. You are my chief witness.'

'It has never occurred to you, I suppose, that I might not be willing to give evidence?' I said, exasperated by her manner and angry at being involved in the unsavoury business.

'Not give evidence!' exclaimed Elise, opening her blue eyes wide. 'But of course you must give evidence. I shall see that you are subpoenaed.'

'You seem very sure of me and the evidence I would give.'

'Do you mean to say that you intend to tell lies if I call upon you to testify to the scene we broke in on this evening?'

'It's all a matter of interpretation. Rachel and Robert are old friends, after all, and colleagues, too. That they were alone together does not necessarily mean that they were making love.'

'So you mean to rat on me?'

But I did not know what I meant to do exactly. I was simply tired of being pushed around by Elise.

'I very much resent having been tricked into this situation,' I said.

'You, with your nose for gossip, you ought to be in your element,' she retorted contemptuously. 'You were in no hurry to leave when you might have done so. However, whether you support me or not, you have served my purpose. Robert knows that there was an outside witness to his little love-scene. He knows the game is up and it will not be difficult now to get evidence against him. It's in my power to ruin him at last, and I mean to do it – with you or without you,' she added, fingering her cheek.

'Elise,' I said, 'why are you so vindictive? You don't love Robert. You don't even want him around. What good will it do to you to get him struck off the register? Why don't you simply divorce him quietly? For Rachel's sake, I don't think he'll defend himself. If you do that I will support your story because I think you two are better apart.'

To my surprise, Elise smiled.

'All right,' she said, 'it's a bargain. You give your evidence and I'll drop the unprofessional conduct charges.'

Was this what she had angled for with her show of vindictiveness? I don't know. All I know is that I was no match for Elise, with her tortuous mind. And so, the bargain was struck.

I offered to stay the night with Elise if she was afraid to be alone in the Big House, but she refused my offer brusquely and I realised that all her former unwillingness to be left alone had been part of a deliberate plan, a plan to drive Robert and Rachel to desperation by keeping them apart and then to trap them as she had now finally done.

I waited until I had heard Robert descend the stairs, bang the front door and drive off in his car, and then I, too, left, by the terrace. The last I saw of Elise she was standing in front of the piano running the back of one finger thoughtfully along the keys and, as I made my way across the lawn, I heard the sound of her playing. The music that she had chosen was the Mephisto waltz.

Music greeted me again as I opened our own front door, for Andy was sitting with his eyes shut listening to a record on his ancient gramophone. He looked up in surprise when I came in.

'Back already, Meg? How was the concert?' he asked.

I realised then with astonishment that it was still early, barely half-past ten, and that Andy, of course, knew nothing of the dramatic happenings at the doctor's house. He listened in silence while I told him of my adventures and, only at the end of my tale, said anxiously, 'Meg, I wish you hadn't become involved in this.'

I said I wished so, too, but that, having promised, I must go through with it.

'Tell me again,' he said then, 'about Elise's illness on the road – every detail that you can remember.'

I looked at him in surprise but did as he asked, adding very considerably to my first account in which I had passed very lightly over that particular episode. Andy was silent for a long time after that, obviously thinking deeply, but at last he said, 'Yes, perhaps it would be as well to let things go on. The sooner those two are divorced the better. A divorce might prevent another tragedy. It all fits in, I can see that.'

'Fits in to what?' I asked.

'Why, to Newton's murder, of course.'

But, in spite of all I could do, I could not get him to elucidate this cryptic statement.

Chapter 12

DIVORCE PROCEEDINGS

After the evening of the abortive concert, events began to move fast. Next morning Elise was on our doorstep before nine o'clock demanding a lift into Carne in order to see her solicitor.

'I want you to come with me, Meg,' she said, directly her request had been made, 'to make your statement at once. That way I shall be sure of you and you will not be able to back out of the bargain we made last night.'

I was, of course, annoyed at being bounced into things in this way but, at a gesture from Andy, I agreed to come as soon as I had put some order into the house. Elise and Andy both followed me into the kitchen and Elise seated herself, with an impatient gesture, on one of the wooden chairs. She did not, of course, offer to help me with the washing up of the breakfast dishes. Meanwhile, Andy, in an effort to be helpful, decided to polish my town shoes in readiness for the visit to our local metropolis. All he succeeded in doing, however, was to hinder me yet further, for in his search for the shoe polish he somehow managed to empty the whole contents of the kitchen cupboard onto the floor and it took me a good five minutes to pick everything up and re-stow it where it belonged. The polish, as Andy ought to have known, was in the dresser drawer. After this there was the bed to make and myself to tidy. Elise's impatience grew with every minute but, at last, I was ready and we set off.

Elise was in one of her silent moods, obviously deep in

thought, her unfocused gaze fixed blankly on the road ahead. What devilry was she planning now? I wondered uneasily. It was another broiling day. The white-hot light of the sun and the blanching dust that lay thickly over verges and hedgerows combined to take the colour out of every growing thing. Only the gleam and glitter of the river, glimpsed between trees, heavy with dark August foliage, gave a little life to the landscape. Carne was a hell of heat, dust and petrol fumes. We left the car in the main square and started to walk to the offices of Piggling and Pritchard, Solicitors, which are situated in a small, cobbled cul-de-sac running down one side of the George Hotel, whose half-timbered facade occupies almost the whole east end of the square. As we were about to cross the road to the front of the hotel a woman stopped me and asked me the way to the Pump Room, one of the chief attractions for the summer visitors to Carne. The woman appeared to be particularly dim and, by the time I had succeeded – or thought I had succeeded – in making my directions clear, Elise had crossed the road and a stream of traffic, released by the lights at the top of the square, had flooded between us. It was several minutes before I managed to dodge my way across, by which time I expected that Elise would have made her way to the solicitors' office, without waiting for me; it would have been quite out of character for Elise to wait for anyone. To my surprise, however, she was standing outside the main door of the George. I was about to hail her when I noticed that she was talking to a man whose face and figure seemed vaguely familiar but whom I could not immediately place. As I watched them he put out a hand

and grasped her by the arm and seemed to be urging her to come with him into the hotel but she shook her head and, putting her free hand on his, lifted it from her arm. For a moment they stood hand in hand, looking intently at each other and obviously quite oblivious of their surroundings. Then Elise, putting her other hand also on his, said something earnestly to him, at which he nodded and, turning abruptly on his heel, vanished into the hotel. Elise watched him go and then, seeming suddenly to come to herself, looked almost furtively around her, and at once saw me standing at the kerb and came hurrying towards me. The whole episode had not taken more than a few seconds.

When Elise reached me I could see immediately that she was angry: her cheeks were flushed and her lips set. Whether her anger was at me or the strange man it was hard to tell, but it was I who got the benefit of it.

'Where on earth did you get to?' she said. 'I've been waiting for you. How long have you been dawdling around here?'

'Only a second or two,' I said, and explained about the summer visitor and the Pump Room and then about the difficulty in crossing the road.

'My God! You need a nanny to hold your hand. Let's get a move on now, for heaven's sake.'

As we hurried along the pavement together I debated with myself whether to ask the identity of the stranger at the George. I knew that I should get my head bitten off if I asked but at last, as we came to the entrance of the cul-de-sac, my curiosity got the better of my discretion and the question popped out before I could prevent it.

'Who's your boyfriend, Elise?' I ventured.

Elise's answer was no less tart than I had expected: 'Really, Meg,' she said, 'I think you have the most ... the most ... vulgar mind of any person I know. If by "boyfriend" you mean the man I was talking to at the George, I haven't the slightest idea who he is. Like your nit-wit woman he was merely asking the way to somewhere.'

Well that's a lie, I thought, and a clumsy, hastily fabricated lie at that – probably suggested by my own encounter in the square. Nobody comes out of a hotel well-staffed with receptionist, hall porter, manager, not to speak of several waiters – all bulging with information about the town – in order to ask the way of a stranger, and then turns straight back into the hotel again.

However, I said no more. It was none of my business, I supposed. Good-looking fellow, though; and, as I recalled the stranger's well-groomed appearance and black, shining hair, I suddenly knew who he was: of course, Mr Brown, whom I had twice seen before, once at Newton's inquest and the second time on the river bank near Llantossy; the very Mr Brown whom Cliff Price suspected of being a poaching buddy of ours. At the thought of Cliff's suspicions I could not help smiling to myself. Anything less like my idea of a poacher than the immaculate figure on the steps of the George it would be hard to imagine. What possible connection could he have with Elise, I wondered, and why had she told a lie about him?

I had reached this stage in my reflections when Elise turned into an entry leading off the cul-de-sac. We had arrived at the premises of Piggling and Pritchard. Thereafter, my thoughts were so concentrated on Elise and her divorce that I forgot Mr Brown. I have often wondered since whether, if only I had given utterance to my thoughts during that short walk down the cobbled cul-de-sac, I might not have averted a death, indeed, two deaths, for the second followed from the first.

A board just inside the entry into which Elise had stepped directed us to the first floor and we mounted a flight of stone stairs to a narrow landing at the far end of which was a glass-panelled door inscribed with the names, Piggling and Pritchard, Solicitors. On opening this door we found ourselves in a small, stuffy office with a window facing us and a second door in the right-hand wall. Two wooden chairs stood near the window and the rest of the wall space was occupied by a large filing cabinet and tiers of shelves, bearing deed boxes and dusty files of old law magazines. Cramped into the space between the second door and the window was a desk at which a fat girl with glasses sat and clattered away at a typewriter. She asked us our business in a tone that suggested that most of Piggling and Pritchard's clients must be drawn from the criminal classes, and obviously she did not consider us to be exceptions to this general rule.

Had we an appointment? No? Well, Mr Evans never saw clients without an appointment. If we would state our business she would fix a suitable time. Had I been alone I should have slunk, chastened, from the office; but not so Elise.

'I think you must be new here,' she said, turning her extraordinary eyes on the opaque lenses of the girl behind the desk.

'Otherwise you would know that I am an old client of the firm. Would you kindly inform Mr Evans that I am here and wish to see him immediately on an urgent matter. My name is Mrs Landon.'

For a moment there was a battle of wills between the fat girl and Elise, then the eyes behind the thick lenses wavered and turned away.

'I'll ask Mr Evans when he will be free,' muttered the girl, and rising from her chair went through the door in the right-hand wall of the office. In under half a minute she was back and there was a dull flush on her pasty cheeks. Obviously she had received a raspberry from her employer.

'Mr Evans is busy,' she said sullenly. 'He can't see you before this afternoon.'

Elise gave her one incredulous look and strode to the door from which the girl had just emerged. As she reached it she turned to me and said, 'Wait there, Meg. I'll call you when I want you,' and with that she was through the door into Mr Evan's sanctum – and, what's more, there she stayed.

'Bang goes a good job!' murmured the poor fat girl with a resigned sigh.

I was sorry for her, but there was nothing I could do and I went and sat on one of the wooden chairs by the window to await Elise's pleasure.

'Who is Mr Evans?' I asked conversationally as I sat down.

'Mr Evans? Why, he's the boss, of course. Senior partner,' replied the girl, surprised that anyone should be ignorant of a fact which loomed so large in her own life.

'What about Mr Piggling and Mr Pritchard?' I went on, in order to divert her mind from her troubles.

'Dead for donkey's years. Firm ought to be called Evans and Skrimshank, by rights. Skrimshank, he's junior partner. Ever so nice he is, ever so thoughtful. Not like *him*,' with a jerk of her head towards the inner door. 'But he's on holiday, Mr Skrimshank is, worse luck. Before he comes back I shall be out on my ear, looks like. Oh, well, that's life, that is,' with which philosophical reflection she removed her glasses, gave them a brisk polish on a dirty handkerchief, and fell to again upon her typing.

It was stuffy and hot in the little office, even though the sash window was open at the bottom and the sun was on the other side of the building. The perspiration gleamed on the fat girl's nose and forehead and my thighs were sticking to the wooden chair. A little band of house flies droned round and round beneath the ceiling. The typewriter clattered and thumped and screeched and minute after minute passed, and I was bored. I put my elbows on the windowsill and leaned out to try and get a breath of air. The window gave onto what were obviously the back premises of the George Hotel and a row of three lock-up garages faced me across a sunlit courtyard in which a troupe of sparrows squabbled and dusted and made love. Two of the garages were closed but the roll-up door of the third was open, exposing a small grey saloon car. When I was tired of watching the sparrows my eyes turned to the car and I examined minutely what I could see of it. I am much given to doodling mentally with the registration numbers of cars driving ahead of me and I did this now with the number of the car in the garage. Its registration letters, I was mildly amused to note, were MEG and its number added up to my own age, minus Curly's. I had just done this futile sum in my head when, to my surprise, the car started to move. There had obviously been some person sitting in it all the time that I had been examining the yard and, presently, that person's head came into view as it craned out of the driving seat window to watch the car's backward progress. It was the head of Mr Brown. No mistaking that black, shining cap of hair. He backed expertly out, turned the car's nose towards the yard gate, invisible to me, and was gone, leaving behind him a thin, blue cloud of exhaust fumes to taint the shimmering air. The sparrows, disturbed by his exit, now returned, one by one, and resumed their interrupted gossip in the deserted, sunlit yard, but their antics soon palled. What on earth was Elise up to all this time? I longed to be out of this dusty, stuffy office and wading the cool river with a trout rod in my hand. With a sigh I turned back to the room. The clatter of the typewriter had ceased and the fat girl was surreptitiously consoling herself with a bar of chocolate while she checked over her recent labours. The flies droned on and on, performing their aimless exercises under the ceiling. At last – at long last – when I had just about decided to leave a message for Elise and go out and get myself a cup of coffee in the town, a bell rang on the fat girl's desk. Hastily stowing away in a drawer the last of the chocolate and wiping her hands and mouth on the same none too clean handkerchief with which she had wiped her spectacles, she vanished through the inner door, to return in a moment with the information that Mr Evans would like to see me now.

Mr Evans turned out to be a dapper little Welshman with a long, pointed nose and a thin, ever-smiling mouth. His manner was courteous, almost fulsome, and his soft voice retained more than a trace of his native Welsh. I disliked and distrusted him instantly – perhaps out of sympathy for the poor fat girl or, perhaps, because of his cold, unfeeling eyes which never shared in the smile on his lips. I could imagine him looking on at some gruesome torture with no more emotion than that of an entomologist watching a beetle slowly turning on a pin. To him, I felt sure, all his clients were beetles – on or off pins – whose curious antics he had acquired the skill to interpret – to his own considerable profit.

'Ah, Mrs Marsden!' he greeted me, rising from behind a large, old-fashioned desk and placing a chair for me beside it. 'Pray be seated.' (He pronounced it seat-ed, giving full value to the second syllable). 'I trust the time of waiting has not been too long. Mrs Landon and I had a little business to dispose of before coming to the sad object of your visit.'

I sat down and found myself facing a large window, looking east, from which nothing was visible but a wedge of house wall and a wide expanse of blue sky and sunny air which again made me long for the cool river. Elise, who had not acknowledged my entry by so much as a glance, was seated in the usual client's chair with her elbow on the desk and her chin in her hand, gazing out at the empty view, her expression quite blank. Mr Evans, of course, was sitting with his back to the window and I could feel, rather than see, his cold eyes appraising me.

'Well, now, Mrs Marsden,' he began, 'I understand that you are a friend and near neighbour of Mrs Landon.'

I assented.

'And she has told you that she wishes to divorce her husband, Dr Robert Landon?'

'Of course, that's why I am here.'

'Quite so, quite so. Mrs Landon tells me that you were witness to an unfortunate scene yesterday evening at Dr Landon's house ...'

'A fortunate scene,' interrupted Elise abruptly, bringing her gaze back from the window.

'That, madam,' said Mr Evans softy, 'depends on the viewpoint.' Then turning to me: 'Would you be so kind, Mrs Marsden, as to give us your account of this ... ah ... scene.'

'Elise – Mrs Landon – has already told you of it?'

'Certainly, but I would like your account in order that I may form a judgement as to the value of your testimony in our case.'

'I hope you are going to take this down, Mr Evans,' said Elise.

Mr Evans turned his head and looked at her and there was a longish pause before he said very gently: 'I am not a stenographer, Mrs Landon. I think a general statement will suffice us at this stage.'

'Nevertheless, I should like you to make notes at once,' insisted Elise. 'I know Meg. She is quite capable of backing out of the whole thing unless you pin her down at once.'

'As you wish,' said Mr Evans, still softly, still smiling, but with eyes as hard as agates; and, taking a pad of paper from a drawer and a silver pencil from his waistcoat pocket, he prepared to note down the salient points in my story.

'Since we are to have a full statement we had better begin at the beginning,' he said. 'Your full name, address, age and occupation, if you please, Mrs Marsden.'

When I had given this information he had other questions to ask in order, as he said, to supply some background to the scene of the previous evening. For instance: How long had I known Elise? Did I know Robert? And Rachel? Had I on any previous occasion noticed anything in the behaviour either of Dr Brading or of Dr Landon that might indicate that an improper relationship existed between them? This last I found hard to answer, remembering Robert's birthday party and the windy evening I had spent with Rachel at Weir Cottage. However, in the end I said that any familiarity I had noticed between them I had put down to the fact that they were childhood friends.

'You did notice a familiarity between them, then?' he asked quickly.

'Not in any improper sense,' I said firmly, and from that I would not budge.

At last we came to the scene of the previous evening.

'Now, I would like this in your own words, Mrs Marsden, if you please. Just tell me what occurred from the moment you met Mrs Landon yesterday evening. You met by previous arrangement, I understand.'

'Yes, that is so. We arranged to go to a concert in Carne together.'

'The tickets were presented to you by Dr Landon?'

'Yes. At least so Mrs Landon told me.'

'Quite so. Pray go on from there.'

So I told him, as shortly as I could, about our visit to Carne, about Elise being taken ill, about our return to the doctor's house in the dark and on foot, about cutting across the lawn to the terrace and, finally – mumbling and, I believe, blushing – about the tableau that met our eyes beyond the French windows. Elise listened impassively to my tale until I had finished describing, with as little detail as might be, the positions in that tableau of Robert and Rachel. Then she burst out: 'Is that all you are going to say?'

'Yes, that's all,' I said.

'My God! You make it sound as though the two of them had been caught playing cat's cradle instead of –' and she used a word which caused even Mr Evans to raise his eyebrows and lose, momentarily, his perpetual smile.

'And what about later, when Robert struck me in the face?' she went on. 'Aren't you even going to mention that?'

'He only struck you under extreme provocation,' I said, red now with anger. 'If you ask me you only got what you deserved.'

'*I* got what I deserved! You speak as though *I* were the guilty party. You think, perhaps, it's the right and proper thing for a husband caught in the act of adultery to turn and beat his wife?'

'Now, now, ladies,' said Mr Evans soothingly. 'Please do not let us have any unpleasantness here. Mrs Marsden has said quite enough for our purposes for the moment. We have a long way to go yet before a petition can be filed. We shall get the evidence, bit by bit, when you two ladies are both in a calmer frame of mind. Now, if you will excuse me, I have another appointment in,' looking at his watch, 'just two minutes.'

'And Mrs Marsden's statement – as far as it goes? asked Elise. 'That must be typed out and signed before I leave this office.'

'My dear Mrs Landon,' said Mr Evans, gently but emphatically, staring at her with his stony eyes, 'you ask for the impossible. My confidential clerk will make out the statement at the earliest opportunity and you will be notified in due course that it is ready for signature,' and, so saying, he rang a bell on his desk and indicated that the interview was definitely over.

Elise opened her mouth to protest, but was prevented by the entry of a tall, pale, elderly man with glasses and lank, greying hair obviously the confidential clerk.

'You rang, sir?' he said.

'Ah, Mr Truffitt. Kindly see these ladies out, then return here for a moment.'

There was nothing for it but to leave; even Elise could see that. Silently, like a farm hand driving two difficult cows, Mr Truffitt herded us through a second door which opened onto the narrow landing at the top of the stone stairs and firmly, but quietly, shut us out.

It was not until we had reached the sunny square that either of us found anything to say. Then Elise broke the silence between us: 'Meg,' she said, 'I believe you're angry with me,' and I really think she did not know how outrageously she had been behaving and was genuinely surprised to find that she had given offence.

'Of course I'm angry with you,' I burst out. 'First you trap me into the extremely uncomfortable position of witness to your matrimonial troubles and then you drag me into an unpleasant scene before a stranger.'

'Come and have a cup of coffee with me,' she said placatingly, 'and let's talk it over.'

'I must be getting home to Andy,' I said, but, in fact, I was already mollified, as I always seemed to be by any show of softness on Elise's part and, before many minutes had passed, I found myself sitting in a corner of the Regency Coffee Room with Elise opposite me.

Then there ensued a rather curious conversation, in the course of which I learned more about Elise and the workings of her mind in half an hour than I had previously done in all the four months of our acquaintanceship.

'Meg,' she began, when we had been served with our iced coffees, 'why are you so much against me?'

'I don't like being tricked into taking sides in your quarrels with Robert,' I said. 'It was all a fake, wasn't it, that business of your illness yesterday evening?'

'Did it look like a fake?'

'No, it was most convincing.'

She was silent for a long time, staring with her elbows on the table at her un-tasted cup of coffee. At last, she said, 'You know, Meg, underneath his mild abstracted manner, Robert is a ruthless man and my death would be very convenient for him at this moment – for more reasons than you know.'

'You are not seriously suggesting that he tried to poison you last night?'

'I leave you to draw your own conclusions.'

'I don't believe it. I think your "illness" was an excuse for you to go home and find Rachel and Robert together.'

'Well, I certainly outwitted Robert there. You are right, at least, in thinking that I laid a trap to catch him. I knew that he and Rachel were desperate. I had managed to keep them apart for weeks by going with Robert on his rounds and keeping Rachel company when Robert was called out late. I knew that the minute I relaxed my watchdog act they would fly to each other. Robert thought he was being so clever in giving me those tickets and getting me out of the way for an evening. He bought them himself, of course – all that tale about a present from a patient was a lie. He little knew that he was playing right into my hands, that it was just the thing I had been waiting for.'

'But Elise, why do you go about things in such a tortuous manner? I'm sure Robert would have let you divorce him if you had asked him.'

'No, no, he would not. That's where you're wrong. You don't know Robert, Meg. He's clever and dangerous and I'm afraid of him. He thinks I did him an injury once, long ago, and he has never forgiven me. I think he enjoys torturing me and he'd rather die than give me my freedom. There was nothing for it but to lay a trap for him – a trap out of which he could not wriggle.'

'But why drag me into it? Why not have employed a private detective? That's what other people do. They don't drag their friends into it. Mr Evans would no doubt have provided you with someone discreet and efficient.'

'And have enquiries dragging on for weeks and months and bills mounting up! Who was to pay for all that? Not me. I'm penniless.'

'So you did it on the cheap, through me!'

'You were the only person I knew. I've had to do the best I could and all alone with no-one to help me or give me advice. Oh, Meg, if you only knew how I hate the life I'm compelled to lead. I must – I simply *must* – get away from Coedafon. If I do not, I shall go berserk one fine day and start laying about me with an axe, like the wretched Lizzie Borden whom the Americans made a ballet about. Everything about the place is evil. Robert – to begin with – who has never been faithful to me since we were first married and who has the mind of a reptile, mean and cruel. And then, the village people with their sly faces, smiling and staring and whispering behind one's back. And the place itself, shut in and secretive and half-dead, like the people. And then the river – the hateful river with its mud and its mists and its horrible dark pools. I can sense it all the time, lying in wait there, biding its time – whispering and chuckling and waiting – waiting until it can snatch another corpse to feed on and bury in its slime. I hate it, hate it, hate it.'

She stared at me with blazing eyes and distended pupils. Then before I could think of any comment on this surprising outburst, she went on: 'You never knew Newton, did you?'

'Well, yes,' I said, 'I met him once.'

'You did!' she exclaimed, brought up short by the unexpected statement. 'When was that?'

'On the afternoon … he died,' I said with hesitation.

'You never told me that. Tell me about it.'

Her eyes searched my face with a curious, intent eagerness. So I told her about Curly and the torn trousers, watering down greatly – out of consideration for Elise's feelings – Newton's unpleasant part in the affair.

'I knew your dogs were dangerous,' she exclaimed, as I described the episode on the river bank, and I noticed that her right hand was clenched till the knuckles showed white.

'Curly had been hurt,' I said defensively. 'There was a gaping wound in her haunch, probably caused by the gaff. Any dog, even one as good-tempered as Curly, will retaliate if it is hurt.'

'Yes, that's true. Even a dog will retaliate when it is hurt,' she agreed, turning my words slightly. 'That's when they are dangerous. Go on, what happened next?'

'I took Newton into the house and cobbled up the tear in his trousers for him.'

'And he let you do that?'

'Yes – a little unwillingly.'

'They were a pretty colour,' said Elise, and it was a second or two before I realised that she was talking of the trousers.

'Yes,' I said, 'I noticed that particularly, and uncommon, too. You don't often see that shade of blue in corduroy.'

'I saw them in a shop window when I was staying with Jo-Jo. So you mended them for him!'

She was staring at me still but now she did not seem to see me and a long, awkward silence fell. To break it I said feebly, 'I gave him some toffees.'

'You did what?' exclaimed Elise, bringing her thoughts back from far away.

'I gave Newton some toffees – because he had been frightened by my dog,' I explained lamely.

And then, Elise began to laugh and the tension went out of her.

'Meg, you're a caution,' she said. 'Come on, let's get home.'

In the car we were silent. The heaviness of an August noon lay over everything and the little car, even with all the windows open, was like an oven. I felt that my face was scarlet with the heat and the palms of my hands on the steering wheel were slippery with sweat. But Elise, sitting beside me, seemed to feel no discomfort. There was no flush on her face, in fact, she looked paler than usual and her skin looked as cool as a river nymph's; no, not a river nymph, I thought, she hates the river. As cool as … as … a zombie, a walking corpse. I was startled and a little frightened at my own fancy, but, indeed, when she fell into an abstraction, as now, she did have a curiously lifeless air. What was she thinking of? I wondered. With her tortuous mind it was impossible to tell. Was she thinking of Newton, that unattractive changeling, whom it seemed she had really loved in her own way? Or of Robert whom she hated and who hated her? Or did he hate her? He was another whose thoughts it was impossible to fathom. Where had he gone, I wondered, after he had walked out of his own door on the previous evening? Had he spent the night in Carne, or had he gone to Rachel?

As we turned onto Coedafon bridge I broke the long silence to ask Elise whether she knew of his whereabouts. But she did not.

'Sharing Rachel's bed and board, I expect,' she said. 'But I don't know and I don't care. I suppose he held his morning surgery as usual, because of course he could not let his sacred patients down, but I was out of the house before nine so I didn't see him.'

It was under very dreadful circumstances that eventually I got an answer to my question and the answer, when it came, sank into insignificance in the welter of events. The violent happenings which preceded the discovery and which involved us personally now began to crowd so thick and fast upon us that Elise's matrimonial troubles soon ceased to occupy the forefront of our thoughts.

Chapter 13

COSHED

It all began with a poachers' raid on Llantossy water, the day, or rather, the night after our visit to Piggling and Pritchard in Carne. It was a Thursday, I remember. The weather had again been sizzlingly hot – too hot to move from the house. The dogs lay all day like logs on the stone flags under the kitchen table. In the afternoon I made a show of gardening, sowing seeds of savoy and winter lettuce and then going round languidly with a bagging hook cutting the long grass along our fences but, by the time I had reached the bottom hedge beside the river path, I had had enough and, sitting in the crotch of an old cob-nut tree that grew in the corner, gave myself up to uncomfortable idleness. Not a soul seemed to be astir in the village – even old Milly Piggott was invisible. The only living things to be seen were the pigeons coming down from the woods to drink at the river's edge and the only sounds were the murmur of water and the crooning of the pigeons as they rested themselves briefly in the willows before winging their way back to their shady woodlands. It was altogether too hot. The heat was oppressive, menacing – and Andy was in one of his moods. He sat all afternoon under the pear tree with a battered copy of Hill's *The Golden Fish* on his lap, but whenever I passed behind his deck chair the book was still open at page 69. Something was worrying him but I knew from past, bitter experience that it was useless either to try to cheer him up or to make any enquiry concerning his worry. In his own good time he would come out of his mood and until then it just had to be borne – by both of us. By six o'clock I, for one, could bear it – and idleness – no longer and, calling the dogs, I strolled off up the lane to fetch butter and eggs from Trev Price's farm. As I closed the front door behind me Robert Landon passed the gate in his car, on his way, I supposed, to six o'clock surgery. He was driving too fast for safety in the narrow, rutted lane, and so carelessly that he grazed the gate-post as he turned into his own drive. Scarcely had the sound of his engine ceased than I heard another car nosing its way slowly up from the village and, as it passed me, I recognised Joseph Ellis' opulent vehicle with himself in the driving seat and I surmised that he must have been summoned by Elise to advise and support her in the matter of her divorce.

The farm lane was steep and I was in no mood to hurry so that it must have taken me close on half an hour, dawdling and picking honeysuckle on the way, to cover the mile to the farm. Once there I had a chat with Mrs Trev about the harvest and with young Rodney Price – the same who had found Newton's body – about eels. He had caught a monster, he said, the previous evening behind the Crib and to prove his statement he insisted on showing me the eel's cat-gnawed head, while his brother, Gwilym, looked on, nodding in admiration at Rodney's cleverness. All this took time. On the way back I stopped at the watersplash, where the brook crossed the lane, to dabble my hot feet among the brooklime and it was while I was here, sitting on a stone in the shade of an elder bush, that I saw Elise emerge from the water-meadow and turn down the lane towards her own house. I was hidden from her by the bush and the dogs were busy in Price's hay meadow on the other side of the lane and consequently invisible. Elise was hurrying, and carrying in her hand a large linen bag with wooden handles. For some reason I got the idea that she did not want to be seen and therefore did not call out to her. As she reached a slight bend in the lane which hid the gate of the doctor's house from us, she stopped suddenly and stood listening and I heard the sound of a car emerging from the drive. Only when the noise of the engine had receded towards the village did Elise continue on her way. Her whole behaviour suggested that she was avoiding someone – her brother, Joseph, presumably, though why she should do that I could not imagine. My supposition that she had summoned him must be wrong and his business must have been with Robert and not Elise. The time by now must have been just after seven o'clock, for the French clock was chiming the first quarter as I reached home.

Andy was still in a mood but, after a silent supper, to my relief he took himself off to consume his nightly pint at the Ferryman. When he returned, soon after closing time, his bad mood had gone and he was full of animation, almost excitement.

'There's a poaching scare on,' he told me with glee as he entered the door. 'PC Jones is lurking under the bridge with a monstrous great Alsatian chained to his wrist and one of the bailiffs from Carne is keeping him company. They've been there since dark. It's supposed to be a secret but old Tom Todd has been smuggling tankards of ale out to them all evening – MacAlister's Boy being the go-between. Everyone in the village knows all about it, of course. The only thing they don't know is Cliff Price's whereabouts. He's been very cagey and mysterious, it seems, but it's thought he's probably at Llantossy, keeping an eye on the footbridges there. All the bridges and all the roads coming down to the river along a five-mile stretch are under observation and there's a motorcycle patrol along the Carne road.'

'How do they know there will be a raid tonight?' I asked.

'Seems Cliff Price got wind of it in some way. Says he's not going to be made a fool of like Taffy Evans on the Tovey. Somehow he's managed to persuade the police to co-operate, just on suspicion. Says he knows where he would go if he was a poacher, but won't tell anyone where that is – except the police, of course, I suppose.'

'Where do you, yourself, think they'll strike? You know the river pretty well by now.'

'Well, it won't be here. The Crib pool is too open and too near the village. Besides, there aren't the fish in it to make it worthwhile. Llantossy Church pool is crammed with fish, but again, I should say, it's too near the village. Perhaps the weir pool would be the best bet. The fish there are jammed head to tail in this drought. The only habitation near the pool is Rachel Brading's cottage and the sound of the weir would cover any noise – if they use the poisoning method, as they seem to have done before. The only problem for them would be where to park the car – or whatever it is they use for the getaway.'

'Inside one of the field gates along the Carne road between the Weir and Llantossy might be a possible place.'

'It might, but the river bank is pretty hard to negotiate on that stretch – rocky and overgrown. Too tough going, I should say, with a few hundredweight of fish to be transported.'

'The best place to leave a car would be the old gravel pit a little downstream from the church at Llantossy. It has its own track up to the Carne road.'

'Meg, you've got it,' said Andy excitedly. 'The church knoll and the trees would hide them and their activities from the village which all lies upstream from there. They'd never need to go near the village at all and the footbridges by the island would enable them to work on both sides of the river. I don't mind betting that's where they are. Come on, Meg. I'm going up there to see the fun.'

'Andy, no. No, no. Cliff Price already thinks we've got some hand in this racket and if we turn up now he'll be certain of it.'

We argued the matter for some time but, at last, Andy gave in.

'Perhaps you're right,' he said sadly, his excitement ebbing. Then after a pause: 'I'm not much good in the rough house these days. Better leave it to tougher folk.'

With that, he relapsed into his gloom of earlier in the evening. I suggested bed, but was ignored, so I found myself a book and tried to read, but it was no good and, as midnight struck on the French clock, I could bear it no longer.

'Oh, come on, Andy, snap out of it,' I burst out suddenly. 'You're behaving like a sulky child. If you won't come to bed, why don't we take a turn down the river bank with the dogs to see what sort of night it is?'

Andy brightened at once.

'Yes, all right. Come on. We might see something,' he said eagerly.

So rousing the dogs and turning down the Aladdin, we were soon on our way down the garden to the river path. As we left the house, Andy snatched a coat off the hook behind the back door and handed it to me, saying, 'Put that on, Meg. You'll catch your death of cold with those bare arms.'

But it was another sort of death entirely that he nearly brought upon me by his thoughtful action.

I was first through the hedge and as I stepped out on the other side I heard Andy call out: 'I can't see a damn thing. I'll have to go back for a torch,' and then his limping footsteps retreating towards the cottage.

I thought he would re-join me in a minute and I strolled on slowly up the river path, then round the end of the doctor's orchard and so to the footbridge over the stream. My thoughts were far away, remembering the days when Andy would not have needed a torch to see his way on a summer night and when his footstep was firm and quick. It was a perfect poachers' night: dark, but clear and not too still. There was no moon, but no mist either and a slight wind was rising, making eerie rustlings and creakings in the willows and sending small scuds of cloud across the starlit sky. As I set foot on the planks of the footbridge I realised suddenly that I was alone. There was no sound of the dogs in the undergrowth. They must have followed Andy back to the house and Andy, himself, had not yet caught me up. I stopped to wait for him, straining my ears for the sounds of his approach, but there was nothing to be heard except the soft rushing of the river and the tinkle of the stream under my feet and, from time to time, a slight fluttering of the willow leaves as the breeze riffled them. It was darker here on the bridge than on the open bank and even the water was scarcely visible, enclosed and overhung, as it was, by trees. The pathway beyond the bridge where it entered the alder spinney was a tunnel of blackness, quite impenetrable to the eye. Suddenly, I was afraid. I did not know of what; certainly not of the darkness, for I have always loved the night, but of something indefinably evil which seemed to emanate from this spot – the bridge where Newton Landon had died. A smell of corruption, of drowned flesh and rotten weeds seemed to rise from the invisible backwater. I was cold and the hair seemed to crawl and rise on my scalp. I tried to call out to Andy and to step back off the footbridge and run for home, but found that I could do neither. Then, when my causeless terror was at its height, I heard a sound – a long-drawn, eerie creaking. For a moment my heart contracted and I thought I should faint, but almost at once relief flooded over me; for I knew what made that sound. It was the rusty hinge of the gate leading into the doctor's garden. Elise, or possibly the doctor himself (I forgot for the moment that Robert was no longer at home), must be taking a stroll along the river, perhaps, like us, to see what they could see of the night's anticipated excitements.

'Elise,' I called out, 'is that you?'

But there was no reply and the next moment a dark shape seemed to materialise out of the blackness. I felt a sharp blow on the head, a sensation of falling, an icy coldness and I knew that

I was in the river struggling for my life. Fortunately, the blow on the head had not entirely stunned me and the cold water soon restored me to my senses. Even so I should have had a hard time of it with the coat Andy had thrust upon me encumbering my arms and dragging me down, had not my flailing right hand suddenly come in contact with an overhanging willow branch. Desperately I grasped it and there I clung, spluttering and choking, and quite incapable of making any further effort on my own behalf. Even to cry out was beyond my powers, for the foul-smelling river water, clotted with slimy leaves, clogged my throat and nostrils. But rescue was at hand; the sight of a torch, first, on the bank, and then Andy's voice calling, 'Meg! Meg! Where are you?' And then urgently addressing the dogs, 'Where's your missus? Go seek, go seek. Seek out, Squelch. Seek out, Curly.' Thus encouraged the dogs soon found me and, guided by their excited yelps, Andy, blind eye, gammy leg and all, was able to crawl far enough along the willow bough to reach out a hand and drag me ashore, where I lay retching and gasping for a minute or more.

'My God, Meg,' Andy said, as I sat up at last, 'you gave me a fright. What on earth were you doing to fall into the river like that?'

'I didn't fall in,' I said crossly. 'I was pushed. Didn't you see whoever it was who pushed me?'

'I didn't see a thing,' said Andy. 'I just heard you yell, and then the splash as you hit the water.'

'And you saw nothing?' I asked.

'Not a thing.'

'Well, somebody came out of Robert's garden and hit me on the head as I was standing on the footbridge.'

'Hit you on the head? Are you sure?'

'Of course I'm sure,' I snapped.

'Here, let me see,' said Andy in a worried voice. 'Are you hurt? Let me look at your head.'

'No, no. I'm all right,' I said.

'Did you get a look at this person?' Andy asked.

'Never saw a thing. I heard the gate creak and I thought it was Elise. I called out to her and the next thing I knew I was in the water.'

'Well, he – or she – must have run up the river through the alder spinney.'

'She?' I said. 'Female salmon poachers are a bit rare, aren't they?'

'How do you know it was a poacher?'

'Well, who else?'

Andy made no reply to this.

'Come on home, Meg,' he said. 'Your teeth are chattering. We can discuss things further when you are safely in bed with a hot water bottle and a warm drink.'

Which is what we did. But our discussion led nowhere. We had neither of us seen my assailant, and that was that.

'Why were you so long in coming on the scene?' I asked Andy.

'When I got back to the cottage,' he explained, 'the Aladdin was flaring and I had to put it out. Then I couldn't find the matches to light a candle with. Then when I found my torch, the battery was finished and I had to rummage about for yours.'

'Lucky you came when you did, anyway,' I said, 'or I'd have been a corpse.'

'It couldn't have been an accident, could it?' asked Andy. 'Somebody running across the footbridge and jostling you into the water?'

'Nobody was running,' I said. 'I should have heard them. And nobody jostled me. Somebody hit me deliberately on the head.'

'And you had just called out, you say?'

'Yes, to Elise, as I thought.'

'So your voice might have been recognised. In other words, it might have been a deliberate attack on you – on *you*, Meg Marsden.'

'On *me*? But why should anyone want to hit *me* on the head? It was just some poacher who lost his head when I disturbed him.'

'And what do you suppose a poacher was doing in the doctor's garden?'

I had no logical answer to that one and we both relapsed into thoughtful silence, which Andy was the first to break.

'What did you do with those trousers?' he asked me suddenly.

'Trousers?' I said, all at sea.

'Yes, yes,' said Andy, impatiently. 'Newton Landon's blue corduroys that Curly fished out of the river.'

'They're in the kitchen cupboard, as far as I know,' I said.

Andy went off downstairs at once to look for them and I heard the sounds of carnage as he emptied everything out of the cupboard onto the floor.

'They're not here,' he called up after a moment or two.

'They must be,' I said.

But they were not, as I soon verified for myself. They weren't in the cupboard and they weren't anywhere else either. We searched the house from top to bottom with the enthusiastic help of the dogs, but of that wretched muddy rag there was no sign. Andy seemed quite upset about it and kept urging me to try to think when I had last seen the trousers, but I couldn't remember. I hadn't thought of the things for weeks.

'Did you show them to anybody? Or mention finding them?' he asked.

'Only PC Jones that time – weeks ago,' I said.

'PC Jones – yes, of course,' said Andy thoughtfully. 'But that doesn't make sense,' he added after a moment or two.

'What doesn't make sense?' I asked.

'Never mind, Meg,' said Andy, coming briskly out of his abstraction. 'You get off to bed. You ought not to be running around after that crack on the head. I'll join you soon, but first I must go down to the bridge and report your adventure to the poacher-watchers. They won't be able to do much about it because whoever it was must be miles away by now, but it'll put them on the alert. And, besides, I think the police ought to know about it.'

'Are you proposing to leave me all alone in the house?' I asked indignantly. 'At this time of night? And just after someone has tried to murder me?'

'You're not afraid, are you?' asked Andy, in apparent surprise.

'Yes, I am,' I said frankly.

'But there's nothing to be afraid of, Meg. I'll leave the dogs with you and lock the front door behind me and take the key so that I can let myself in without knocking and frightening you. You can sneck the windows and lock and bolt the back door yourself. And, just to be on the safe side, let nobody in while I'm gone. Nobody at all – not your dearest friend, not the police – nobody. You'll promise me that, Meg?'

'Of course. What do you take me for?' I snapped.

'That's all right, then,' he said cheerfully, quite unmoved by my tartness. 'I shan't be long.'

In another moment he was gone. I heard the key turn in the front door and then the sound of his limping footstep retreating up the front path.

The hour that followed was one of the worst of my life. I am not normally of a nervous disposition, but that night, suffering from shock as I must have been, and with a splitting headache from the blow that I had received, I was on the verge of panic. Every sound seemed sinister: the tick of the French clock on the mantlepiece; the lowing of a cow in the field across the lane; the distant barking of a dog; the faintly heard susurration of the wind in the boughs of the pear tree. At first, I stood petrified in the middle of the living-room floor, where Andy had left me, listening to these sinister sounds and quite unable to summon up the resolution to follow Andy's advice and return to bed. But soon the black stare of the naked window forced me into feverish activity, pulling curtains upstairs and down, locking windows, bolting the back door; and, when all that was done, I found I could not stay still. I tried getting into bed again, but the bedclothes seemed to stifle me. The blood throbbed in my aching head and my heart leaped and thumped. The draught from the open bedroom door made the oil lamp smoke and flicker so that the lighted patch on the landing dimmed and wavered as though a shadow had been cast on it – the shadow of some watcher lurking in the darkness beyond my range of vision. But, when at last I managed to screw up courage enough to shut the door and turn down the lamp sufficiently to stop its smoking, things were no better, for in the dim light the brass handle of the door seemed to be stealthily turning. I held my breath and strained my ears to hear the click of the tongue disengaging in the lock, but the thrumming of the blood in my ears masked every other sound. At last, in desperation, I gave up all thought of rest and, lighting a candle, spent the remainder of the waiting time roaming from room to room. And a strange perambulation it was – which I shall never forget – with the shadows leaping and darting before me and the two dogs, who seemed to sense my terror, padding after me, their heads drooped and their tails between their legs.

Once, as we approached the front door, Squelch darted ahead of me with a low growl and stood quivering with his nose pressed against the crack along the floor. Slowly the hair rose along his spine and his ever-wagging tail was still, held rigid as he listened. Instantly I was as tense as he and it seemed to me that I heard a faint fumbling and rustling against the outer door panel.

'Who's there?' I called desperately. But there was no reply and in a moment Squelch's tail began to wag again and, after a series of snuffs worthy of a vacuum cleaner, he turned a re-assuring glance on me, as much as to say, 'OK, nothing there.' But there had been something there. A rat? A cat? One of the village dogs? Or, a would-be murderer?

And once, just as I was leaving the kitchen, there was a small, sharp crack behind me, followed by the clatter and rush of something falling. I whirled round, spattering warm candle grease onto my hand and wrist. At first, in the wildly leaping candlelight, I could see nothing, but then I noticed that the kitchen cupboard was open and its contents had cascaded onto the floor. Weak with relief, I sank onto a chair and at that moment heard the joyful sound of a key turning in the lock of the front door and Andy's voice calling softly. 'Meg, are you awake?'

Oh, blessed deliverance!

'Here, Andy,' I called. 'In the kitchen.'

'Why, Meg, what's the matter?' he exclaimed as he came through the door and saw me sitting there, slumped on a wooden kitchen chair, a guttering candle clutched in my hand.

'You look like Lady Macbeth in one of her weaker moments. What is it? What's happened?'

'Nothing,' I said, giggling with relief. 'Everything suddenly fell out of the cupboard and frightened me nearly out of my wits. I thought I was about to be murdered. It's all your fault for cramming things in so untidily.'

'All right, old girl, you're a bit overwrought,' he said. 'And no wonder! You've had quite a day. Go on up to bed while I stuff this junk back into the cupboard. I'll be with you in a moment.'

He stooped to give me a fleeting kiss, then bent a little

further to pick up a tin of boot polish that had rolled nearly to my feet. Muzzily, I watched him and a vague idea came into my mind that the polish was significant in some way and that I ought to concentrate my thoughts upon it. But my head ached so abominably that I could think of nothing but my own tiredness.

'What are you staring at?' asked Andy, pausing for a moment in his task of bundling the contents of the cupboard back onto the shelves.

'Nothing,' I stammered. 'Only, there's something I ought to remember, I'm sure there is.'

'You look too far gone to remember so much as your own name,' said Andy, briskly. 'Come on, Meg. Off to bed.'

So I let the vague idea slip out of my head again – more's the pity – and reeled off to bed, thus putting an end, at last, to this eventful evening. As Andy finally blew out the bedroom candle I remember muttering, sleepily, 'Well, thank goodness that day's over.'

Little did I know what the next twenty-four hours held in store!

Chapter 14

MR BROWN'S CAR

I slept late the next morning and the first I knew was when Andy brought me up a cup of tea at about ten o'clock. He seemed disgustingly cheerful.

'How's the head, old girl?' he asked, seeing my sour looks.

I shook it gently to find out and started up a small ache at the back of the eyes. Then, feeling gingerly behind my right ear, I discovered a lump about the size of a walnut.

'All right,' I said glumly, 'but I expect I shall develop delayed concussion.'

'Oh, come now, old girl, it's not as bad as that, I hope. I've asked Robert to call,' he added.

'Oh, *no*, Andy, you *haven't*,' I said, sitting briskly up in bed. 'I don't need a doctor. I'm perfectly all right. You can just go and put him off again.'

'Can't disturb him in the middle of surgery,' said Andy ostentatiously folding his pyjama legs and avoiding my eye. 'You just see him, like a good girl. He said he'd be along about eleven.'

'Andy,' I accused, 'you've got some game on. What is it?'

'No game. Just anxious about you, dear.'

'Nuts!' I said. 'Come on, what is it?'

But Andy wouldn't be drawn.

'Boiled egg, tea and toast for breakfast,' he called back over his shoulder as he shut the bedroom door behind him. 'I'll bring it up in a minute.'

But that was going too far and the moment the door was closed I was out of bed and dressing. My legs were a bit wobbly, I found, and my head had to be moved with care, but I was – as I well knew and Andy well knew, also – really, on the whole, none the worse for the night's adventure. I met Andy on the stairs with the breakfast tray and took it from him and we both returned to the kitchen where the sun was just coming round to shine through the south window. It was another wonderful day, but cooler than the day before, with a stiffish breeze blowing dazzling clouds across a dark-blue sky.

'Now,' I said, as I sat down to my egg and tea and toast, 'just tell me all about it.'

'About what?' asked Andy innocently.

He was sitting on the window seat in a patch of sunlight with his blind eye turned towards me. Seen like this in profile his scarred face was a mask – a death mask, I thought, with the old clutch of pity at my heart.

'Well, about last night, to start with,' I said. 'You were gone a long time. What were you up to?'

He turned his good eye towards me and I saw by the interest, and even excitement, in it that my instinct had been right. He had seen or heard something last night – or, he was planning something now.

'As a matter of fact,' he said slowly, 'I had rather an interesting walk down to the bridge and back.'

'Did you find Constable Jones all right?'

'Yes. He and the Tovey bailiff and the Alsatian were still lurking about behind the Ferryman.'

'Had they had any excitement?'

'No, they hadn't seen a soul all evening, so your assailant obviously didn't try to gain the main road by crossing Coedafon bridge.'

'Well, I told you, he went the other way.'

'If he broke back, meaning to use the Llantossy footbridges, he must have run into trouble, because directly I had told Jones about your little adventure he rang up Llantossy Police Station – got Gloria out of bed to use the post-office telephone – and the constable in charge at the station told him there was a considerable shemozzle on at Llantossy at that moment. One poacher had been caught and was in the cells and the sergeant and Cliff were in full cry after another one.'

'Perhaps one of those was the one who coshed me.'

'Unlikely, I think. He couldn't have got there in time. But Jones warned them to look out for him anyway, then, leaving the Tovey bailiff and me to keep an eye on the bridge, in case the man was lurking in the woods waiting his chance to slip across, he took the Alsatian up river to the gate into Landon's garden to see if he couldn't get onto the trail from there. In about half an hour he was back. Seems the dog picked up a scent at the gate all right which led over the footbridge past where you were standing and through the alder spinney, but when they got into the long meadow they ran into that herd of young steers Trev Price put to graze, and the beasts were so skittish and troublesome that they put the poor dog right off his stroke. He'd do nothing but sniff along the hedge round the doctor's garden, pretending to work, but really afraid of all those lowered heads and side-kicking feet. Or so Jones thought. After taking the dog back to the exit from the alder spinney a couple of times and each time being headed off up the hedge by the cattle and nearly gored into the bargain, he gave up and came back to us at the bridge. By that time I thought I had left you alone long enough and came home, leaving Jones and the bailiff confabbing together as to whether they'd disturb poor Gloria again to ring Llantossy and see how the hunt was going that end.'

'It was very noble of you to leave before your curiosity was fully satisfied,' I said sarcastically, 'on *my* account.'

'Yes, it was noble of me,' Andy agreed, 'but my virtue was rewarded, because I saw something rather interesting on the way back.'

'Not somebody trying to force our front door, by any chance?' I asked.

Andy looked startled.

'Did someone try to force our front door? You never said anything about it last night.'

'I'm not sure about forcing the door,' I said, 'but there was somebody or something snooping round the front. Squelch and I both heard a noise.'

'When was this?' asked Andy, suddenly serious.

'About ten minutes before you got back,' I said.

Andy looked thoughtful, studying the floor in silence.

'No, it can't have been,' he said to himself at last.

'What can't have been what?' I asked in exasperation.

But at that moment the front door bell rang.

'Might tell you later,' said Andy hurriedly. 'There's Robert. And Meg?'

'Yes?'

'Not a word to him about anything but your crack on the head.'

'Why not?'

'Never mind. But, please, Meg, promise.'

'Oh, all right,' I said, 'if you want to be so mysterious.'

When I opened the front door I found Robert Landon standing on the path with his back to the door, apparently studying his own feet. Every line of him spoke dejection and when he turned towards me, I saw that he was very pale and his eyes were red-rimmed and glittering, as though he had not slept for a week. He looked at me blankly and silently stepped past me into the living room. It was an embarrassing moment, considering the circumstances under which we had last met. I wanted to explain how I had been tricked by Elise into being a witness of the unfortunate domestic scene of two nights ago, but I could not find the words.

'Andy got you here on false pretences,' I began awkwardly when I had shut the door. 'I don't really need you. You see ...'

But he did not let me finish. I suppose he must have been as embarrassed as myself because, still without a word, he reached for the door handle and would have been gone had not Andy put a hand on his arm and stopped him.

'All the same, Robert, I'd like you to have look at her,' he said. 'She got a pretty nasty crack on the head last night and was nearly drowned, into the bargain. Anyone but Meg would have been in bed for a week after such an experience.'

'All right,' said Robert, turning his back and breaking his silence, at last. 'Let's have a look at this crack.'

Not a word of sympathy; not a single question as to how I had come to acquire a sore head. But he had a look at the bump behind the ear and told me what I knew already – that there was nothing to it.

'Keep quiet. Don't sit or run about in the sun and take a couple of aspirins if your head aches,' he said, 'and by tomorrow you ought to be as good as new.'

So that was that, and again Robert made to go, but again Andy detained him.

'No need to rush off, old chap. Sit down a minute and have a drink – or a cup of tea if you'd rather. You look as though you needed it.'

To my surprise Robert turned back at once and let himself drop heavily into our one easy chair.

'I do need it, and that's a fact,' he said with a sigh. 'You wouldn't have a drop of whisky about by any chance?'

'Whisky it is,' said Andy, turning to the sideboard and silence fell again while he poured a stiff peg and splashed a drop of soda into it. 'There!' he said when that was done. 'Drink that down. You look as though you've been up all night.'

'Awake all night, yes,' said Robert.

'See any poachers?' asked Andy.

'Poachers? No. How should I see any poachers? I was in bed by eleven.'

'In bed!' I exclaimed. 'I thought you said you were up all night.'

'Not up, but awake. I couldn't sleep. I had a wretched night.'

Wretched, indeed, he looked sitting hunched in the big chair staring at his now empty glass with the withdrawn look that was so typical of him.

'Robert,' I said suddenly, taking my courage in both hands. 'I do want to apologise for the other evening and explain how I came to intrude on you the way I did. You must believe me when I tell you ...'

But that was as far as I got. At that point Robert rose slowly to his feet, put the empty glass on the sideboard and walked out of the house, leaving Andy and me looking at each other with our mouths open.

'Well, you don't seem very popular with your doctor,' said Andy at last, laughing.

But I was furious.

'What right has he to treat me like that,' I said. 'You would think it was he who had caught me in the act, instead of the other way round. We'll change our doctor tomorrow. And I'm washing my hands of the whole Landon family from now on.'

Fate, however, had other plans, but that is by the way.

'You know, Meg,' said Andy, after I had calmed down a little, 'that was really a very interesting visit. You asked me what I saw on my way back from the bridge last night. Well, what I saw was some person walking in an extremely furtive manner up the lane from our front gate and I could almost swear that person was Robert Landon.'

'But he said he was in bed by eleven o'clock.'

'I might have been mistaken, but I don't think so. And if I wasn't mistaken, then Dr Robert Landon is telling lies – for some reason best known to himself.'

'Andy! Are you suggesting that it was Robert who hit me on the head last night?'

'I'm not suggesting anything. I'm just curious. That was why I was so anxious that you should see Robert this morning. I wanted to find out what he had been doing lurking around so late last night. But you frightened him off too soon.'

'He probably had a late call and had to go up to the surgery to fetch something.'

'On foot? And, in that case, why a cock and bull story about being in bed by eleven?'

I could think of no plausible answers for those questions. We discussed the affair for a little but I could see that Andy's thoughts were not entirely concentrated on the subject in hand. It was as if there were some wider problem on his mind into the solution of which he was trying to fit this fact of Robert's somewhat odd and disingenuous behaviour. But he would not tell me what the problem was.

It was our day for the Llantossy water – being a Friday – but of course, in view of my sore head, there had been no thought of going out. After a leisurely lunch, however, I could see that Andy was beginning to get restless.

'How do you feel, old girl?' he said, after we had been sitting for about ten minutes under the pear tree.

'All right,' I said.

'No headache?'

'No.'

'Ate a pretty good lunch, I was glad to see.'

'Yes, I did.'

'Not feeling tired?'

'No.'

'You wouldn't feel up to a spot of fishing, would you?'

Although I knew quite well what he had been leading up to, my heart sank at the words.

'No, not today, Andy,' I said with what I hoped was sufficient firmness to put a final stopper on the notion.

Silence for another five minutes or so while Andy absent-mindedly scratched Curly under the chin.

'Dogs are getting a bit restless,' he said at last, carefully keeping his eyes from the recumbent form of Squelch who was snoring behind my chair. 'What about taking the car up to Llantossy and getting the latest news about last night's affair?'

'Oh, all right,' I said, 'you win.'

As a matter of fact, I was quite glad to move as long as I could sit in the car and not have to exert myself unduly. The heat in our garden was beginning to make my head ache again but outside the shelter of our hedges there was a cool breeze blowing which would soon blow the headache away.

It was pleasant driving along beside the glittering river. The giant balsams, known as policemen's helmets, were in bloom along the water's edge and the wind scurried and flurried among the tall red stems making them toss their heads of pink, pendant flowers. We were near enough the water from time to time to see the flashes of silver as salmon leaped boredly in the tepid pools. It was all very peaceful, and far removed from the terrors of the night before which now, in the sunlight, seemed in the highest degree unlikely, like a dream, or a tale told on a winter's night to make one's flesh creep. Beautiful river, I thought, nothing evil there, surely. But it was the last time I looked with pleasure on the waters of the Tossy.

As we approached Llantossy Police Station, we saw Constable Jones just emerging and I drew the car up beside him so that Andy could enquire the latest news.

'Did you get your other poacher, Constable?' Andy called out as I switched off the engine.

'Ar, we got en. The sergeant did, that is.'

'He did! Good work! Where did the sergeant catch up with him?'

'Near to Weir Cottage, 'twas. Turned down river, 'e did, thinking to clamber up the bank, look, and across the rough to the gate on the Carne road, this side of the cottage. The Land Rover was there, see. Well, 'e got along too far, seems, and found 'isself under the weir wall. Trapped. And no way to turn. Sergeant took 'im easy. In the cells at Carne, 'e is, and 'is mate with 'im. But another one, 'e got away.'

'There was a third man, was there?'

'Ar. Cliff Price, 'e chased en down t'other bank, but lost en at the finish. Slim chap, quick as an eel, Cliff says. One time 'e thought 'e 'ad 'im and the next moment 'e was gone, like 'e was snatched away by devils, Cliff says. In a rare taking, Cliff was, when 'e come back. Gone two hours and more, 'e was, and when 'e come back, what with the running and the stumbling about in the dark and the rage 'e was in, look, 'e was fit to pass out. White as a sheet, 'e was, and blood on 'is 'ands and face where the briars 'ad got 'im. Sergeant give 'im a tot of first-aid brandy to bring 'im round.'

'Where did he lose the man?'

'Coupla miles downriver, near the boathouse, where them trees come close down. Reckon the chap slipped into the wood, meself.'

'Is anybody watching the bridges for him?'

'Ar. And the forest road to Carne. Constable Timms from Carne, 'e's up in the forest and Cliff, 'e's at Coedafon.'

'And Llantossy footbridges?'

'I'm on my way there now to relieve Bailiff Evans.'

'Well, we won't keep you. Hope you get him.'

'Funny,' I said, as Constable Jones proceeded on his way, 'that they didn't use the old gravel pit to park the Land Rover in. It seems such an obvious place.'

'They don't know the river as well as we do,' said Andy reasonably.

'No, but they must have reconnoitred beforehand.'

'Perhaps they did use it,' said Andy, and then, excitedly: 'Yes, yes, perhaps they did. Possibly another car was parked there and that's what the man got away in last night. If he doubled back at the boathouse he could have got across the temporarily unguarded footbridges ahead of Cliff and then, while everyone was fussing around Cliff, made his getaway along the cart track to the gravel pit which comes out on the Carne road well out of sight and hearing of Llantossy village. The cart track to the Carne road is so overgrown that probably no guard was put on it. Let's go and see whether we can find any traces.'

That was how we came to find the car with the registration letters, MEG and the (to me) memorable number, the car which I had last seen from Piggling and Pritchard's office window on Wednesday morning, the car belonging to, or at least driven by, the mysterious Mr Brown. It was well hidden behind a bramble-covered spur in the gravel pit which was, perhaps, why it had not been discovered the night before – if, indeed, it had been there all the night before. There was nothing to prove that it had, of course. Mr Brown might have parked it there within the last hour and be at that minute strolling down the bank and enjoying the beauties of nature. He did not quite seem that sort of man, however, and there was no other conceivable occupation in the neighbourhood of the gravel pit.

Eventually, after a good deal of talking to and fro between us, Andy and I decided to report the presence of the car to Llantossy Police Station. The sergeant who, in the absence of his constable, was sitting behind the desk with an enormous ledger open in front of him, seemed sceptical as to the car in the gravel pit having any connection with the previous night's affair. No-one had seen the car then, but he admitted that it was just possible that it had been overlooked. He would have an eye kept on it until it was collected, as he seemed perfectly sure it would be, in due course by its owner.

'This Mr Brown who owns the car,' I ventured tentatively as we were leaving – much deflated, 'I believe he would repay investigation. Cliff Price knows, or suspects, something about him. Would it be a good idea to ask Mr Price what he knows?'

'I'll do that, Mrs Marsden,' said the sergeant politely but with complete lack of interest. 'Good day!' and he slammed shut the giant ledger as a sign that the interview was closed.

'Well. I feel a proper fool.' I said to Andy, as we started up our own battered vehicle and made for home.

'No need,' said Andy. 'I've an idea it's the sergeant who will feel the greater fool in the end.'

And Andy was right.

Chapter 15

THE BOATHOUSE

'You know, there's something very queer about last night's happenings,' I said to Andy, as we drove homewards along the Carne road.

'How do you mean "queer"?' asked Andy.

'Well, nothing seems to hang together. Here's me hit on the head – quite pointlessly, as far as I can see – at Coedafon. And miles away on the other side of the river near Rachel's cottage there's a Land Rover, said to be a poacher's getaway car, but most inconveniently placed for such a purpose, unless the weir pool was to be the scene of operations – which it was not. Then Mr Brown's car parked where the poachers' vehicle ought to have been. And, finally, the problem of three vanishing men ... are you listening, Andy?'

'Three vanishing men,' repeated Andy, coming out of his own thoughts with a start.

'You haven't heard a word I said.'

'Yes, yes. Three vanishing men. You mean the one who pushed you into the river, the one Cliff Price chased along the bank, and Mr Brown.'

'Yes. Can you explain them?'

'Not all of them, but I have my ideas. This chap, Brown, though, he seems a bit of an enigma. I took no note of him at all on the only occasion we ever met, but you've seen him several times, Meg. What does he look like? What sort of age would you put him at?'

'Age? About thirty-five, I should say and, as to his appearance – tall, dark and handsome, in a flashy sort of way.'

'Pretty much of a city type, would you think?'

'Very much of a city type.'

'Then what's he doing hanging around down here? He's been here, off and on, since May, at least, which seems far too long simply to reconnoitre a river with a view to poaching it.'

'Perhaps he has business – or friends – down here and has nothing whatever to do with the poaching. And now I come to think,' I added, 'Cliff told me once that he had seen his car parked by Weir Cottage. Perhaps he's a friend of Rachel's. After all, we know nothing of Rachel's friends or family.'

'Doesn't sound her type.'

'Any man is any woman's type, if she happens to fall in love with him,' said I sententiously.

'Meg!' exclaimed Andy, laughing. 'What are you hinting at, now? I should have thought Rachel's love affairs were tangled enough already without introducing Mr Brown into them.'

'Perhaps he's her ex-husband.'

'Come back into her life under the romantic name of Brown in order to woo her back into his arms?'

I laughed. 'No, well, he needn't be her ex-husband, but it may be an explanation of his car being parked in the quarry at Llantossy that he has been to see Rachel at her surgery.'

'Wrong time of day,' said Andy shortly, and relapsed into silence. But there was obviously something working on his mind, for presently he said, apropos of nothing, 'You know, Meg, if only we could get Leslie Jones to talk we could go places. There might almost be enough evidence to lay before the police.'

'Les? Whatever has he got to do with it? He was in bed and asleep, presumably, long before anything started up last night.'

'I'm not talking about last night. I'm talking about Newton Landon's murder.'

'Am I going mad, or are you? What on earth has Newton Landon's murder – if he was murdered, which I don't now believe – have to do with salmon poaching on the Tossy?'

'I believe there is a kind of connection. Meg ...'

'Yes?'

'Would you get hold of Leslie and try to make him tell you what it was he saw the afternoon Newton was drowned? It's no use my asking him. He's terrified of me because of my appearance, but he likes you and you might be able to winkle it out of him.'

'What do you want to know?'

'I just want to know what it was that almost frightened him into a fit. I'd rather not tell you what I think it was in case you put the idea into his head without meaning to – in which case his evidence would be worthless.'

'Well, I'll try. But he's as near inarticulate as makes no difference and I don't want to frighten him into another fit.'

'Have a go.'

'All right. The next time I see him.'

As it happened, the next time I saw Les was almost immediately, for, as we were putting the car away at the Ferryman, his unmistakable form appeared, trotting downhill from the direction of Constable

Jones' bungalow. He was flopping along with his usual ticky-toed gait, slapping each foot down in turn, with his head wobbling back and forward at every step and his mouth, as usual, wide open. Over his arm was a brown cloth shopping bag and, tightly clasped in one hand, a scrap of paper – evidently a shopping list.

'There he is. Go to it, Meg,' said Andy. 'I'll stroll on home with the dogs.'

The boy was obviously making for MacAlister's shop and I timed my approach to meet him at the door.

'Hello, Leslie!' I said brightly. 'Doing the shopping for your mam?'

'Ar,' he said, a gleam of pride appearing in his heavy-lidded eyes.

'Bread,' he added. 'All gone.'

'You look hot,' I said, cudgelling my brains for some reasonable approach. 'Would you like an ice-cream?'

He looked at me silently with his mouth open, obviously wondering whether he had heard right.

'I'm hot, too,' I went on desperately. 'We'll both have an ice-cream. You go and get the bread for your mam and afterwards I'll buy you an ice-cream and I'll buy one for myself, too.'

Still without a word he shambled into the shop and tendered his scrap of paper to Gladys. I followed him in.

'Lovely day, Mrs MacAlister,' I said. 'Here's Leslie to get bread for his mam and after that we want an ice-cream each to cool us down.'

''Tis the day for it, indeed,' said Gladys. 'Strawberry, is it, or vanilla?'

'Strawby,' said Les, suddenly and firmly.

'Make it two strawberry cones, then,' I said.

'Never thought to see you here today, Mrs Marsden,' said Gladys, leaning over the steaming ice-cream bin.

'Oh?' I said. 'Why not?'

'Some fairy tale the Boy come home with that you was near drowned in the river last night.'

'No fairy tale,' I said. 'I *was* nearly drowned in the river last night.'

'We-ell! Well, I never!' she exclaimed, her bright brown eyes opening wide with astonishment. Then handing Leslie a strawberry cone: 'They do say as you were pushed. Poachers, was it?'

'Yes, I was pushed,' I said, and proceeded to give her a short account of my adventures. As I approached the end of my tale my ear caught the biscuity sound of Leslie's ice-cream cone falling to the floor and when I turned to look at him I was surprised to see on his face a look of such extreme terror that I broke off in mid-sentence.

'What's the matter, Leslie?' I exclaimed. 'Don't you feel well?'

Immediately the poor boy broke into a torrent of unintelligible mouthings and mutterings, shaking his head and flapping his hands as though warding off a swarm of bees.

''Tis one of his queer turns, poor creature,' whispered Gladys. 'Best take him home, Mrs Marsden.'

My heart sank at the thought and I called down a malediction on Andy's head for getting me into such a predicament. However, there was nothing for it but to follow Gladys' advice, so, grasping the boy's arm with one hand and taking his mam's shopping bag, full of bread, in the other, I started off for Constable Jones' bungalow on the hill. To my relief, Leslie began to calm down almost as soon as we were out of the shop. His mutterings became less excited and more intelligible, until at last I could make out a word or two here and there: 'pushed', 'river', then again 'pushed', then 'Newt' and, finally, with great distinctness 'pushed him in the river'. The words stopped me in my tracks.

'Leslie, what are you saying?' I exclaimed. 'Who was pushed in the river?'

'Newt,' he mouthed.

'Who pushed him in?' I asked urgently.

But, at that, all the boy's excitement returned and, snatching the brown cloth bag from my hand, he set off up the hill at a shambling run, muttering to himself as he ran. I wondered whether I ought to follow him and try to force an answer out of him, but decided in the end that I should probably only succeed in pushing him finally over the edge into an epileptic fit. Besides, my head was aching again, my mouth was as dry as the desert sands, the hill was steep, the sun hot and my whole being ached for a nice cup of tea. I watched until I saw him turn in at the constable's gate and then, with a sigh, made for home.

My thoughts were in a turmoil. Had I really heard what I thought I had heard? If so, did it mean what it seemed to mean? Was the boy imagining that Newton had been pushed into the river, or had he really seen it done? Had he, perhaps, done it himself?

Or, had he, in his twilit mind, confused the two episodes of Cliff Price's ducking by Newton and Newton's own drowning? This last was the most likely hypothesis, I decided. But Andy, when I expounded it to him over a life-saving cup of tea, disagreed.

'That boy saw something, I could swear,' he said, 'and what you have just told me is ample confirmation. What a pity he didn't let slip any name! You're quite sure, Meg, that there was no name identifiable among all his ramblings?'

'Quite sure,' I said firmly. I would not even allow myself to think back over those disjointed mouthings in order to try to identify a name. I did not, I realised, want to know. I wanted, as long as possible, not to have to believe in Newton's murder. But Andy believed in it, and not only believed in it, but knew already the name of the murderer – or so he said.

'But, the proof. How can I prove it?' he muttered in exasperation, staring at the ground between his knees as we lingered over our tea in the garden.

'Oh, forget it, Andy, do,' I said. 'Let sleeping dogs lie.'

But he seemed not to hear me and, getting abruptly to his feet, started pacing our small square of lawn. I watched him uneasily seeing, as he limped to and fro, first the stony, death-mask side of his face and then the other, un-scarred side – alive, intent, implacable; and as I watched him I was afraid, overwhelmed by a sense of impending disaster, of horrors to come which would destroy the peace of our life beside the river.

At last to my relief he stopped his pacing and, turning to me, said, 'It's no good, Meg. The problem of proof has got me beaten for the moment. I think I'll take my trout rod and fish the stretch above the boathouse. I've seen some good-sized trout there and, perhaps, when my thoughts are at peace, as they always are when I'm fishing, my mind will work out the answer for me. Come along with me, Meg. It's a lovely evening and the stroll will do you good.'

He was right about the evening. The long shadows of the pear tree lay across the grass, dense and almost motionless, only wavering a little at the edges as an occasional breath of wind stirred the branches overhead. The sky was a pale, pearly blue, except in the west where it was suffused with gold by the blazing August sun, now sinking towards the valley rim. Nothing could have been more peaceful.

'All right, I'll come with you,' I said.

But if I thought I should be soothed and refreshed by the walk along the river bank which I knew and loved so well, I was mistaken. Today the path seemed sinister. The scent of honeysuckle in the hedges reminded me – for some reason – of the heavy perfume of lilies on a coffin and every rustle in the bushes, made by the breeze or by the snuffling dogs, caused my heart to contract and my head to turn stealthily in the direction of the sound. And this in broad daylight with Andy not three paces in front of me. As we approached the end of the doctor's garden a sound of music came to our ears. Elise – for, of course, it must have been she – was playing with a fierce emphasis some thunderous and inharmonious modern composition with which I was quite unfamiliar and which jarred my nerves and seemed actually to disorder the beating of my heart. To its discordant and loud accompaniment – Elise must have been playing with the windows wide open – we approached the footbridge: Newton's bridge as I had come to call it in my mind. With my thoughts full of the unpleasant associations of the spot – Newton's death and my own shattering experience of the night before – and with Elise's neurotic music disturbing the peace of the evening, it took me all my strength of will to force myself across the shadowed planks and into the dark tunnel of the alder spinney beyond. Only the presence of Andy gave me the necessary courage. Once through the spinney and into the sunlit meadow beyond, however, things went better. Here the sound of music was muffled and, at last, extinguished by the dense belt of alders, and the evening breeze, given free play by the wide meadow, blew round my aching head with a pleasant coolness.

Upstream of the boathouse was a short, gravelly run where the river shallowed and quickened its pace before deepening again into the slow-moving pool on the bank of which the boathouse had been built. It was here, in the lively, well-aerated shallows, that trout lay in the warm evenings, watching for drowning river flies and other titbits carried down by the stream, and it was here that Andy meant to lure them if he could with his synthetic trout flies.

When we reached the boathouse I allowed Andy to walk on alone to his trout run while I settled myself in my favourite place with my back against the boathouse wall. The dogs, as they had been trained to do, stayed with me, lying beside me or doing a little discreet hunting in my immediate neighbourhood. Andy's form soon disappeared down the bank, but I could still hear the occasional churr of his reel as he lengthened line to cover the rise; a safe and peaceful sound. Now, at last, I could relax and let the beauty of the summer evening soothe my overwrought nerves. With half-closed eyes, I watched a small cloud of midges rising and falling in the shadow of an alder, deliberately emptying my mind of all unpleasant thoughts and allowing the pleasant sounds of water, of Andy's reel, of the twitter and flutter of small birds in the bushes to occupy the whole forefront of my mind. I was almost at peace. But, at that moment, Squelch, returning from a short foray down the muddy bank, came to sit beside me. Arranging himself, as his habit is, on one haunch and leaning with all his weight against my thigh, he settled down, nose twitching, bright eyes alert, to wait for the exciting screech of the reel which would mean a fish on the hook. Normally, Squelch's leaning habit is endearing and companionable, but today he was wet from a swim in the river and stank of rotten mud. I sat up to push him away from me and, as I did so, I heard behind me a creak from the boathouse door. For some reason I was immoderately startled and, jumping to my feet, whisked round the corner to see who or what had made the sound. There was nobody there, but I was just in time to see the end of Curly's tail disappearing into the gloom of the boathouse. Trev Price must have forgotten to lock the door, in spite of the fact that his young bullocks were in the meadow. Better secure it, I thought, or there would be an accident; but first to extract Curly. Pushing the door as wide as it would go and calling the dog's name, I peered inside. The west sun shining through the doorway flooded three quarters of the interior with a crimson light, but a wedge of shadow still lay over part of the dock and in the dock was Curly, her fore-paws threshing up and down as she paddled to and fro. She seemed excited and the noise of her splashing reverberated in that narrow space.

'Curly, come out,' I called, but she took no notice of me. Then my eye caught a glimpse of something white floating just under the water on the edge of a patch of shade. Curly saw it, too, and dipping her head seized it in her jaws and brought it to the surface. It was a man's hand. On one of its fingers was a ring which glinted in the red evening light – a ring which I thought I recognised.

I ran out of the boathouse and I suppose I must have screamed because almost immediately I saw Andy's hobbling figure hurrying towards me.

'What's the matter, Meg?' he called as he came. 'Have you hurt yourself?'

'It's a hand, it's a hand!' I shouted hysterically. 'Curly found a hand. Make her drop it, for God's sake. Make her drop it.'

'Pull yourself together, girl,' said Andy, throwing down his rod and trout net and shaking me by the arm. 'Pull yourself together and tell me what all the commotion is about.'

So I told him, as best I could, and we went back to the boathouse together. Squelch had joined Curly by now and between the two of them they had managed to drag the hand and part of the arm to which it was attached onto the landing stage. In so doing they had dragged a face to the surface of the water – a bloated and mutilated face; not so mutilated, however, but that I was able to recognise it at once as the face of Mr Brown. I felt as though the world were spinning round me and there was a humming in my ears. I was about to faint. But Andy forced me to sit on the ground and shoved my head down in the nick of time.

'This is no time for fainting, Meg,' he said. 'Sit with your head as far down as you can for a moment while I get the dogs. Then I want you to run and fetch the police. Do you think you can?'

I nodded and, breathing deeply, tried to get a grip of myself. In a minute or so Andy was back, leading a dripping dog with each hand.

'Now, Meg,' he said, 'go as fast as you can to Constable Jones' bungalow. Ask him to ring Llantossy Police Station and then to come here as quickly as possible. I'll stay and see that no-one interferes with anything until the police arrive. Not that anyone is likely to do so, but you never know. Once you've told the constable, go home and wait for me there – but lock and bolt the doors.'

'I shall come back here with Constable Jones,' I said firmly, thinking of the horrors of the night before when I had had my fill of sitting alone behind locked doors waiting for Andy.

'All right,' he agreed, 'I think that would really be the best thing, but I thought you might be tired.'

I was tired all right, but anything was better than being left alone.

'Get going then, Meg old girl,' said Andy, pulling me to my feet and giving my shoulder an affectionate squeeze. 'You'll be all right. There's nothing to be frightened of. It won't be dark for a long time yet and on the way back you'll have the constable for company. By the way, don't forget to bring torches. Ask Jones to bring the most powerful one he has. Good luck!'

Then, as I started reluctantly down the river, he called after me: 'Don't go through the alder spinney, Meg. Cut up through the meadow and into Trev Price's farm lane. You'll be more or less in the public view that way.'

I had already decided on this route, without Andy's advice, for nothing in the world, I thought, would induce me to cross Newton's bridge again that night.

Chapter 16

WAITING WITH ELISE

I remember little of the journey to the village, except that I kept as far as possible from the river and gave all bushes and trees a wide berth. On my way across the meadow Trev Price's bullocks joined me, snuffling down my neck, then cavorting off with their tails in the air, then, led by an insatiable curiosity, coming up behind me again to repeat the performance. They followed me all the way to the gate into the lane and, in spite of their wildness, I felt their presence as a protection. As I passed the Landon's front gate the sound of the piano came to my ears again. It was Liszt this time played, as I noticed, despite my agitation, with such astonishing virtuosity that once again, as many times before, the thought crossed my mind that Elise was really quite wasted in this country dump.

The sun had set and dusk was falling as I panted up the hill to the constable's bungalow. Mrs Jones opened the door to me.

'I want to see Constable Jones at once,' I said breathlessly.

But at first sight of me, I noticed that the blood rushed to Mrs Jones' face. She stared at me silently for a moment with pursed lips and angry eyes.

'We-ell, of all the sauce!' she managed to bring out at last, while I gazed at her with astonishment. 'To come here after what you done to my Leslie. You just take yourself off, Mrs Marsden, afore Les sees you again. Near frightened him into a fit, you did and the sight of you'll just about finish 'im. Come on now. Out of here. I'll talk to you in the morning at your place.'

'I'm sorry about Leslie,' I said desperately. 'I'll explain about that tomorrow, but just now I must see your brother. It's murder. A man has been murdered. Please, Mrs Jones, call your brother quickly.'

At the word "murder" Mrs Jones' jaw dropped and without further ado she vanished into the back premises to emerge a moment later with her brother, a newspaper in one hand and his braces hanging down his back. In a few breathless sentences I told him of the dead man in the boathouse..

'And hurry, please,' I finished, thinking of the half-blind and crippled Andy waiting alone in the dark on the river bank. 'And bring your torch, and one for me, too. But first, I suppose, you will have to telephone the police station at Llantossy.'

'Ar, I'll do that,' said Constable Jones who had so far not uttered a word, but had stared unblinkingly at me throughout my tale, his mouth open and his prominent teeth gleaming in the dusk of the doorway.

'And Dr Landon, too,' he added.

'Couldn't you leave that to the Llantossy police?' I asked impatiently. 'The man in the boathouse is quite dead. There's no hurry for a doctor.'

'Got to do me duty, ma'am,' he said heavily. Then raising his voice: 'Bring a light, Blodwen, do, and look lively.'

There followed an endless wait while Mrs Jones brought and lit an oil lamp, the constable meanwhile retiring into another room to don his uniform – an indispensable preliminary, it seemed, to ringing up his superiors at Llantossy. I was not invited into the house nor did Mrs Jones address another word to me. The lamp lit, she withdrew into the kitchen and left me to cool my heels on the doorstep and watch the dusk turning minute by minute to dark night. Presently I heard the rumble of the constable's voice as he used the telephone in his sitting room; I could even hear something of what he said. There seemed to be some doubt as to the whereabouts of Dr Landon and the conversation dragged on and on until I thought I should scream. However, at last it was done and the constable emerged, in full police rig with a torch in his belt and his helmet in his right hand. He was extracting a pair of bicycle clips from his left-hand jacket pocket and seemed surprised to find me still standing there.

'No use for you to wait, Mrs Marsden,' he said. 'I'll get right down to the boathouse on me bike. Go home now and I'll take your statement on me way back up.'

'I'm coming with you,' I said.

'Not with me, you're not,' he retorted, closing his front door and walking off towards the back of the bungalow to fetch his bicycle.

I was definitely *persona non grata* to the Joneses, it seemed. So what to do now? I started down the hill and the constable soon zipped past me, his front lamp blazing – for it was black dark by now. With every weary step I felt less and less inclined for the long trek up to the boathouse and the terrors of the way loomed ever larger and larger. But what to do, and where to go? Our own cottage, after the experience of last night and without even the dogs to keep me company, was out of the question. Had I been a man I could have gone to the Ferryman, but unaccompanied women – especially female "gentry" – were frowned on by Tom and his customers alike. Milly Piggott, then? No; impossible in my present frame of mind to parry her endless questions, and I felt curiously reluctant even to mention my horrible discovery in the boathouse. There remained Elise – if she would let me in. She was at least of my own kind and, besides, would almost certainly be, as usual, so absorbed in her own affairs as to be quite incurious as to the reason of my visit. So with dragging steps, I walked past the lighted windows of the village and up the dark lane to the Landon's house.

The piano was silent now, but I saw that a lamp had been lit in the sitting room. A thin beam of light streamed through the curtains of the French windows, which were ajar and I went up the terrace steps towards it, thinking that, by going straight to the sitting room instead of to the front door, I would save Elise a dark journey into the hall.

'Elise, are you there?' I called as I approached the windows, and I heard her startled voice from inside exclaiming, 'Who is it?'

'It's me, Meg,' I said, stepping into the room.

'You! What do you want?' she said with rather more than her usual lack of cordiality.

She was sitting at a desk set between the windows, with a standing lamp at her elbow and a mass of papers before her, which she attempted to cover with a blotter as I entered – a secretive movement which inevitably directed my attention towards them. A single glance was sufficient to tell me that they were legal documents of some kind and I assumed – quite wrongly, as it turned out – that they had some connection with her impending divorce action, though it did cross my mind vaguely that Piggling and Pritchard must have been quick off the mark.

'I hope I'm not disturbing you,' I said uneasily, feeling, as usual, foolish and inadequate under her hostile stare.

'Yes. You are disturbing me,' she said uncompromisingly.

'Oh, I'm sorry,' I said and turned to leave, as I had come, through the French windows.

'No, stop! You can witness a signature for me, now you're here,' she said.

As I turned to face her again I saw that the hostility had gone from her expression and that she was studying me with a considering look. There was a slight smile on her lips, a gleam of amusement in her eyes.

'You'd like to know what is in these papers, wouldn't you?' she asked.

I disclaimed – with truth – any such desire.

'Of course you would,' she said, brushing aside my disclaimer, 'and I'll satisfy your curiosity, if you like. But, my dear Meg, you ought to curb that curiosity of yours. It'll be the death of you one day.'

Elise had long since decided that I was another, but more persistent, Milly Piggott and that my one object in life was to pry out the secrets of my neighbours and gossip about them in public places. There was no disabusing her of this notion and I did not attempt to do so now.

'I suppose your papers have to do with your divorce,' I said.

'They have nothing to do with my divorce,' she replied. 'They are documents in connection with a settlement made by my father many years ago. I expect you would like to know the provisions of the settlement, but I do not intend to satisfy your curiosity quite to that extent. Jo-Jo brought them with him when he came down yesterday. He is staying here, as I expect you have already found out. At the moment he is in Carne dining with my precious husband in order, as he says, to get the other side of the story.'

So that was why the police seemed to be having so much difficulty in contacting Robert. I wondered whether they had managed to track him down in the end, or whether some other doctor had been summoned in his place. Thinking my own thoughts and picturing to myself the macabre scene that must at this minute be taking place on the river bank, I lost the thread of Elise's discourse, but I returned to my present surroundings in time to hear her say 'On Sunday I go home with him' – Jo-Jo presumably – 'and shake the dust off Coedafon for ever from my feet. That will be the day!'

As she said this Elise rose from the chair in front of the desk and started pacing up and down the room.

'I feel like I used to as a school-girl on the last day of term,' she went on, working herself gradually into a state of excitement. 'By this time the day after tomorrow I shall have closed this horrible chapter of my life and can start afresh. Fourteen wasted years shut in this stifling valley among the clods of Coedafon, with no company but a mad boy and an unfaithful husband. Wasted,

wasted years! It doesn't bear thinking of. But it's nearly at an end now. Only another thirty-six hours and I shall be free. How they crawl, though, the last hours! Everything is done already. My trunks are packed and locked – nothing left open now but my small suitcase. If it were not for Jo-Jo and his business – he has business of some sort in Carne besides his interview with Robert – we could leave tonight, walk out of this horrible house now and never see it or any of its contents again.'

Infinitely weary, dizzy in the head – possibly as a result of delayed shock – my heart as though staggering in my chest, I sat slumped in an easy chair, listening with only half an ear to Elise's monologue. For once, her long, egotistical ramblings could not hold my interest and, after thinking with a small flicker of amusement how right I had been in supposing that Elise would feel no curiosity as to the purpose of my visit, I allowed my thoughts to return once more to the scene in the boathouse. I was anxious about Andy and afraid that he, too, for his part, might be anxious about me, since I had not returned with PC Jones, as I had said I would do. I wished that I had had the courage to face yet once more, even though it were alone and in the dark, the terrifying walk along the river path. I ought to be at Andy's side, to be his eyes and ears as I had become accustomed to being these last few years. While Elise talked on – about Robert's iniquities, about Jo-Jo's lack of understanding, about the drabness of life at Coedafon – I closed my eyes the better to picture, first, Andy's lonely figure waiting on the bank with the dogs at his feet and the dusk slowly falling until it was dark; then the arrival of PC

Jones and the contingent from Llantossy; torches flashing, cutting brilliant green swathes through the bushes, reflecting from the sluggish waters of the boathouse pool and lighting red gleams in the eagerly watching eyes of Curly and Squelch; the dank smell of the river at night; the sound of low-voiced questions and answers and the creaking of the boathouse door being opened wide; then a huddle of dark figures bending over the torchlit dock; the scrape of boots on planks; quick exclamations and directions; the metallic clink of water drops as searching hands dipped and lifted from the dock; and, finally, a mighty surge and splash, reverberating hollowly as though from a subterranean pool, as the hands found the object of their search and, with a concerted heave, hauled it out onto the planks. But at this point I could go no further. Even in imagination I could not bear to look at the gruesome thing that had been brought up out of the water and, turning my head sharply as though to avoid looking at the image forming in my mind, I opened my eyes – to find Elise seated once more in front of the desk and staring at me intently.

'What's the matter, Meg?' she asked.

'I have a headache,' I said quickly.

It had been a mistake to give in to my weariness and preoccupation. Even someone as self-absorbed as Elise could hardly fail to notice by my slumped attitude and closed eyes that I was not my usual cheerful self. She sat considering me for a moment.

'Where's Andy?' she asked.

'On the river,' I said.

'Fishing? At this time of night?'

'Best time for sea-trout,' I mumbled disingenuously.

Why was I so unwilling to mention the body in the boathouse, even to Elise, with whom I had been in the habit of gossiping daily? I don't know. Perhaps it was from a feeling that once the discovery was mentioned and discussed it would take on an added and more horrible reality, and partly from a vague fear I had that Elise was somehow acquainted with Mr Brown. She had certainly talked to him on the morning of our visit to Carne and her explanation of the conversation had not been convincing. Whatever the reason, I was stubbornly determined to make no mention of the matter unless absolutely driven to it.

'Why aren't you with him?' Elise continued with her inquisition.

'Why should I be?'

'I thought you never let him fish alone.'

'I'm not his keeper.'

There was a pause while Elise stared at me with a curious intensity.

'You've quarrelled,' she started flatly at last.

'We have not quarrelled,' I said. Then searching round desperately in my mind for some diversionary subject of conversation: 'Wasn't there some document you wanted me to sign?'

But she was not to be diverted.

'Never mind that,' she said. 'Does Andy know where you are?'

'No,' I said.

It was quite unlike Elise to reject a subject concerning herself in favour of one concerning me – or anyone else. I could not make out her sudden and uncharacteristic interest in my affairs and I tried once more to deflect it.

'When will your brother be back?' I asked.

'Jo-Jo? I don't know. Not before ten o'clock, I imagine,' she answered with a preoccupied air. 'I suppose Andy is fishing at that place below the village – the Crib, or whatever you call it?'

'Actually, he went upriver,' I said. 'Why? Do you want to see him?'

'It's hot,' said Elise, avoiding my question, 'and I feel restless. It's all this waiting about before I can leave this horrible house. A breath of air would do us both good. We'll stroll along the bank to meet Andy.'

So saying, she opened a drawer of the desk, took a torch out of it – a heavy spotlight torch with a big, bulbous head – and prepared to leave the room by the French windows. She had not – as you may notice – asked me whether I should like a stroll along the river; she had merely stated that we were both about to take one.

'You can go if you like,' I said. 'I'm staying here. I'm tired and I have a headache.'

'Then the best place for you is in your own home,' said Elise. 'I'll take you there. It will give me a short walk, at least,' and with her curiously spatulate forefinger she beckoned me to precede her through the window.

I was too tired to argue. Besides, if Elise accompanied me home, I thought I should, perhaps, be able to keep her with me on some pretext until Andy arrived. Or, perhaps, Andy might even be sitting at home already, waiting for me and wondering anxiously about my whereabouts. When he saw that I had not turned up with Constable Jones he must have been worried in view of the previous night's attack on me. He would surely have hurried back as soon as possible. As I stepped past Elise out of the window I had fully persuaded myself that, of course, Andy would be waiting for me at home by now.

Elise closed the window so that a sudden draught should not set the lamp flaring in her absence and, tucking my arm under hers – a most unusually friendly gesture – and clicking on the torch, led me across the terrace and down the steps. And then, instead of turning left towards the gate into the lane, she turned right in the direction of the river.

'Where are you going?' I asked, tugging at my arm to free it from hers.

'We'll go through the garden and along the river path,' she replied. 'It's longer and will give us both more time to clear our heads. I have a slight headache, too.'

As she said this, she pressed her left arm to her side so as to prevent me freeing myself. It was not worth struggling to release my arm and so I resigned myself to facing yet once more the terrors of "Newton's" bridge and the path by the river. At least I should not actually have to cross the bridge nor penetrate the darkness of the alder spinney. The doctor's garden gate would lead us out onto the river bank just below both of these. Besides, Elise and her torch would be sufficient protection against all but superstitious terrors.

So I allowed her to lead me across the neglected lawn, ankle-deep in uncut grass, then through an overgrown kitchen garden where the path was bordered by a rank growth of docks, sow thistles and cocksfoot grass, among which gleamed the large, white convolvulus flowers of the strangling bellbine whose ineradicable roots, I thought as my eye distinguished the flowers in the darkness, would cause years of future trouble to the Landon's successors in the house. The sound of the stream that bordered the garden and joined the river at "Newton's" bridge could now be heard, tinkling and gurgling, away on our right. Beyond the kitchen garden lay a belt of fruit trees, heavy with late summer foliage, and from the dense darkness under their boughs came the acrid, waste-land smell of nettles – giant nettles, crowding so close to the path that more than once I felt the tingling pain of stings on my cheek and hands. I urged Elise to go ahead of me so that, by walking in single file, we should have more chance of avoiding these unpleasant contacts. But she would not.

'We're just there,' she said.

Indeed, at that moment the beam of the torch picked out the overhanging bough of a plum tree, laden with ripening fruit, and beneath it a small wooden wicket gate set in an overgrown hedge.

Elise released my arm in order to open the gate and usher me through ahead of her. The eerie creak of the hinges brought back with unpleasant vividness the events of the night before and it was all I could do to force myself forward into the darkness beyond the gate. The small tinkling of the stream had swelled now into a steady rushing murmur as the waters of the brook met the deeper waters of the river. Where the two joined was "Newton's" bridge, and, as Elise took my arm again to urge me on, I could not prevent myself from exclaiming 'I don't know how you can bear to come here. Newton's ghost must haunt this place for you. It does for me'.

At the first word I felt the muscles of Elise's arm contract. Then she withdrew it and, seizing me above the elbow with fingers that dug into my flesh like iron rods, she swung me round to face her and, shining the torch into my eyes, exclaimed in a strangled voice, 'What's Newton to you? My feelings about Newton are no affair of yours. He was my son, not yours. Keep your prying little mind off my affairs.'

Then switching off the torch, she pushed me before her down the slight slope to the river path. On reaching the path I stood still for a moment to allow my eyes, dazzled by the torch, to become accustomed to the darkness, and here a fresh terror assailed me. There was a rustling in the alder spinney beyond the footbridge. It was not loud – indeed, it could hardly be heard above the rush of water – but it was certainly louder and more purposive than any sound the faint night wind could cause. Then a twig snapped sharply. Elise heard it, too, and we both froze in our tracks.

'Someone in the spinney,' I breathed in her ear.

'Keep still,' she whispered back. 'He may pass without seeing us.'

'Unless he is lying in wait for us,' I quavered, shivering in every limb.

'What nonsense,' hissed Elise. 'Pull yourself together.'

At that moment a dark shape seemed to materialise on the footbridge: the shape, apparently, of a crawling man. Then for a brief moment, it was silhouetted against the paler waters of the river and instantly I recognised the characteristic outline. It was not a man. It was a dog. It was Curly. I would know that silly topknot anywhere, and that stringy tail. Then I managed to distinguish the click of a dog's paws on planks, and the dark, sausage shape of Squelch glided onto the bridge and, behind him from the alder tunnel, the bobbing light of a torch appeared, held, almost certainly, in the hand of my dear, dear Andy.

Oh, the exquisite relief!

'Curly, Squelch, Andy!' I shouted, and soon I was surrounded by leaping dogs and Andy was saying anxiously, 'What on earth are you doing here, Meg?' And I was explaining incoherently that Elise was seeing me home.

But, when I turned to look for Elise, she had gone.

Chapter 17

PATTERNS IN THE DUST

Of the rest of that evening I have little recollection. My one idea, after being reunited with Andy, was to get home as quickly as possible, take a couple of aspirin for my throbbing head, and fall into bed. I was, for the moment, quite incapable either of taking an intelligent interest in Andy's adventures since I had last seen him, or of answering his questions concerning mine. I do remember, however, that as we were approaching our own garden, we met Robert trudging up the river path with his bag in one hand and his torch in the other. It appeared that he had not been in the George Hotel in Carne when the police rang through, but that a message had been left for him to the effect that a man had been found in the river near the boathouse and that he was to proceed there as soon as possible.

His voice, as he told us this, had an exhausted ring and Andy had no difficulty in persuading him that his presence at the boathouse was no longer required as the police doctor from Carne was already on the spot and had done all that was necessary for the moment. The body had been removed from the dock and placed on a stretcher and was even now, doubtless, on its way downriver. Finally, Andy suggested, to my annoyance, that Robert should come into the cottage and have a drink before returning to his hotel. After a long hesitation, Robert gave an apathetic assent to this suggestion. But I was beyond playing the hostess for that night and, on our arrival at the cottage, left the two men to their drinks and stumbled up to bed, where I remained, sleeping like the dead, until Andy awoke me next morning – for the second day running – with a cup of tea.

'Sorry to wake you, Meg, old girl,' he said as he handed me the cup. 'I'd have let you sleep on, but PC Jones is due at any moment now to take our statements – or rather, your statement. He took mine last night.'

'Was he here last night?'

'Yes. On his way home, mainly to see you but I wouldn't let him wake you. He'll be here again at ten sharp and it's nine-thirty now.'

'Heavens! I must have slept like Rip Van Winkle. I never heard him, nor Robert leaving, nor you coming to bed.'

'How do you feel now? How's the head?' asked Andy anxiously.

'All right. I feel fine. That good sleep was just what I needed. Toast me some toast, like a darling, and I'll be down in a minute for some breakfast.'

It was true, I did feel fine and, apart from a tender spot behind the ear, completely restored to normal, both mentally and physically. As I finished my toast and butter the front doorbell rang to herald the arrival of Constable Jones. He was very portentous this morning, very conscious of his position as the law's representative. His lips were closed as far as possible over his prominent teeth and he did not permit himself to smile as he greeted me formally.

'Good day, madam,' he said, keeping a careful watch on his diction. 'I think you was expecting me.'

'Yes, yes, Constable,' I said. 'Come in. You want a statement from me, I understand.'

'That is so, madam,' he assented ponderously as, removing his helmet from his head and wiping his feet on the mat, he followed me into the sitting room. 'If you will be so good,' he added with what I think was intended to be sarcasm.

Then, finding himself a hard chair by the window, he placed his helmet under it and himself upon it, produced a black notebook and pencil from the breast pocket of his tunic and was all ready for the fray. He was enjoying himself – no doubt about that – and I suspect that he hoped to find some opportunity to harass and annoy me if he could. Ever since I had shown him Newton's trousers and he had refused to take any action with regard to them, our relationship had been far from cordial and the episode of Leslie's fit the afternoon before had, I suppose, still further blackened me in his eyes. However, if he had hoped to distress me or score off me, he was disappointed, for today I was perfectly mistress of myself. Even when I came to relate how the dogs had raised that terrible face from the waters of the dock my voice hardly faltered, though it took all my resolution to keep it steady; the more so as the constable seemed ghoulishly interested at this point and made me go over my story more than once while he laboriously recorded my answers in his little black book. He questioned me as to the appearance of the face and what injuries I had observed, hoping, I think to force me to show some sign of distress. But here he went beyond his powers and Andy, who had taken a chair by my side, said suddenly and firmly, 'That's enough,' at which Jones exclaimed angrily that he was but doing his duty. However, he did not persist.

The interruption must have rattled the constable and put him off his guard, for in his next questions he let slip a piece of information that, almost certainly, he had not intended to divulge. At one point in my statement I had said that I had recognised the face in the water, but had been stopped by a question before I could mention a name. Now Jones, turning back a leaf of his notebook to refresh his memory after Andy's interruption, resumed his interrogation – for interrogation it was – by saying, 'This face in the water, now – not injured so bad but what you knew who 'twas?'

'Yes, I recognised the face,' I said.

'How come you knew this man, Daniel Carstairs?' he asked then.

'Daniel Carstairs!' I exclaimed. 'You mean the dead man?'

'Yes, yes,' said the constable testily.

'That wasn't the name I knew him by,' I said, 'if we mean the same person. Brown, he called himself when my husband and I met him some months back on the river bank. Mr Price, the bailiff, introduced him to us, as he'll tell you, if you ask him.'

'Brown. Yes. My error,' said the constable, looking confused.

'I always thought it was a false name,' chipped in Andy at this point. 'You managed to ferret out his real name very quickly. How did you do it? There were no papers on the body which could have given it away – that I know. The man was only wearing a shirt and trousers and I saw the trouser pockets emptied out last night. There was nothing in them but a handkerchief and a little loose change. So it was through the car, I suppose – the car that my wife and I found yesterday in Llantossy sand pit.'

'That's as may be,' said the constable sulkily. 'And now, if Mrs Marsden has nothing to add to this here statement, I'll be on my way. Sergeant, he'd be obliged if you two was to call in at the station to sign your statements, as soon as convenient.'

'We'll do that,' said Andy, as Jones rose to leave. 'But wait – just one question, Constable – was this man, Daniel Carstairs, known to the police?'

'He might a bin, or he might not,' retorted the constable, shortly.

'Come, come,' said Andy good-humouredly, 'why all the secrecy? I suppose he was concerned in this poaching affair two nights back?'

'Sergeant reckoned he were,' muttered Jones.

'And with similar affairs before that?'

'Done a stretch for currency smuggling, ten years back, and wanted for the theft of a lorry load of cigarettes from Carne in May. On our wanted list, he was – him and his gang. His photo's in the cage in front of Llantossy Station where you could a seen it any day. That's how we come to identify him so quick.'

'And the car in the sand pit was his?'

'Ar. Finger prints all over, and his driving licence made out to Carstairs.'

'Well,' said Andy, when the constable had taken his leave, 'that's another bit fitted into the jig-saw. The picture is beginning to get a little clearer now.'

'Clear as mud,' I said. 'About as comprehensible as "Woman with a Guitar" by a vorticist painter.'

'Woman with a lover, more like,' said Andy.

'Woman with a lover? What does that mean? The only woman with a lover in this picture is Rachel – or would be, if she were in the picture at all, which she isn't.'

'Oh yes, she is.'

'What do you mean? You laughed at me when I suggested that this Brown – or Carstairs – might be a friend of Rachel's.'

'I laughed at the idea that he might be her ex-husband,' corrected Andy.

'Well, what do you think his connection with her was?' I asked.

'That needs thinking about,' said Andy, and would not be drawn further.

'There's one of your three vanishing men accounted for, at any rate,' resumed Andy, after a pause.

'Two of my vanishing men, because I suppose "Mr Brown" was one and the same as the poacher whom Cliff Price pursued and lost in the dark.'

'No, I think not. There must have been two separate people involved because Daniel Carstairs certainly did not inflict those terrible injuries on himself and then throw himself in the dock. Someone murdered him.'

'Perhaps Cliff Price isn't telling the truth. Perhaps he caught up with Carstairs when he was running down the river bank and killed him by accident with some piece of commando jujitsu. Or, perhaps even, he murdered him for some reason of his own. He always seemed to have some grudge against "Mr Brown".'

'And who hit you on the head? I think it must have been the same person as killed Carstairs, because it's unlikely, to say the least, that there could have been two homicidally minded persons running around the banks of the Tossy that night. It certainly was not Cliff Price who attacked you, because he couldn't have been in the right place at the right time.'

'Why was I attacked at all?' I said. 'I can't understand it.'

A cold shiver went down my spine as I said it and as it dawned on me suddenly for the first time that the hand that was responsible for the terrible face in the dock had been lifted against me, also. My mutilated head might well have been lying at that moment beside that of the unfortunate Daniel Carstairs on the mortuary slab in Carne. But why? Why? Daniel Carstairs had obviously led a fairly dangerous life and might well have made hosts of enemies, but I? Nothing could have been more sedate and less eventful than my life up to the present. I had never borne ill-will nor aroused it in others, as far as I knew – at least not to the point of murder. And what possible connection could I be supposed to have with "Mr Brown"? Apart, that is, from meeting him once months ago with Cliff Price on the river bank and seeing him twice in Carne? In whom could we both have aroused such hatred or fear that we had to be got out of the way? My mind was in a maze of bewilderment and the more I thought the more hopelessly confused and then frightened I became. Because this unknown and apparently motiveless enemy was still at large and might strike at any time. Who was he, for God's sake?

'Andy,' I burst out at this stage of my cogitations. 'Did you find anything in the boathouse last night which could give a clue as to who killed Daniel Carstairs, and for what purpose?'

'Yes. Yes. I think so. I saw some interesting things last night after you had left me and before the police came and mucked everything up. Of course, by the time they came it was dark and they could not have seen what I saw, and by this morning there will be little enough to see, I imagine, although I warned them to trample about as little as possible. I was lucky to be on the spot when I was. Would you like to hear about it?'

'Yes, yes, of course,' I said.

'Well, the first thing I did when you were gone was to push the door open as far as it would go – until it lay flat against the right-hand wall. I used the net handle to push with, along the bottom of the door, so that any possible fingerprints would not be blurred. The door faces west, so this let the sunlight into nearly the whole of the floored-over part of the boathouse. Only the dock and a small triangle behind the door were in shadow. You remember how strongly the sun was shining in last night?'

'Yes, indeed I do. Blood-red and low, making enormously elongated shadows,' I said, shivering slightly at the memory. 'I remember my own shadow when I first looked in, stretching right across the floor and climbing up the sliding doors giving onto the water at the far end of the boathouse.'

'Yes, exactly,' said Andy. 'Well, with the light so strong and at such a slant, not only was the whole interior brightly lit, but every inequality in the floor stood out like brass rubbings on soft paper. Actually, the only inequalities in the floor were those made by the varying thicknesses of dust that lay on it. And a very interesting pattern they made. Listen! Along the edge of the dock was a clear patch, about six feet by three, where there was hardly any dust at all. The only marks that showed on it were the dogs' wet paw marks and splashings and splatterings made by Curly and Squelch when they shook themselves after coming out of the water. Then, in the far corner, in the angle made by the right-hand wall and the water door there was a rectangular patch, about two feet by three feet, whose shape was outlined by thick ridges of a particularly fine white dust.'

'Where the empty fertiliser sacks were piled?' I interrupted to ask.

'Fertiliser sacks? There were no fertiliser sacks in the boathouse last night.'

'Weren't there? No, of course not. How silly of me,' I said. 'It wasn't last night that I saw them but a long time ago – one evening in May. It was the first and only other time I ever was in the boathouse and it gave me the creeps even then. Don't you remember? Actually, it was the pile of white sacks looking ghostly in the gloom – that and the dank smell of the place and the stealthy lapping of the hidden water – which frightened me then. And I must have looked frightened, too, because you asked me when I came out whether I had met a tiger and I said 'No, only a ghost'. Don't you remember?'

'That's very interesting,' said Andy. 'Not the psychic part of it but the pile of fertiliser bags. They would be exactly the right shape to make that rectangle on the floor and the thick ridges of white dust round the edges would be fertiliser from the sacks. I wonder what happened to those bags. It would be worth getting the police to drag the dock for them, I think. We'll try to get the sergeant at Llantossy on to it when we go in later.'

'If the police found the bags in the dock what would that prove?'

'It wouldn't prove anything, but it might go some way towards explaining something that has been puzzling me quite a bit.'

'What's that?'

'The absence of any struggle in the boathouse. If the man was killed in there you would expect blood, and plenty of it from those frightful injuries. But there was no blood, as far as I could see, and I searched pretty carefully. Or, if the man was killed outside you would expect drag marks in the dust, but the only marks made in the dust, besides a few vague scuffings between the door and the dock made by the dogs' feet and by the feet of the murderer and his victim, of course, were the two clearish areas I have told you about. And one other mark, or rather, pattern of marks.'

'You seem to have seen a lot with your one gammy eye.'

'Not so gammy as all that. My near vision is pretty good now and the strong, slanting sunlight was a help. If these marks hadn't happened to lie just within the illuminated portion of the floor I don't think I should have seen them.'

'Well go on. What were these marks?'

'They were the imprint of ten toes and of the balls of two feet.'

'You mean ten bare toes?'

'Bare, wet toes. You could see where the dust had caked. They were situated directly under a bracket on the long wall of the boathouse – one of a series of four brackets which must have been used for the stowage of oars. I told the police about the toe prints.'

'And what did you and the police deduce from them?'

'That someone with bare, wet feet had stood on tip-toe at that spot, facing the wall, perhaps in order to reach for something off the bracket.'

'Probably one of the village lads after bathing.'

'Possibly – but probably not. It's not a very salubrious spot for bathing.'

'Whose toe-prints do you think they were, then – the murderer's or the victim's?'

'The murderer's.'

'Were those all the clues you collected?'

'Yes.'

'Not very enlightening.'

'Oh, I wouldn't say that.'

'You found them enlightening, did you?'

'Well, they indicate how the murder was committed.'

'Oh, they do, do they? And how was that?'

'I think Daniel Carstairs either was lured into the boathouse in some way, or went there by appointment. His murderer got there before him and set the scene. What scene exactly I don't know except that it involved laying the paper sacks along the edge of the dock. Once inside Carstairs was induced to lie down on the sacks.'

'Sounds a bit difficult.'

'Oh, I don't know. Supposing there were some object – some valuable object – that Carstairs had come to collect. And suppose that valuable object was, by accident or design, lying in the dock, where it would be perfectly visible and not impossible to retrieve since the water is really quite shallow there, not much more than an arm's length deep. Carstairs, who had no coat – he must have left it in the car – and was wearing nothing but a short-sleeved shirt and trousers would then lie down on the edge of the dock and plunge his right arm into the water in an effort to reach the hypothetical object. Lying there he could be easily knocked out by a few clunks on the head with something really heavy.'

'Such as an iron weight?' I interrupted.

'Yes. Why do you say that?'

'Because there was a big weight behind the door that time when I saw the ghost. Must have been used as a drag anchor for the boat.'

'That would be just the thing. After being hit on the head he could have been tipped into the water where, if he were not already dead, he would very soon drown. Any blood would fall on the sacks which would then be gathered up and pushed into the mud at the bottom of the dock, and the weight could be disposed of in the same way. It is possible that the murderer was barefoot and was compelled to wash away blood marks after the deed – which would explain the wet toe-prints by the wall.'

'That's just a story you've made up, isn't it? You've no proof of any of it?'

'It's a story that fits the facts. I'm not saying it's true in detail, but I think it is in outline.'

'What about this valuable object? Did you find any such thing?'

'No. If it ever existed it would have been retrieved of course by the murderer. Actually, I'm very doubtful whether it did in fact exist. I just invented it to show you that it would not have been impossible to induce Carstairs to lie down on the sacks.'

'Why must he have been lying down? Couldn't he have been hit on the head while he was standing up?'

'It's possible but, if so, he must have been neatly felled by the first blow so as to fall tidily on the sacks. He could not have been knocked straightaway into the dock because there was more than one blow, which it would have been very difficult to administer once he was in the water.'

'I see. Well, you seem to have the method pretty well taped. What about the wielder of the "blunt instrument"? Have you any idea as to who it might be?'

'More than an idea. I know the murderer.'

'You know him?'

'Yes.'

'Have you told the police?'

'Not yet. You can't go about accusing people without some proof.'

'But you can tell me?'

'No, I'd rather wait. Excuse me saying so, dear Meg, but you're not one of the most discreet individuals in the world, and you're not very good at hiding your feelings either. It's safer that you shouldn't know.'

Then, seeing my hurt expression, Andy got up and tapped me on the cheek.

'It's for your own safety, darling,' he said. 'Now,' he went on, changing the subject, 'tell me how you came to be on the river path last night with Elise.'

So I told him about my evening's adventures, much as I have told it here, while Andy listened in silence.

'Typical Elise,' he said when I had finished. 'Did you ever sign her document?'

'No. In the end I think she was unwilling that I should see it. She obviously shares your poor opinion of my discretion.'

'Dear Meg! I'm glad you're not the cagey, cautious kind. I'd never have married you if you had been. But this document – did you see what it was?'

'No, but I've an idea it had something to do with her late father's will. And brother Joseph is in it somewhere. It seems the purpose of his present visit is mainly to settle up some family affairs.'

'Jo-Jo – yes,' said Andy thoughtfully. 'He was discussing business with Dr Robert last night, I understand.'

'Divorce business, yes,' I said. 'Possibly the financial provisions of the marriage settlement. There was a document on Elise's desk last night on which I made out the word "Marriage" in florid lawyer's script.'

'It would be interesting to know the provisions of the

settlement and of the Will and what, if anything, brother Joseph has to gain from either – or Robert.'

'Well, we shall never know,' I said.

'I think we shall know,' said Andy, 'in due course.'

And he was right.

Chapter 18

CLIFF DETAINED

In the early afternoon we drove over to Llantossy Police Station to read over and sign our statements, and on our way Andy gave me an account of Robert's visit of the night before.

'He's taking this divorce affair very hard but the reason for his attitude is not very clear. He obviously dislikes his wife, in fact hatred, I think, would not be too strong a word to describe what he feels for her. You would think he would be glad to be rid of her at almost any price.'

'Almost, but not quite any price,' I said. 'If there's anything in Elise's story of goings-on with patients, his career and his livelihood may be at stake.'

'Yes, or it may be that he is worried on Rachel's account. If he really loves her and is not merely amusing himself with her – which is far from certain, by the way – he must find the thought of her being cited in the divorce court extremely unpleasant, to say the least of it.'

'Which reminds me,' I said, 'that we haven't seen or heard of Rachel since the night of the rumpus. Why don't we call in on her on our way back this afternoon?'

'On what pretext?'

'No pretext needed. Just out of sympathy and friendship. And a most heartfelt sympathy it is on my part,' I said.

'A most heartfelt curiosity, you mean,' said Andy unkindly.

'Now that's not fair,' I protested. 'I'm really fond of Rachel and I think she has had a very raw deal all round. Though, mind you,' I added, 'I'm not saying I wouldn't like to know her reactions to the situation.'

Andy smiled.

'I bet you would,' he said, 'and as a matter of fact I shouldn't mind making her better acquaintance myself. It's about time I did in the circumstances.'

'Well, we'll stop on the way back and see if she's in,' I said. 'It's Saturday afternoon and Robert and Rachel take turn about to be on call at the weekends so there's a fifty-fifty chance she will be.'

We were lucky. As we turned in at the gate of Weir Cottage, after having duly signed our statements at Llantossy, I saw Rachel at once. Although the sky was overcast for the first time for many days and an intermittent mizzle of rain had been falling off and on since morning, she had taken an ancient deck chair out onto the little plot of grass under her sitting-room window and was lying slumped in it with her eyes closed. Wearing a dirty pair of slacks and an old sweater, with her hair in a bird's nest and her drawn features yellow in the unflattering light, there was no vestige left of her old attraction. For a second, with all the horrors of the last few days lying very near the surface of my mind, I thought she was dead and my heart missed a beat. But as soon as I called her name – rather breathlessly – she opened her dark eyes and stared at me for a long moment, obviously without recognition. Then, as it dawned on her who I was, she leaped to her feet and a slow flush spread upward from her neck to her hairline. She never said a word – just stared – and my heart was so wrung by her look of absolute wretchedness that impulsively I ran forward and putting my hands on her shoulders kissed her on both cheeks.

'You poor darling!' I said. 'I wish I had come before to tell you how sorry I am about the other evening. I was tricked into it. You know that, don't you?'

'Yes,' she said in a low voice averting her eyes from mine. 'I'm sorry you should be mixed up in the filthy business.'

Then, shaking my hands impatiently from her shoulders, she turned to the front door and muttered without looking at me, 'I expect I can find you a cup of tea. Come in, won't you – and your husband?'

All my curiosity had by now evaporated, leaving nothing but a sense of shame and discomfort at having, like a fool, rushed in where I was so obviously not welcome, and I opened my mouth to say that we must be on our way when Andy forestalled me.

'Thank you, Dr Brading,' he said, 'a cup of tea would be very refreshing. I'm sure poor Meg must be dying for one.'

So I closed my mouth again and we followed Rachel into the cottage and sat silently and awkwardly in the stone-flagged living room listening to the rattle of crockery and the opening and shutting of cupboards in the kitchen as Rachel put a kettle on the oil stove and found cups and plates. When she came out at last she had combed her hair and put some powder on her face and looked altogether more human. There was an uncomfortable pause while she set the tea out on a small table and to break the silence I said, with that false brightness such embarrassing social occasions always engender, but which was quite inappropriate both to the present situation and to the remark I was about to make: 'I suppose you've heard about the latest murder?'

I imagine I used the word 'latest' with the death of Newton Landon in the back of my mind, forgetting that, except by Andy and myself, no suspicion of murder had ever been attached to his death.

At first Rachel did not answer and, thinking that perhaps she had not heard me above the rattle of the teacups, I was about to re-phrase my remark when I heard her say, as though to herself, 'Latest − yes,' then raising her voice and looking at me: 'You mean the unknown man who was found dead in the boathouse last night? Yes, it was all the gossip in the village this morning. They were saying that you found him, Meg.'

'Yes, I found him,' I said. 'Or rather, it was Curly really. But the man was not unknown, you know. The police identified him almost at once.'

'His name,' said Andy, breaking in on me suddenly and looking intently at Rachel, 'was Daniel Carstairs.'

I thought Rachel was about to faint. A cup which she was holding in her hand fell and was smashed to fragments on the stone floor as she groped her way to a chair that was standing behind her.

'No, no,' she said wildly. Then crouching forward and putting her hands over her face she burst into tears.

I was stunned and quite out of my depth.

'Do you know him?' I asked with astonishment.

But she could not answer. So I drew another chair up to hers and, laying a hand on her knee, said as gently as I could, 'Rachel, Rachel, what is it? *Do* you know this man? What is it that's troubling you so much? Tell me and perhaps Andy and I can help you.'

But with an impatient movement she jerked her knee from under my hand and shouted in a voice almost inarticulate with sobs, 'Go away. Leave me alone, can't you. For God's sake.'

I looked helplessly at Andy, but he had no eyes for me. He was still staring fixedly at Rachel and now he said in a stern voice such as I had never heard from him before, 'Pull yourself together, Dr Brading. If you know something of this man – and it's clear from your behaviour that you do – it's your duty to go immediately to the police with your information. I think you know that, don't you?'

There was no answer from Rachel and for a long five minutes which seemed like hours Andy waited patiently but inexorably for the violence of her emotion to subside. At last when her sobs had diminished he said, 'Do you hear me, Dr Brading?'

A slight nod from Rachel, but with her hands still covering her face.

'You will go to the police, then?' asked Andy.

'No, no, no,' said Rachel fiercely, snatching down her hands and turning her large eyes, brilliant with tears, towards him. 'Never, never, never.'

'In that case, I'm afraid I must tell you, Dr Brading, that I shall be forced to report this scene to the police myself. You see, they must know of it – though it would come better from you.'

Rachel made no answer, but stared at Andy with an expression of desperation, bewilderment, despair, like a cornered animal. I could not bear to see it.

'Come on, Andy,' I said. 'Leave her alone. She's had as much as she can take. Come away, do.'

'I'm coming,' said Andy impatiently, 'but first I want to say this.' Then addressing Rachel again he said solemnly: 'Dr Brading, you must realise your position and mine. Every piece of information relating to this man, Daniel Carstairs, is of importance at this moment to the police. He was horribly murdered and if you know anything concerning him or concerning his murder it is your duty to communicate it to the police at once. I am in a similar position to yours and I mean to do my duty. If I do not hear from you by this evening that you have made up your mind to tell the police what you know, I shall be forced myself to report your conduct here to them. You see I am giving you time to think. I shall give you until eight o'clock – no longer.'

With that he turned and limped slowly out of the door with me trailing shamefacedly after him.

We were silent until we reached the car and then I could contain myself no longer.

'Andy,' I said furiously, 'why were you so brutal to Rachel? If you had been a bit kinder and more sympathetic she might have confided in us.'

'She would never have confided in us ...'

'You didn't give her much chance.'

'... and, in any case, it is not her confidence I want.'

'What *do* you want?'

'I want her to go to the police.'

'Why? What concern is it of yours? You're not the keeper of her conscience.'

'My dear Meg, you don't know what you're talking about. What has conscience got to do with it?' said Andy testily. 'I'm merely trying to ensure against another murder being committed. Now shut up and let me think.'

Another murder! I was indeed out of my depth.

For the rest of the afternoon Andy was on tenterhooks. He could not settle to anything. His books and his beloved fishing tackle lay neglected, and when I suggested a short stroll with the dogs he snapped my head off.

'You know I can't leave the house,' he said.

I did not know it, but I forbore to argue.

Every car that passed in the lane took him to the front door to peer short-sightedly after it.

'Who was that?' he would ask me impatiently.

Once, it was Trev Price's ancient rattletrap with Trev himself driving and Billy and his cousin, Les, mouthing to each other on the front seat beside him. Another time it was Dr Robert Landon on his way to the surgery, or perhaps for a last interview with his wife before she left him for good. Lastly came the sleek limousine of Joseph Ellis driving up, I supposed, to fetch Elise and take her home with him. I wondered whether she would call in and say good-bye to us on her way down the lane again. If so, had we any drink in the house? I thought not and I called out to Andy that I would take the dogs and nip down to MacAlister's shop for a bottle of cheap sherry, if Gladys would let me have it out of hours.

As I reached the garden gate Milly Piggott "happened" to emerge from her front door, having evidently observed my three expeditions into the front garden to peer after passing cars.

'Expecting summun?' she called out with the false brightness of curiosity.

'Can't stop,' I called back gaily, waving to her. 'Got to get down to the shop before it closes.' I was hurrying past when she brought me up short by shouting, ''Eard about Cliff Price?'

'No. What about Cliff Price?' I asked turning back slowly to Milly's gate.

By this time she had reached the other side of the gate and, leaning over it conspiratorially, she said in a hushed voice but with much emphasis, 'Police got 'im.'

'The police have got him! Got him for what?' I asked confusedly.

'Murder!' said Milly with relish. 'That 'ere poacher as 'e said 'e was chasing after, same one you found with 'is 'ead bashed in. Well, 'e done it. Cliff Price done it.'

'Cliff Price! Well! Is that really true, Miss Piggott? Has he confessed?'

'True as I stand 'ere, Mrs Marsden. Police come and took 'im into Carne, not an hour gone.'

'And he confessed?' I insisted.

'Well, as to that I couldn't rightly say,' admitted Milly reluctantly, 'but Evan Jones 'e arrested 'im when 'e come in for 'is tea.'

'Well, I'm sorry for it,' I said, 'but I mustn't stop to gossip now, Miss Piggott,' and I went thoughtfully on my way.

Cliff Price! Was it possible? Certainly he was on the river bank that night and he had openly stated that he had seen and chased a man but had declared that the man had evaded him in the end. Would he have owned to seeing the man at all if in fact he had caught and killed him in so brutal a fashion? And why in any case should he have killed him? Cliff, an ex-commando, would have known many methods of rendering his opponent harmless without going to the length of bashing his head in in so bloody and amateur a fashion. On the other hand, it was perhaps not as a poacher that "Mr Brown" had been murdered. Perhaps he had done Cliff some injury quite apart from his poaching activities and Cliff had seized upon this apparently heaven-sent opportunity for getting his own back. According to Constable Jones he had returned to Llantossy that night in a state of collapse and covered with blood. And certainly he had known "Mr Brown" before, as I could testify and, moreover, had seemed to have a grudge against him. I remembered in this connection a conversation we had had together one hot day in summer – a ridiculous conversation in which Cliff had not only openly displayed his dislike and distrust of "Mr Brown" but had also hinted at a nefarious connection between him and us – Andy and myself. What was the motive of his dislike? In our case I was pretty sure it was prompted by a suspicion that we knew of his pilfering propensities. Could it be the same motive in the case of "Mr Brown"? And was it a motive strong enough for murder? Then a great light dawned on me. Of course, of course! Such a theory would not only explain the murder of Daniel Carstairs, but would also cover the attack on me on the night of the poaching affray. Cliff, taking advantage of the night's confusion had decided to shut all dangerous mouths. The poachers would be blamed for the deaths. It was the act of a madman, but the motive, too, was scarcely sane. I shuddered slightly at my thoughts. Thank goodness that the police, for once, had been really quick off the mark and had put Cliff under lock and key before he could complete the job on Andy and me.

Mrs MacAlister allowed me to take away the sherry for which I had come since it was, by now, only twenty minutes before opening time and Constable Jones was known to be in Carne with weightier matters on his mind than minor infringements of the licensing laws.

'How did the police get on to Cliff Price?' I asked as I picked up my bottle from the counter.

'Get on to him!' exclaimed Gladys in her sing-song Welsh voice. 'Well, he was there, look you, being as he's bailiff, like. Bound to be there when it's waiting for poachers they were.'

'But how did they know he had committed the murder?' I insisted.

'Who says anything about him committing a murder?' exclaimed Gladys with her black eyes round with astonishment.

'I was told that Cliff Price had been arrested by PC Jones and taken into Carne,' I said.

'No such thing,' said the good-hearted Gladys indignantly. 'No indeed. The very idea! 'Tis helping the police, he is, with their enquiries. 'Twas Blodwen Jones her own self, look you, standing where you're standing now not an hour gone said them very words: "Cliff's gone to Carne with Evan," she said, "to help the police with their enquiries." Cliff to murder a man! The idea!'

So Cliff had not yet been actually arrested, but the form of words quoted by Gladys was surely that employed by the police when suspicion was so strong as to be practically certainty. After a little further chat I put my bottle under my arm and strolled thoughtfully homeward. I found Andy still limping restlessly about the living room.

'You didn't see a car passing in the lane in either direction, did you, Meg?' he greeted me as I opened the door.

'No, but surely you would have heard it if there had been one?'

'I might have missed it,' he replied anxiously. 'Nearly six and still no word from Rachel.'

But bursting as I was with my own news I had only half an ear for Andy.

'What do you think,' I said excitedly, 'Cliff Price has been arrested for the murder of Daniel Carstairs – or at least, as good as arrested.'

That caught Andy's attention.

'Cliff Price has!' he exclaimed.

'Yes, yes. And don't you see, it fits in beautifully,' and I went into a long exposition of my cogitations concerning the events of the night of the poaching affray and concerning my conclusions on Cliff's motives.

'And finally,' I finished, 'Cliff would fit the part of Newton's murderer, too, though the motive there would be a little different. In that case it must obviously have been revenge for his ducking.'

'Obviously,' commented Andy, but by the tone of his voice I knew that he was laughing at me and my theories.

'You don't agree with me?' I asked somewhat crestfallen.

'Well, well, never mind that,' said Andy. 'But tell me. Is this gossip about Cliff's arrest all over the village?'

'I imagine so,' I said. 'Though some people seem to think that Cliff has not yet actually been arrested and has merely been detained for questioning.'

'Would they know of it up at the doctor's house? I wonder.' Andy was talking to himself rather than to me. 'They might if Robert has been gossiping with his patients. I hope they do. It may give us more time.'

With that cryptic statement he returned to his restless pacing and would not be drawn into further comment or discussion. Finally, I gave up trying to draw him and retired to the back premises to start the preparations for supper. A salad would be nice, I thought, and I wandered off into the garden to find a lettuce and some Welsh onions. The intermittent drizzle of the day had quite cleared off but the grass was still pearled with drops like dew. The clouds were breaking as they slowly moved off to the north-east and the sinking sun lit their summits with a golden light. It was a beautiful, calm evening and I thought that after supper I would take my small trout rod and try to catch a nice breakfast of trout for Andy and myself. But fate had other plans for me.

Chapter 19

RACHEL'S STORY

As I picked a lettuce, cold and crisp with rain, I heard a car in the lane and it seemed to stop at our door. With a farewell visit from Elise in my mind I hurried in. But it was Rachel. When I arrived at the living-room door she was already installed in Andy's chair and he was unwrapping the sherry preparatory to pouring out drinks for himself and her. Rachel, though haggard still, looked calmer and, in fact, quite mistress of herself. She had changed into a linen suit of a warm brown tint which brought out the tawny lights in her eyes, and she had even touched her lips and cheeks with colour. She smiled at me as I came in, 'Sorry about this afternoon, Meg,' she said. 'My nerves seem all to pieces these days.'

'That's all right,' I said, smiling back. 'I understand and it seems to me that we owe you an apology too, for barging in as we did. I hope Andy has said sorry for his rudeness.'

'No, I have not,' said Andy uncompromisingly, handing us each a glass of sherry. 'However, let's drink to a happy outcome to this whole miserable business.'

We all drank but none of us, I must confess, with any appearance of enjoyment. The present occasion hardly seemed one for jollification. Moreover, Gladys' sherry turned out to be even nastier than I had anticipated.

'I hope, Dr Brading,' continued Andy, 'that you have come to say that you are on your way to tell the police what you know of Daniel Carstairs.'

'Well, no,' replied Rachel slowly, 'not exactly. Really I am here to ask your advice.'

'Well, you know what my advice is,' said Andy tartly. 'I made it clear enough this afternoon, I should have thought.'

'You did,' agreed Rachel, turning a hostile glance on him, 'but then, you see, you didn't know the facts. I want to tell you a story. It concerns Elise and Bob, and Newton and Daniel Carstairs – and myself a little. I think it's very unlikely that you'll know any of it. And when it's all told I want you to advise me as to how much or how little I should tell the police. I am so near everything myself that I can no longer judge what is relevant and what not, and you, Meg,' pointedly omitting Andy, 'are the only friend down here who could advise me.'

'I still think you should go straight to the police,' said Andy, 'and tell them all you know. But, all right. We'll listen and give you the best advice we can.'

'Thank you,' said Rachel.

She was silent for a couple of minutes, obviously marshalling her thoughts, and then she began. 'To start with,' she said, 'Newton Landon was not Bob's son …'

'So that was why,' I could not help interrupting, 'he was so unlike Robert and why Elise always makes such a mystery of her courtship and marriage. Was she "in trouble", as they say, when Robert married her?'

'I shall be coming to that,' said Rachel, 'but I want to begin at a point much earlier than the marriage of Bob and Elise. You know, I think, that Elise was at London University when she was a girl. It seems she was a very clever child with a special talent for mathematics and, as you know, music. Her father, who was a stock broker and a self-made man, thought the world of her. He was one of those men, I gather, who held education, intelligence, knowledge – and especially scientific knowledge – in absolute reverence, chiefly, I suppose, because he had never had very much education himself, nor any opportunity for exercising his intelligence in any but the severely practical way of making money on the stock exchange. His gods were Newton, Einstein, Rutherford, hence poor Newton Landon's name. On the other hand, he really abominated the arts – music, literature, painting – which he considered decadent and useless. I have all this from Bob, of course, because old Mr Ellis was dead long before I knew Elise. When Elise left school her father insisted that she should give up her music and take a science degree at London University. That was where Bob met her. He had rather an unfortunate childhood of which I know very little after he moved away from the house next door to ours. I think his father went bankrupt soon after that and it was not until Bob had completed his National Service that a bachelor uncle came up with the fees necessary for Bob to study medicine, as he had always wanted to do. He had already been up four years when Elise arrived so that, what with one thing and another, he was a good deal older than she was.'

At this point I shifted perhaps a little impatiently in my chair and reached for the sherry bottle, and Rachel turned to me and said, 'I'll keep it as short as I can, Meg, but all this does really have a bearing on events because, you see, it was Elise's mood of rebellion that made her such easy prey for Daniel Carstairs, and it was Bob's comparative age and experience that made her turn to him when she was in trouble. At least, that was Elise's tale to Bob – though there is a different interpretation of her actions, as you will see later.

'Well, to come to Daniel Carstairs: he was a no-good even then, but very attractive to women in a tough, masculine way. He was a war orphan, both his parents having been killed in the Blitz. He was brought up by foster-parents – in Harrow, I think – and he also had done his National Service before coming up to college on a county scholarship in the same year as Elise. The minute he set eyes on Elise, which he did at a dance in the first term, he fell quite genuinely and madly in love with her. She was a most beautiful creature at that time, Bob says, with a look of dewy innocence about her which simply sent a certain type of man – such as Carstairs was – crazy with a desire to possess and deflower. But fundamentally she was completely frigid and her biting tongue belied her innocent look and enabled her to hold off all the – to her – undesirable men, including Carstairs.

'Bob met her first at a party towards the end of her first year and he, too, fell a victim to her blue eyes and seraphic looks, but was treated to no more favour than the rest of her male followers of whom the most persistent at the time was Carstairs. At least this was the case at first. Then quite suddenly her attitude seemed to change towards him, Bob says, and she began to single him out for favours – began to allow him to take her out to theatres and concerts and even to accompany her home afterwards to her Bloomsbury flat. She had stubbornly refused to become a resident at any of the women's colleges and her father had been compelled to take a small attic flat for her in Coram Street. Well, to cut a long story short, it's my opinion that she deliberately set out to seduce Bob, though Bob didn't realise this at the time, for he was genuinely in love with her. Elise's version of the affair was that she turned to Bob for protection against the frightening attentions of Dan Carstairs and that Bob abused her trust in him. However that may be, the fact is that they were intimate together and very soon Elise announced that she was about to have a baby.'

Rachel fell silent, obviously lost for a moment in her own bitter thoughts.

'So then he had to marry her?' I said to rouse her.

'Yes,' said Rachel heavily. 'That was what Elise had been planning for, as I firmly believe, but her scheme did not succeed as easily as she had expected, because Bob, in his way, you know, is as tough a character as Elise herself. An even tougher character perhaps,' and Rachel shuddered slightly, then continued.

'At that time he had absolutely no thoughts of marriage. For one thing he had no money and for another he was ambitious. He had no intention of living a life of obscurity as an overworked GP. He had the brains and the character to specialise and set up eventually in Harley Street, and the uncle was willing to finance the extra years of study required. If he were to marry before he was even qualified all financial support would certainly be withdrawn immediately. He refused absolutely to marry Elise.

'There then took place a little scene very reminiscent evidently of the one you assisted at, Meg, the other night, only in this case the chief actors were Bob and Elise, and the interrupting witness was Elise's father, old Ellis. It is this episode that makes me certain that my interpretation of Elise's actions is the true one. Bob has never been willing to tell me what occurred exactly, but the outcome was that he and Elise were married within the month. Old Ellis never spoke to Bob after that day and never forgave his daughter, but he supported the young couple until Bob could earn his own living and he settled money in his will on the baby.

'Well, things were bad enough for Bob with all his ambitious dreams shattered, but at least he had Elise whom he really loved, and he looked forward with pleasure to the thought of a child. And then came the final blow. The baby was born prematurely and Bob was present at its birth. Up to that moment he had never had that slightest doubt as to the child being his own, but now, as he held the newly born infant in his arms and looked into its red, crumpled face, he suddenly knew with absolute certainty that the child he held was not his son but had been fathered by Daniel Carstairs. These startling resemblances to one or other parent are often to be seen in the first few days after birth, though they may fade rapidly soon afterwards and may never be permanently established. Bob says that if the nurse had not come in at that moment he would have strangled the baby there and then.'

Rachel fell silent and leaned her head against her hand.

'That's the story,' she said.

'How terrible,' I murmured. 'Poor Bob!'

'But there's something more on your mind than this old story?' said Andy looking keenly at Rachel.

'Yes, there is,' said Rachel slowly, then after a pause: 'Oh don't you see. Don't you see? I'm terrified of what Bob may have done. When he first found out about how Elise had tricked him he was almost insane with rage for a time. He told me so. His whole life was in ruins because of that bastard and his rage was directed not against Elise so much – because he was still then as though hypnotised by her beauty – as against the child and its father. He spent weeks and months, he told me, looking for Daniel Carstairs and if he had found him he would have killed him, he said. But luckily he could not find him. He had been sent down from the university for some scandal connected with a girl at Westfield College and had disappeared without trace. But then he turned up again about a fortnight ago. Bob saw him in Carne. And then he overheard Elise on the telephone one day and was sure she was talking to him, and in the last few days Bob has got it into his head that Elise and Carstairs were plotting together to ruin him through me. To ruin his life a second time. Don't you see, don't you see? Then the night Carstairs was killed Bob was supposed to have come to me at the cottage, but he never turned up. Where was he? Where was he? Why doesn't he tell me where he was? *Must* I go to the police? Mr Marsden, advise me. I am no longer able to see things sensibly myself.'

But instead of answering her directly Andy, peering intently at her with his one good eye, said slowly, 'Dr Brading, I have a question to ask you: How did Newton Landon die? Do you know?'

An absolute silence fell. It was getting dusk now in our northward-facing front room. Rachel and Andy were sitting in the window and I watched their motionless profiles facing each other with an intent and frozen stillness. We all three seemed to hold our breaths. Even the sleeping dogs were inaudible and the only sound to be heard was the hurried ticking – like the beating of a frightened heart – of the little French clock and then, suddenly, its musical chime as it struck the hour – seven o'clock. The sound seemed to rouse Rachel.

'He was drowned,' she said tonelessly. 'It was an accident. There was an inquest. The verdict was "drowned". Accidentally.'

'But you know better?' persisted Andy.

'No, no, no, no,' protested Rachel violently. 'He was accidentally drowned, I tell you. You know that. Meg was at the inquest. Why should you question the verdict? What is it to you?'

'Never mind that,' said Andy, 'but my advice to you, Dr Brading, since you asked for it a moment ago, is to go to the police *at once*, and tell them everything you know. *Everything.*'

Rachel rose stiffly from her chair.

'You treat me like a criminal,' she said. 'I thought I should find more friendship here.'

'Will you go to the police, *now*?' persisted Andy, rising also.

'Yes,' said Rachel bitterly. 'Having told you so much there is now no possibility of keeping it from the police. I was a fool to come here. Good-bye.'

'You will go at once?' insisted Andy again as she opened the front door to let herself out.

'Yes, yes,' called back Rachel impatiently, and she was gone without a word to me.

'Poor Rachel!' I said as Andy turned back to the sitting room. 'Why are you so unkind to her?'

'I'm not unkind, Meg,' he protested. 'You're too soft-hearted. Come on, old girl, let's light the lamp and have some supper.'

While I busied myself with feeding the dogs and then washing the lettuce and setting out our simple meal on the sitting-room table, my thoughts kept turning to the tale we had just heard and trying to fit it into the facts we knew. I remembered the first time we had met Dr Landon on the afternoon of Newton's death when he had nearly run Andy down in the lane and I remembered his agitation which, even at the time, had seemed disproportionate. If Newton was drowned at about 3.30 in the afternoon, as Andy and I had established by our deductions long ago, then Robert Landon could have had a hand in it. He had been out, ostensibly on his rounds, all that afternoon. And then I suddenly remembered another thing. Last night when the police had tried to contact him they had been unable to find him. Daniel Carstairs was dead by then, of course, and Elise had said something about Robert dining with Joseph Ellis, but it was unusual surely for a doctor to go off without leaving some address or telephone number where he could be contacted. Even Rachel did not seem to know where he had been. Was he perhaps, for at least part of that time, engaged in disposing of blood-stained clothing? His motive for killing both Newton and Carstairs appeared to be strong. Then again, he could well have been the person who had hit me on the head at the end of his own garden, though here the motive was obscure. I shuddered again at the thought of my narrow escape. And to think that Andy had actually called him in next day to minister to my sore head!

'Not very pleasant,' I said as we sat down at last to eat, 'to have a murderer for a doctor.'

Andy laughed.

'So that's where your cogitations have led you, is it?' he said.

'Don't you think Robert Landon is a murderer?' I asked.

'Rachel told a good tale,' he said evasively.

'Don't you believe her?'

'We have only her word for it, remember. And didn't it strike you, Meg, that her whole behaviour couldn't have been better calculated to throw suspicion on Robert?'

'She's in love,' I said with anxiety. 'She hardly knows what she's doing.'

'Maybe you're right, at that,' said Andy.

Chapter 20

WEIR COTTAGE

The table had been cleared and I was drawing the curtains across the night-blackened window panes when suddenly the darkness outside was brilliantly lit and I realised that a car had just turned out of the doctor's gate and was heading down the lane. Andy saw the lights, too, and limped to the window.

'Who's that?' he asked, peering out.

But it was impossible to make out anything definite against the glare of the headlights.

'Joseph Ellis and Elise,' I said, 'or the doctor. It's too dark to see which.'

'Hasn't Elise left yet?' asked Andy and his voice sounded anxious.

'I don't know,' I replied. 'I saw the car go up but I haven't noticed it come down again. It might have done, though, while Rachel was here. We were all too absorbed then to notice anything that was happening outside.'

Andy stood for a long time after the curtains were drawn with his face to the window and his head bent – obviously deep in thought.

'I don't like it,' I heard him mutter at last, and then turning to me, 'Meg, old girl, would you mind if we got the car out and called on Rachel again?'

'Oh, dear,' I said, 'must you bother her again? She's not in a fit state to be badgered, Andy.'

'Oh, come on, girl,' said Andy, suddenly irritable. 'There's really no time to waste in argument. Don't bother with locking the house up. The dogs can come with us in the back of the car.'

So before I knew where I was we were hurrying down the lane with Squelch frisking delightedly round us and the more sedate Curly trotting to heel. It was not yet black dark and a greenish glow still lingered in the western sky, making it easy for me to see my way. For Andy it was more difficult, and when he had stumbled twice I took his arm and we hastened on together. As we approached the village we could see that Tom Todd was doing good business in the Ferryman. The door to the public bar was open and among the sea of faces crowding it I picked out that of Cliff Price. So Gladys was right and Milly Piggott wrong; he had not been arrested. With a mug of beer in one hand and the other elbow propping up the bar he was holding forth to the assembled company.

'… along the mortuary to 'dentify him, see,' he was saying as we passed and I should have liked to stop and hear more, but Andy hurried me on.

'No time, Meg,' he urged. 'Not a moment to lose.'

So I extracted the car from the boat store as quickly as I could and we all piled into it – Andy and I and the two dogs – and we were on our way. The greenish glow was darkening now in the west and a thin crescent of moon, like a paring from a silver nail, was floating in the sky, bright and clean among the pale stars. As we reached Rachel's cottage we saw the red tail light of a car parked outside her gate.

'My God! I hope we're not too late,' said Andy, and before

I had even switched off the engine he was out of the car and hobbling up the path. The dogs in a wild scramble followed him and I was left to bring up the rear.

Surprisingly, there was no light visible in the cottage as we approached. When we came to the front door we found it standing wide open and beyond it, blackness – a cavern of blackness without a glimmer of light – and out of the blackness there wafted a strong smell of paraffin oil. On the threshold Andy paused and leaning against the side of the door he peered into the gloom. As I came up he motioned to me with his hand to keep quiet and I seized the dogs by their collars and crouched down beside them listening. The voice of the weir seemed very loud in the still night, a long sighing roar, not unlike the sea-swell heard in a shell held close to the ear but magnified a thousand times. It seemed to fill the cavern of darkness before us as the noise of breakers fills a sea cave and with the same resonance. Impossible to detect any smaller sound of movement, of breathing, of human activity of any kind against the ear-filling roar. I held my breath until the blood drummed in my ears but could distinguish nothing except the quiet panting of the dogs close to my head. Then, as I let my breath out slowly at last, I thought I heard a very faint clink from the depths of the darkened cottage. Andy obviously had not heard it, for he made a movement at that moment as though to step through the doorway, but I straightened quickly and laid my hand on his arm, and he realised by my tenseness that I had heard something. And then it came again, more pronounced this time – a slow metallic scraping. Another pause while I listened with every muscle tensed, and for the third time I heard it, no louder, no nearer than before, and no further away. And suddenly I knew what it was.

'It's the window,' I whispered. 'The kitchen window.'

Then the scraping sound came again and I realised that it was almost certainly not made by any human agency. In spite of the stillness of the night, I felt sure that it was either a light breath of wind or, perhaps, the updraft from the weir, which lay immediately beneath the window, which was causing the unlatched casement to swing very gently to and fro and to drag its iron stop bar across the sill.

'Only the wind,' I whispered.

Andy put his hand in his pocket and brought out something which I realised by the small rattle it made was a box of matches. He was about to strike one when he evidently thought better of it – perhaps because of the strong smell of paraffin.

'There's a torch in the car,' he breathed in my ear. 'Fetch it and at the same time shut the dogs in the car. Make them stay to heel down the path.'

So I whispered fiercely 'Heel,' first in Curly's ear and then in Squelch's and set off down the pathway. The journey to the car was not a pleasant one. Scarcely daring to breathe I tip-toed down with eyes and ears straining for any sign of movement. But there was no movement except the quiet padding of the dogs and I reached my destination safely and found the torch – a lantern type model with a powerful beam – and motioned the dogs into the back seat and closed the door on them without daring to sneck it for fear of the noise. That done I was cautiously making my way back to the cottage again when my attention was caught by the car still standing in front of ours with its rear light glowing steadily in the darkness. Perhaps it was Rachel's car, I thought. Perhaps she was sitting in it stunned and needing help. Perhaps, even – I scarcely dared formulate the thought – perhaps she was dead: murdered. Anything was possible after the nightmare of the evening before when I had found a battered face in the water of the boat dock.

But it was not Rachel's car; it was Robert Landon's, and it was empty. I breathed a sigh of relief. But my relief did not last long. Almost immediately anxiety began to mount again. Where *was* Dr Landon, then? And where was Rachel? I hurried back up the path and thrust the torch into Andy's hand. At once he switched it on and its powerful beam cut a swathe of light across the living room and, through the open door beyond, into the kitchen, revealing a scene of complete confusion. The little table on which Rachel had set out the tea things that afternoon was lying on its side and beyond it, overturned, the chair on which she had sat and wept. Not far from the table a large, dark stain covered much of the floor. For a moment I held my breath, but it was only paraffin oil, as I saw when Andy swung the torch a little to the left and lit up the Aladdin lamp lying with a shattered chimney on the far edge of the stain. In the kitchen, too, was chaos. A heavy iron saucepan lay on the floor and a tin kettle was cocked precariously on its side on the oil cooking stove with a pool of water on the tiled floor under its spout. Broken shards of crockery, obviously swept off the dresser, lay scattered everywhere and a wooden kitchen chair leaned crazily on two legs against the sink. But a Primus lantern, hanging from a bacon hook in the middle of the ceiling, was still intact. Of Rachel and Robert Landon – dead or alive – there was no sign.

'Better look upstairs,' whispered Andy.

So after pausing for a moment to listen intently at the bottom of the little spiral flight of stone stairs and, hearing nothing but the unending roar of the weir, we made our way cautiously, step by step, to the upper floor. Here there was no disorder. In each of the two small bedrooms a single bed stood, neatly made, without a wrinkle on its coverlet. One bedroom, by the toilet articles on its dressing table, was obviously Rachel's and the other, as obviously, had been recently occupied by a man. A pair of hair brushes lay on a small table under a hanging mirror, a man's camel hair dressing gown hung behind the door and, under the bed, the torch beam lit up a pair of masculine bedroom slippers. So Elise had been right; Robert had been sleeping at Weir Cottage. The bathroom – the only other room on this floor – proved to be equally empty and orderly.

'Nothing here,' said Andy in his natural voice. 'Do you think you could light the Primus lantern, Meg, if we go back to the kitchen?'

'If it has been filled and if I can find some methylated spirit to start it with,' I said, following Andy's example and abandoning the strained whisper in which we had so far conversed.

The lantern proved to be full of oil and the small, long-nozzled tin of methylated spirit for starting it was close by on a high shelf above the sink where it had escaped damage. Soon the lantern, pumped to its full brilliance, was hissing away on its bacon hook and we could see the chaos around us in better detail.

It was only then that I noticed the window – the same window whose creaking had startled me on our arrival at the cottage. It was as I had thought then: one half of the large casement was wide open and swinging very gently in the night air and the hinged and perforated iron bar attached to the lower edge of the frame was scraping to and fro on the outer sill. But what drew my eyes was not so much the bar as the windowpane above it. Instead of the expected square of light, darkly mirroring the kitchen, there was nothing but a black and jagged hole and into the top and bottom of the hole protruded long and wickedly pointed spears of glass. From the longest of the cruel points fluttered a strip, about an inch wide and four inches long, of some dark cloth.

With an exclamation of horror I ran to the window, but even before I reached it I recognised in the impaled fragment of material the russet brown linen of the suit which Rachel had been wearing that evening. It was stained with blood and, on both the inner and the outer windowsills, large pools of blood were coagulating slowly. From the pool on the inner sill sluggish drops were still falling with an almost inaudible "plop" into yet another, smaller pool on the floor beneath the window.

I felt the colour draining from my face and my eyes stretching with horror as I turned to Andy and stammered, 'He's … he's … killed her.'

'Or she's killed him,' said Andy slowly. 'What a fool I've

been,' he muttered to himself. 'We should have taken Rachel to the police at once ourselves. It was the only safe thing.' Then turning to me: 'Quick, Meg, ring Llantossy Station and get the sergeant to send someone out at once. And don't touch anything.'

I flew to obey, but once out of the wedge of light shining through the kitchen doorway I was brought up short by the darkness of the living room beyond, and as I was groping my way past the overturned table towards the window sill where the telephone stood, the air was suddenly rent by the strident shrill of its bell.

I stopped in my tracks. What now?

'Probably only a patient,' called Andy from the kitchen. 'Answer it, Meg.'

So with trembling hand I lifted the receiver.

'Weir Cottage here,' I said, with what calm I could muster.

A man's voice at the other end asked angrily: 'Is that you, Elise?'

Elise? Thoughts of a wrong number flashed through my mind.

'This is Dr Brading's cottage,' I said.

'I know, I know,' retorted the man irritably. 'Who is that speaking?' And when I told him: 'Mrs Marsden, yes, yes. Please ask my sister to come to the telephone, will you. This is Joseph Ellis speaking.'

'Do you mean Elise?' I asked foolishly.

'Yes, yes, of course,' he retorted impatiently.

'But Elise isn't here,' I said. 'Did you expect her to be?'

'Not there! But I left her there about an hour ago.'

'Well, she's not here now,' I said.

'Damn and blast! All right, tell her when she comes back that I can't find what she sent me to the house for and I refuse to waste any more time on it. If she wants to be fetched tell her to ring the George in Carne. Whether she wants any dinner or not, I most certainly do and I'm going into Carne for it.'

With that, and before I could get in a word of explanation, I heard the receiver at the other end banged down on its rest.

'Who is it?' called Andy from the kitchen.

'Joseph Ellis,' I called back.

'What did he want?'

'To speak to Elise. He seemed to think she was here.'

No comment from the kitchen. Then: 'Ring the police quickly, Meg. Events are getting too much for us.'

So I rang Llantossy Station and reported that I was afraid there had been an accident to Dr Brading. The constable in charge said that he could not himself leave the desk but that he would get in touch with the sergeant at once and that someone would be at Weir Cottage as soon as possible. As I replaced the receiver there was an urgent summons from Andy.

What now? Oh, God!

I flew back to the kitchen to see Andy, with the un-shattered half of the casement wide open, leaning perilously over the sill.

'What is it? Are you hurt?' I cried breathlessly.

'No, no, girl,' said Andy testily, pulling his head back into the room. 'Come here quickly and tell me if you can see anything lying on the rocks at the tail of the weir. My damned eyes aren't good enough to make it out. Here, take the torch.'

I took Andy's place at the window, avoiding with a shudder the rapidly coagulating pool of blood on the other sill, and shone the torch down onto the seething cauldron of the weir pool. The sight and battering sound of the racing, swirling river turned me giddy and the water's cold, dank breath striking against my face seemed to be sucking me downwards so that for a moment I thought I should fall; but with an effort I pulled myself together and began to play the beam slowly down the near bank. At first, I saw nothing but rock and water with, lower down, an occasional half-drowned willow bush hanging on for dear life to its precarious root-hold, and I was about to shift the torch beam to the further bank when suddenly at the extreme limit of the torch's range I saw something gleaming palely. The object, whatever it was, lay on a slab of rock worn smooth by centuries of floodwater. There was a backwater at that point caused by a small promontory of rock beyond and in the lea of the promontory grew a stunted willow with its branches trailing in the water. I strained my eyes to try to make out the nature of the pale object. Was it a light-coloured boulder? No, it was certainly not a boulder. Or a piece of river wrack? No, not that either. It seemed to me that it was a human face. Yes. Yes. Certainly. It was certainly a human face and part of the body to which it belonged could just be made out.

I tumbled back into the room.

'She's lying down there,' I gasped to Andy. 'On a rock at the tail of the pool. What shall we do? She may still be alive.'

'I'll see if I can reach her – or him,' said Andy, snatching the torch from my hand and hurrying to the door at a hobbling run.

'Stop,' I called after him. 'Andy, stop. You know you can't possibly get down there and in the pitch dark, too. I should only have two corpses on my hands.'

'Damn, damn, damn!' said Andy. 'All right, I suppose as usual I'll have to leave it to you. But Meg, for God's sake be careful. And take the dogs. Curly can probably guard you better than I could anyway. The police ought to be here at any minute now and I'll send them out to help you at once.'

Chapter 21

CONFESSION

Taking the torch from Andy I ran out of the front door and to the car and released the dogs. Then still running and stumbling on the rough ground, I made my way along the garden hedge trying to find a gap. At last I found one in the corner nearest the river. There was a faint track here as though Rachel had used this route from time to time to reach the river bank. It ran along the top of the sloping side wall of the weir and, where the wall ended abruptly, continued, trending gradually downward, along the side of the high, rocky bank. I followed the track as best I could but kept coming to dead-ends of bramble-covered rock where I had to cast around for a possible way through. Once, I turned an ankle, twisting it painfully, and more than once I slipped and fell on my back or knees. Soon I could feel blood trickling down my cheek where a blackberry spray had whipped me savagely, but I kept going desperately, driven as much by the terror of meeting a murderer as by anxiety for the creature lying on the rock at the river's edge.

At last, when it seemed that I had been stumbling and crashing about for an eternity, the beam of my torch picked up the gleam of water. The river was just ahead and I was about to hurry down to the edge of it in order to get my bearings when suddenly I stopped short, frozen in my tracks, for the torch beam had picked out something else besides the gleam of water. It was the figure of a man bending over some object on the ground. As the light disturbed him he straightened and turned his face in my direction. It was Robert Landon. Shouting something unintelligible he came springing towards me, leaping from boulder to boulder. With a cry of terror I snapped off the torch and flung myself sideways behind a rock. I felt myself falling through brambles and nettles and landed with a painful jar on stony ground. In spite of the acute discomfort of my position I lay still and held my breath to listen. I heard Robert blundering by above me, cursing under his breath, and then he must have met the dogs for I heard a yelp of pain from Squelch and an angry snarl from Curly. Then the sound of his stumbling footsteps gradually died away and was swallowed up by the boom of the weir. I continued to lie still for what seemed an age in case Robert should come back, wondering the while whether Curly had just saved my life. When at last I felt certain that Robert would not return to hunt me out but was thinking more of saving his own skin than adding another victim to his list, I addressed myself to the problem of extricating myself from the hollow in which I lay. After a long and painful struggle, in the course of which my hands and face became covered with nettle stings and my fingers full of thorns, I managed to drag myself clear of the clinging vegetation. Then summoning up what courage remained to me – which was little enough – and calling the dogs to my side, I advanced cautiously towards the object over which Robert had been bending and turned the torch, still miraculously unbroken, upon it.

It was, as I knew in my heart it would be, the body of a woman – the body of Rachel. She was lying on her back with arms outspread and her head turned sideways away from me. She had been stripped to her underclothes and the tatters of the brown linen suit lay in an untidy heap at her feet as though it had been torn off her. The body must have been moved from where I had seen it from the cottage window, for the ground under it was not rock but mud and shingle bound together by stunted rushes. I could see no wound, but I dared not touch the body to make a closer examination. Suddenly the weakness of my knees forced me to sit down on a nearby boulder and, sitting there, I burst into tears. It was too much. I just could not take any more horror.

But I was not yet at an end of the terrors of that night.

My moment of weakness did not last long, and I was wiping the tears away with the back of a hand, considering what I must do next, when I heard a dog barking from further down the river. It was unmistakably the voice of Squelch in a high state of outrage. Meg to the rescue once more, I thought hysterically as I rose to my feet and started to stumble towards the sound. As I approached I could hear, mingled with Squelch's maddening outcry, the voice of a woman sobbing.

'Go away, you beast. Let me alone, let me alone, let me alone,' and I shouted to Squelch at the top of my voice to shut up. For a wonder, he obeyed me so that I was able to hear the woman's voice more clearly. It was the voice of Elise. I was past surprise or wonder or even fear and so, without so much as pausing to consider the unlikelihood of my identification, I blundered on with the vague idea of verifying with my eyes the evidence of my ears. Yes; it was Elise. She was, for some reason my mind refused to wonder about, lying on a slab of rock with her legs in the water and a willow bush trailing its branches over her thighs. As my torch lit up her form I recognised in detail the vague picture I had picked out from the cottage window. This then was the body I had seen from above, but it was not a dead body. It was certainly alive, though only just, I thought, as I observed the somehow unnatural and broken attitude, the ghastly face and staring eyes, the wet Medusa locks coiling snakily against muddy cheeks.

'Who are you?' she whispered, staring fixedly into the beam of the torch.

'Meg,' I said. 'It's me, Meg Marsden,' and I lowered the torch beam and scrambled up on the rock beside her.

And then she began to laugh on a horrible note of hysteria.

'Meg!' she gasped between the peals. 'Meg Marsden! Of course. Meg Marsden, the super-snoop! Who else? It had to be Meg.'

'Elise, Elise,' I shouted to try and stop the horrible sound. 'How did you get here? Where are you hurt? How can I help you?'

Her laughter stopped as suddenly as it had begun.

'My back is broken, I think,' she said in a matter of fact tone. And then, with a lightning movement of which I should not have thought her capable in her condition, she shot out a hand and grasped me around the ankle.

'Got you at last, Meg Marsden,' she exclaimed with a note of triumph in her voice. 'I bungled the business two nights ago. That blow should have dislocated your neck like a rabbit's, but it went astray in the dark. But now …'

For a moment the meaning of her words did not sink in and,

even when it did, the full implication of her statement did not strike me at once. I was utterly amazed, but not afraid. I suppose it was hard to connect danger with the broken creature at my feet. I should have remembered that a wounded snake can still discharge a lethal venom.

'But why?' I asked, incredulously. 'What have I ever done to you?'

'You found Newton's trousers, didn't you? Fished them out of the river, I suppose, or found them washed up on the bank. They'd be a sodden rag by then, but nothing is too trivial, too filthy for Meg Marsden to pry into.'

'Newton's trousers!' I exclaimed. 'How did you know I had them?'

'I saw them on your kitchen floor the day we went to the solicitor in Carne. Later that same afternoon I stole them when you and you precious husband were out fishing – so that, at least, you would have no evidence.'

I remembered the cupboard door which had burst open on the night of the attack on me, when Andy had left me alone in the cottage, and I remembered the tin of shoe polish which had seemed to hold some significance that in my dazed condition that night I had been unable to pin down. Of course! That tin had lain on the floor beside Newton's trousers on the morning of my visit to Carne and the two objects had been stuffed into the cupboard together – but the trousers had not been in the cupboard when Andy and I had searched the house for them later. It was then that I understood the full horror of what Elise was saying and I cried out, 'So it was you who killed Newton – you, his mother. And I thought you loved him!'

'Loved him! Loved that toad, that newt, that bastard changeling! I loathed him from the moment he was born.'

The malevolence in Elise's voice made my flesh creep.

'He ruined my life – he and Daniel Carstairs. Because of those two I was trapped in this hideous valley, year after year, seeing my youth wither and my talents go to waste.'

'You could have gone away any time,' I cried with outrage.

'Gone away? Saddled for life with the upkeep and care of that half-witted monstrosity – and with no money? My father's money was left in trust for the boy. I couldn't touch a penny of it until he was dead. I might have gone away and then killed him, but that money was not enough. I had to have more to live in reasonable comfort. It was not until Robert and Rachel fell in love that I saw my way clear. With Robert's alimony and Father's trust money I could be free to live my own life, to meet people to whom I could talk intelligently, to study music and make a name for myself in the world.'

The passionate conviction, without a trace of guilty feeling, with which Elise uttered these appalling confidences showed me suddenly that this was a mad woman with whom I had to deal. Elise was definitely not sane – had never been entirely sane since I had known her, as her colossal egotism should probably have led me to suspect long ago, I suppose.

I was paralysed with horror. I dared not try to remove my ankle from her grasp because I knew she would tip me into the river without compunction, and yet I could not bring myself to use violence against that broken body. What should I do? Where were the police? Why did they not come?

Through the turmoil of my thoughts I heard Elise's voice, like a voice in a nightmare, forcing me to listen: 'Newton was easy to kill. I had it all planned years ago, of course, and then my chance came, at last. He was fishing by the footbridge and he had no suspicion of me when I came up behind him with the gaff. I put the point of the gaff through the waistband of his trousers at the back. Then I jerked him into the deep water and held him under until he stopped struggling. Afterwards, when I was sure he was dead, I pulled him out and stripped him and then pushed his body back into the river. Everyone knew his habit of stripping and diving for his bait and I had encouraged him in it. I had brought a beach bag with me and a set of dry clothes in it, including a second pair of blue corduroy trousers, identical to those he had on. I had bought the two pairs months before with just this object in view. After I had dropped the dry clothes and the wet gumboots and socks on the bank, I fixed a waterlogged branch to the prawn hook which was attached to the fishing line and flung it out into the stream and jammed the rod handle under the bridge. The wet clothes I took home and quite openly hung on the line to dry. It was Monday, washing day, you remember.'

I did remember. The events of that beautiful May afternoon passed rapidly before my mind's eye as she spoke and the story she was telling me fitted the facts as I knew them. So it was the truth she was telling. These were not merely the ravings of a mad woman.

'It was easy. Everything was dead easy, but I made one mistake, which need not have mattered but for you. The wet trousers slipped from my hand into the river and were carried out of reach before I could retrieve them.'

So Andy's reconstruction had been pretty near the truth.

'And Daniel Carstairs,' I asked in fascinated horror, 'did you kill him too?'

'Yes,' she said, without a tremor in her voice. 'He only got what he deserved. He was my evil genius,' she continued, showing signs of agitation for the first time. 'It was his beastly lust that brought me to this. I never liked men – any man. They mean nothing to me. But he wouldn't take no for an answer. He was so sure he was irresistible. In the end he forced me against my will and I was in trouble, like any man-mad shopgirl. Everything has flowed from that. And then that he should turn up again just when freedom was in sight!'

Elise was flinging her head from side to side now in impotent rage at the thought of the cruel twist of fate that had driven her still further into crime.

'I had not seen or heard of him for a dozen years or more and then, on that day of all days, he had to turn up again. He was on the river bank that afternoon on some evil errand of his own and he saw me leaving the river with the bag of wet clothes in my hand. Pure bloody coincidence! He recognised me at once, it seems, but made sure of my identity by enquiries in Carne. Later he attended the inquest and, without a shred of evidence, leaped to the conclusion that I had something to hide. He said he knew me of old. Then he started blackmailing me. You caught me talking to him on the telephone one evening – I think it was on Robert's birthday.'

Yes, I remembered that, too, and Elise's fury with poor old Mrs Rees for her eavesdropping. No wonder she had been angry!

'The disgusting creature said he still loved me – lusted after me would be a better description of his feelings. He did not want money. Only my body. I held him off for months but, although I was certain that he knew nothing and could prove nothing, I was afraid. In the end I pretended to give in.'

She fell silent and her head ceased its restless tossing. A curious stillness enveloped us, broken only by the now distant roar of the weir, swelling and dying on the light breeze, and by the steady rushing of the steam beyond the backwater. At the river's edge the ever-busy Squelch snuffed about among the rushes and I could hear the small sound of his claws scratching on stones. Curly sat on her haunches beside the rock and gazed steadily at us. Now that my eyes had become accustomed to the darkness it seemed quite light here by the river with the moonshine and the faint starlight reflecting from the water. Ever-present in our nostrils was the dank smell of rotting weeds which, it seemed to me, had run like a leitmotif through all this story. I had squatted down on a rock beside Elise. She had not released her grip on my ankle but, for the moment, I no longer noticed the pressure of her hand, lost as I was in the horrified contemplation of her story. At this stage there was some pity mingled with my horror, but the pity was of short duration. I was brought back from my thoughts by a sudden increase of the pressure on my ankle and, turning to Elise and peering into her face, I saw that there was a smile on her lips.

'I enjoyed killing him,' she said softly. 'Shall I tell you how I did it?'

Horrified, yet fascinated, I nodded assent.

'We made an assignation the day I ran into him unexpectedly in Carne – the day you were with me. We were to meet in the boathouse. I arrived first and made my preparations. There were some paper sacks in a corner and I laid them down as a bed, and behind the door there was a heavy old iron weight which I moved to a handy position. I received him naked. When I had let him see the body which he seemed so much to desire I had no trouble in making him lie just where I wanted. I had put my clothes in a beach bag – the same one in which I had carried away Newton's wet garments – and hung it on a bracket on the wall. As he lay down his eye fell on this and he made to rise. I think he knew at that moment what was I store for him. But it was too late. The first blow with the iron weight stunned him but I struck him many times more to make sure. Then I rolled him into the dock and the sacks after him. There was blood on my hands and body – even on my hair – so, to be on the safe side, I got into the dock and, standing on his body to keep my feet out of the mud, bathed myself from head to foot. At last I felt cleansed and pure, body and soul. Afterwards, I dressed at my leisure and walked home. The sun was shining. I felt free at last to lead a new life.'

She described the gruesome scene as one might recall some

golden afternoon of innocent childhood and I realised, with a new shock of horror, that I must have seen her returning, fresh from the slaughter, as I sat dabbling my feet in the watersplash below Trev Price's farm. I remembered that her curls had been wet as though from bathing. All pity for her died at that moment and my only thought thereafter was to keep her talking, if I could, until the police arrived. For the present, she needed no urging.

'But he won in the end,' she continued, her restlessness returning. 'I told him to leave his car in Llantossy gravel pit, meaning to go after dark dressed in Robert's clothes to fetch it and drive it to Ty-Mawr coach house where it might have remained almost forever undiscovered. How was I to know that he had planned a poaching raid for that night? I ran into the thick of it and had to turn back.'

One of the three disappearing men on the night of the raid, I thought, but I said nothing.

'It was then that I saw my opportunity with you,' Elise continued, 'but there I failed again. I tried three times to eliminate you but each time I was thwarted.'

'You tried three times to kill me?' I asked, to spin out the time.

'Later that same night I came to your cottage,' she said impatiently, not interested in her failures. 'I had a scheme, but a man came down the lane – it was your husband, I think – I had to give it up.'

So Squelch had been right. There had been someone at the door the night I had been coshed and Andy had left me so light-heartedly. The figure, which in the dark and with his poor eyesight he had taken for Robert had, in fact, been Elise, dressed in Robert's clothes.

'And the third time?' I prompted.

'Last night, of course, by the footbridge, but your dogs and your husband arrived just a minute too soon.'

'With the car found,' continued Elise after a pause, 'Daniel was identified at once, it seems, and somehow Rachel got to know of it.'

She fell silent again.

'So you killed her, too?' I asked as calmly as I could in order to keep her talking.

'Is she dead?' asked Elise, with a note almost of regret in her voice.

'She is lying twenty yards upstream from here,' I told her, 'and I think she is dead.'

'Rachel dead!' she said. 'Well, she knew too much. Robert told her too much, but I bore her no malice. She was so useful to me – she and Robert.'

'So now there only remains you,' she continued, suddenly closing her spatulate fingers more tightly round my ankle. 'Only Snoopy Meg left, with her curiosity fully satisfied but with no likelihood of ever being able to pass on her gossip. I warned you, didn't I, that your curiosity would be the death of you one day.'

It only then dawned fully on me that she really meant to kill me if she could, useless as such an act would be. Of course, in order to gain time and also, incidentally, to keep myself safe, I should have sat still and kept the macabre conversation going.

In her condition she was powerless against me as long as I stayed solidly seated, but my instinctive and foolish reaction, as I suddenly realised the full extent of her malevolence, was to rise abruptly to my feet and try to escape from her evil presence. This, of course, gave her exactly the opportunity she needed and, with a sudden convulsive heave, she dragged one foot from under me and threw me off balance so that I fell heavily on my back, shattering the torch and nearly knocking myself out. What would have been the outcome I shudder to think had not a furry bomb exploded at that moment between us as Curly launched herself onto the rock and sank her teeth into Elise's arm.

Such a cry as then burst from the lips of the broken-backed woman on the rock I hope never again in my life to hear. It was like the scream of the tortured on the rack or of a damned soul in hell, and it was followed by a terrible outcry of shrieks and imprecations and laughter. At that moment Elise went finally over the brink into raving madness.

Somehow I managed to scramble to my feet and, with hands clapped to my ears to shut out the horrible din, I plunged, sobbing and stumbling and falling, up the bank with the dogs at my heels. Of the rest of that evening and night I have little recollection. At some point I ran into a glaring eye of light which must have been a torch, held in the hand of a policeman. And then, I was babbling out my story to a group of unidentified faces; and, a little later, I was lying on a bench in a moving vehicle, presumably an ambulance, with Andy sitting beside me holding my hand. Then nothing more until I awoke in broad daylight in my own bed in the cottage.

Chapter 22

TIDYING UP

The first thing my eyes fell on was Andy's anxious face. He was standing by the bed with a tray in his hands and it must have been his entry that had wakened me. I smiled at him and instantly the worried look left him and he smiled his crooked smile back at me. Then laying the tray on the side table and drawing a chair up beside me he took my hand in his.

'How do you feel, Meg, old girl?' he asked in a tone of such solicitude that I was quite startled. 'I was a selfish, thoughtless brute to let you go off alone last night. If you had been killed I should never have had another happy moment. More than that – I think I should have killed myself. Can you ever forgive me?'

'Forgive you for what?' I asked in astonishment.

'Dear Meg! I don't know what I've done to deserve you. You know, Meg, I've spent the whole night thinking about things, about us and our life here. What a selfish beast I've been – and a coward, too. Full of self-pity and never thinking of you and of how I have been wasting your life, burying you down here ...'

'Stop, stop,' I interrupted. 'You know I have loved every minute of it, that is, until this horrible business with Elise. Anyhow I am always happy wherever you are.'

'I do believe that's true, Meg,' said Andy wonderingly. 'Though heaven knows why. The sort of wife I deserve is one like Elise who would have come up behind me one dark night when I was fishing for sea-trout and shoved me into the river.'

Elise! I shuddered at the name.

'Have they arrested her, Andy?' I asked.

'No. She's vanished. When PC Jones and the Llantossy constable went down to look for her last night, after listening to your somewhat incoherent story, there was no trace of her to be found. Either deliberately or accidentally she must have slid or fallen off the rock. They're dragging the river now for her body. But don't let's talk about her. Let's talk about us while we drink the tea I brought up before it's stone cold.'

So for a long time we talked very satisfactorily about "us" and as I watched Andy's eager face I thought that one good thing at least had come out of all the horror: Andy was a man again, full of hope and plans for the future – plans which, please God, will be fulfilled.

Afterwards I started to get up but Andy wouldn't hear of it and pushed me back against the pillows with a touch of his old irritability.

'Lie back, girl. Don't you realise you've been suffering from mild concussion? Robert looked in this morning and says you're not to stir from bed for at least three days.'

I relapsed obediently and, I must say, most willingly and watched Andy in a state of dreamy contentment as he busied himself about tidying the room and the bed and stacking the tea things on the tray. The evening sun was streaming through the window and lighting his absorbed face. Now the "good" side and now the "bad" blind side was illuminated and I thought how much I loved them both, the bad and the good equally. How lucky

I was compared, for instance, to Rachel.

'Poor Rachel and poor Robert!' I said giving voice to my thoughts. 'What a terrible time for him. I feel so ashamed when I think of the awful things I thought about him. Is he taking Rachel's death very hard?'

'Good Lord! Of course, you don't know. Rachel is not dead. She's in hospital in Carne and Robert tells me that she is going to be all right. He reached her just in time last night and got her round with – rather appropriately – the kiss of life. He was like a madman when he came bursting into the cottage last night to ring for the ambulance, but he told me that he had met you on the way up from the river and had yelled to you to sit by Rachel until he returned.'

So that was what Robert had been shouting as he came leaping up towards me. I started to laugh and then found that I could not stop laughing and Andy had to give me a good shake and then administer a sedative tablet which Robert had left for me before I could pull myself together. After that I went to sleep again and it was not until six days later that I learned the full details of the action-packed evening and night when I had sat on the dark river bank listening to the confessions of a mad murderess.

Andy knew little more than I did of the events of that evening but he was able to explain many other aspects of the affair to me. He had known, he said, that Elise was the murderer of Newton long before Curly had found Daniel Carstairs' body in the boathouse. That gruesome discovery had confirmed his conviction. He said it was simply a question of logic. In the case of no-one else could one combine opportunity, motive – which he seemed to have fathomed fairly early on – and, above all, access to Newton's wardrobe. Who but his mother could have supplied the boy with two identical pairs of trousers and then seen to it that these trousers were the ones worn on that day? It was conceivable that it might have been Robert but few fathers, especially fathers who disliked their sons, would concern themselves with their wearing apparel. Andy had realised long ago that Elise was not quite sane. It all seemed very obvious when he put it like that! The difficulty had always been, of course, how to prove it. The whole logical edifice rested upon my unsupported evidence to the effect that there must have been two pairs of trousers. Andy, knowing me, believed it but he doubted whether anyone else would have done so.

Cliff's somewhat suspicious behaviour, Andy thought, was almost certainly caused by a guilty conscience connected with his pilfering propensities. It was even possible that he had stolen some part of Newton Landon's tackle when he had first come upon it on the bank.

As to Constable Jones' odd behaviour – this was undoubtedly connected with his unfortunate nephew, Leslie. The boy had certainly been in the vicinity of the footbridge at the time of Newton's death and his uncle, the constable, had obviously feared that he might actually have pushed his tormentor into the river in sly revenge for past ill-treatment. Affection for his dim-witted nephew apart, such a scandal in the family would, to say the least, have done Evan Jones no good. When I showed him the trousers the constable was in a panic lest the whole affair should be raked up again and Leslie implicated.

The small mystery of the "apparition" which I had seen one night at the Crib was easily explained, Andy thought. This was simply one of the poaching gang reconnoitring the possibilities of the Crib pool.

As soon as Rachel was well enough to receive visitors I went to see her in the Carne District Hospital. She was sitting up in bed and looking, for the first time since I had known her, really happy. It was astonishing the difference it made in her appearance. In spite of the harrowing experience she had just been through she looked ten years younger. There was even a faint glow of colour in her cheeks and her large, dark eyes – always her best feature – positively sparkled with happiness. In view of the unhappy circumstances in which we had last met I announced myself with some diffidence, but she seemed pleased to see me.

'How sweet of you to come, Meg,' she said.

When I tried to apologise, somewhat incoherently, for Andy's treatment of her she cut me short by saying, 'Andy was quite right. If I had followed his advice at once, as he urged me to do, all this would never have happened. The thing that held me back, of course, was the horrible – the torturing – suspicion that Bob had killed Newton. He had always hated him so passionately. And then, when Daniel Carstairs' body turned up in the boathouse, I was sure that Bob had killed them both. How could I have been so wicked!'

'What I don't understand,' I said, after I had reassured Rachel that her suspicions had been very natural under the circumstances and that I had shared them, 'is how or why Elise came to visit you at Weir Cottage that night.'

So then Rachel told me the story of that evening's happenings. When she got home after leaving us, she said, instead of going straight on to Llantossy Police Station, she decided to take the night to think things over. She was sitting in the living room in the dusk with the unlit Aladdin lamp beside her and wrestling with her tormenting thoughts, when she heard a car stop at the gate. She says she leaped to her feet with joy, thinking it was Bob come to see her at last and that he would be able to explain away her suspicions. But it was not Bob; it was Joseph Ellis and Elise. As she opened the door to them she heard Elise say to her brother, 'You'd better go back to the house for it Jo-Jo. It's either in the sitting-room desk or in a despatch case in my bedroom wardrobe.'

Then, as Joseph Ellis turned away grumbling something about the idiocy of forgetting the most important document of all, Elise called after him, 'Come back and fetch me in half an hour.'

Rachel said she was appalled at the thought of a tête-à-tête at that juncture with Bob's wife but, before she could close the door in her face, Elise had pushed past her into the living room.

Then the nightmare began. Rachel said it started quietly enough. It seems that Elise had simply come to inform Rachel that she was quite determined to get her divorce, that proceedings were already underway and that Rachel would be well-advised to persuade Bob to let the suit go through undefended. Otherwise Elise would do her utmost to press a charge of unprofessional conduct on Bob's part and that would be his ruin, however it turned out. Evidence of such conduct, Elise indicated, should not be difficult to find in view of the fact that Bob had never been faithful to her but had chased after every pretty patient in the neighbourhood. At this point, Rachel said, she – Rachel – suddenly lost her temper and shouted, 'It's a lie! Who are you to talk – you, Daniel Carstairs' mistress of whom Bob made an honest woman!'

At the name of Daniel Carstairs, Rachel said, Elise seemed to turn to stone. She could not see her face in the dusk, but every movement ceased and there was a long silence. Suddenly Elise made a menacing gesture and shouted, 'What do you know of Daniel Carstairs?' and Rachel shouted back: 'I know that he was your lover and that his body was taken out of the river last night.'

Rachel said she shouted this without the least idea of accusing Elise of murder, but at the words Elise went berserk. She sprang forward with her curious broad-tipped fingers clutching at Rachel's throat. Of the ensuing struggle Rachel remembered little. She heard the table with the lamp on it crash to the ground as she backed against it and then she was free of the clutching hands for a moment and was running for the kitchen, but before she could slam and lock the door Elise was after her. There was a confused struggle round and round the kitchen and then she suddenly saw Elise coming for her with a heavy iron saucepan in her hand. She felt a shattering blow on the side of her neck and must have fallen backwards towards the window. Elise's fingers were round her throat once more and pressing her head against the pane. Some convulsive movement of Rachel's shoulders must have shattered the glass, at the same time lifting the latch of the casement. She felt a searing pain as a spear of glass ripped her upper arm and then for an eternity she seemed to hang there, bent backwards over the abyss and tearing at the iron-fingered hands at her throat. She felt the low windowsill pressing against her thighs and struggled desperately to keep her footing, but suddenly her feet slipped from under her and she felt herself falling, dragging Elise with her. She did not remember hitting the water. She and Elise must have fallen into the deepest part of the weir pool avoiding by a miracle the rocks and the blocks of fallen masonry, and the current must have carried them swiftly downstream and then whirled them round into the backwater.

It seems that Robert, who had come to Weir Cottage to explain his absence of the night before, had arrived just in time to see the two struggling forms falling from the window and had then raced down to the river bank and had reached the backwater just as Rachel's unconscious body was floating within reach. Elise must have retained consciousness and somehow managed to grasp the trailing branches of a willow bush and with their help drag herself up onto the rock where I had found her.

'I owe my life, of course, to Bob,' Rachel finished. 'Without his skill and presence of mind I should certainly have died. And when he was working over me there on the river bank I came to myself for a moment or two and what he was saying to himself then, when he thought I was unconscious, convinced me once and for all that he truly loves me – just as much as I love him. As soon as Elise's body has been found, and when all the horrible business of the inquests is behind us, we shall be married.'

'Dear Rachel,' I said, 'I am so glad and I hope you will be very happy. You both deserve a bit of a break.'

MacAlister's Boy and young Rodney Price, worming for eels early the next morning, came across the body of Elise Landon floating face downwards in the backwater behind the Crib, not five feet from the spot where the naked body of her misbegotten son, Newton, had been found drowned four months before.

THE END